D1563299

MARIA'S GIRLS

Books by Jerome Charyn

MARIA'S GIRLS
MARGOT IN BAD TOWN
(Illustrated by Massimo Frezzato)
BILLY BUDD, KGB
(Illustrated by François Boucq)
ELSINORE
THE GOOD POLICEMAN
MOVIELAND
THE MAGICIAN'S WIFE
(Illustrated by François Boucq)
PARADISE MAN
METROPOLIS
WAR CRIES OVER AVENUE C
PINOCCHIO'S NOSE
PANNA MARIA
DARLIN' BILL
THE CATFISH MAN
THE SEVENTH BABE
SECRET ISAAC
THE FRANKLIN SCARE
THE EDUCATION OF PATRICK SILVER
MARILYN THE WILD
BLUE EYES
THE TAR BABY
EISENHOWER, MY EISENHOWER
AMERICAN SCRAPBOOK
GOING TO JERUSALEM
THE MAN WHO GREW YOUNGER
ON THE DARKENING GREEN
ONCE UPON A DROSHKY

MARIA'S GIRLS

JEROME CHARYN

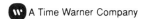

THE MYSTERIOUS PRESS
New York · Tokyo · Sweden
Published by Warner Books

A Time Warner Company

Mysterious Press books are published by
Warner Books, Inc., 1271 Avenue of the Americas, New York, NY 10020

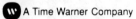 A Time Warner Company

The Mysterious Press name and logo are trademarks of Warner Books, Inc.
Printed in the United States of America

First printing: May 1992

10 9 8 7 6 5 4 3 2 1

Library of Congress Cataloging in Publication Data

Charyn, Jerome.
    Maria's girls : a novel / by Jerome Charyn.
        p.   cm.
    "The Mysterious Press."
    ISBN 0-89296-460-X
    I. Title.
PS3553.H33M37   1992
813'.54—dc20   91-58027
                                                            CIP

To my Monday Morning Club:

Marie-Pierre Bay, Bill Malloy, and Cécile Bloc-Rodot.

Part One

1

His name was Caroll Brent. He was a detective on loan from Sherwood Forest, the precinct in Central Park. The police commissioner had copped Caroll Brent. His own squad was afraid of him. He'd become a man without a country at the NYPD, a floater who belonged to Isaac Sidel.

The PC had a bug up his ass about the Board of Ed. He avoided the schools chancellor, Alejo Tomás, and stepped outside Alejo's own inspector general. Caroll lived in some fucking fourth dimension, where he had to police the schools of New York City behind Alejo Tomás' back. He was on his own. He had no official function. Caroll knew he was going to die, just like Manfred Coen, the PC's former blue-eyed angel.

He could have quit. He was married to the second-richest woman in New York. His wife, Diana, came from the Cassidys, a tribe of Catholics that was close to Cardinal O'Bannon, prince of St. Patrick's Cathedral. The cardinal took pity on Caroll. Somehow he'd uncovered Caroll's fourth dimension, and he marched to Isaac Sidel. Isaac pleaded ignorance.

"I swear to God, Jim. I'm not sure what you're talking about. Detective Brent does small favors for me from time to time."

"Small favors?" the cardinal said, with a cigarette in his mouth.

"He's off the fuckin' chart. He hasn't been to Sherwood Forest in a month. Isaac, you're turning him into a ghost."

"Aint that the truth," Isaac said, adopting a policeman's brogue for Cardinal Jim. "And I suppose this visit has nothing to do with the fact that he's married to the goddess Diana."

"Don't blaspheme, Isaac. You'll rot in hell."

"There are no hells where I come from. It's all one big purgatory."

The cardinal socked Isaac Sidel. And Isaac fell to the floor. He sat on his ass in the purgatory of his own office at One Police Plaza.

"I'm sorry," the cardinal muttered, between bites of the cigarette, and helped Isaac to his feet. "You shouldn't taunt me. I have a temper. I don't want Caroll at One PP."

"Jim," Isaac said. "Have you ever seen him in my office?"

"You know damn well what I mean."

And he walked out of One PP in his cardinal's cape. But it didn't help Caroll. He was doomed to patrolling school yards for Isaac Sidel. He didn't want to work for the Cassidys. He was a cop. He had none of Diana's ambition. He didn't like to mix and mingle. He just wanted to get back to Sherwood Forest.

But he was in the middle of Harlem on a Saturday night. It scared the shit out of him. He had no back-up. He was a one-man task force. A human android in the service of Isaac Sidel. A Martian on Jupiter's twelfth moon. He could have made a couple of collars on the street. But he had nothing to do with conventional burglars and drug salesmen. He was staking out a school near St. Nicholas Terrace, drinking coffee out of a thermos bottle. His feet were cold. He didn't miss the Park Avenue duplex Papa Cassidy had bought for Diana and him as a wedding present. Caroll missed the broken pipes and leaky roofs of Sherwood Forest. The precinct was a former stable, a goddamn firetrap that sucked up wind, rain, and snow. But Caroll had loved it in there until his own squad turned on him, called him the pet of One PP. *Blue Eyes Brent.*

And now he saw a great big ass coming out of the second-story window at the school, along with the legs of a piano. It was a baby grand. *Jesus.* Caroll continued to drink his coffee. The PC had told him about this heist. Sidel seemed to know everything that was going down at Alejo's schools. He could have told the Inspector General's office. And Alejo's cops would have come waltzing into Harlem on this same Saturday night. But Alejo's cops were clowns, according to Sidel. Caroll was here, and he wasn't supposed to make a collar but act like some avenging angel.

He didn't even wave his gun. He called up to the window. "Denzel, is that you?"

The piano legs rocked in the window, without the great big ass. Two heads appeared. They looked very angry, as much as Caroll could tell in the dark.

"Hey motherfucker, what you want with us?"

"I'm Detective Brent of Manhattan North."

The two heads started to laugh.

"You Isaac's little sister."

"Yeah, Denzel. That's me. And if you don't get away from that piano, I'm going to break all four of your legs."

"You got no business here. We borrowing the piano from the school board."

"Well, borrow it back to where you got it, Denzel. And come on down."

He could hear a metallic click and then something that sounded like the popping of a lightbulb. Caroll's pants were wet. Denzel had shot the thermos bottle out of his hand. The ground was sprinkled with silver and glass. A marksman, Caroll muttered. A marksman with a Saturday Night Special. He still hadn't taken out his gun.

"Denzel, I'm getting pissed off."

And then he saw a figure in the shadows behind the schoolhouse wall, and Caroll cursed himself and Sidel and the ghost of Blue Eyes. He'd been set up. He ducked into a very narrow gutter when a shotgun angled at him started to explode. Caroll lost the heel of his shoe. His foot was bleeding. He took a flare out of his pocket. He always carried flares on these suicide missions for Isaac. He lit the flare and hurled it at Denzel's window. The whole of Harlem looked like a Christmas tree. St. Nicholas Terrace could have been Jupiter's thirteenth moon. The sky seemed to break into molten pieces of red and blue.

The piano fell out the window.

Caroll escaped into his fourth dimension, a crazy cover of light.

2

He couldn't run with the Cassidys on a policeman's pay. He had to borrow. He used a Mafia shylock. No one knocked on Caroll's door. He was close to the Commish. Blue Eyes Brent, with the brown eyes.

He had to keep borrowing to pay off the vig. The vigorish alone was a thousand dollars a week. Diana might have cleared his debts, but how could he ask her for the money? He didn't go shopping for an heiress. He met his future wife on the job. Dee had been threatened by a slasher. The slasher had seen her jogging in Central Park. He'd cut her sweatshirt with a hunting knife. He began calling her on the phone. She had all the connections of a Cassidy. Caroll was put on the case, the brown-eyed detective from Sherwood Forest.

She was twenty-nine and had never been married. He escorted her to the opera, the opening of art shows, the New York Film Festival. The department paid for his rented tux. It was a glory assignment, but Caroll didn't like it. He tried to duck out on Diana, invent some crime that would keep him away from her, but she always asked for him. She'd become Caroll's case.

He couldn't bear parties, operas, charity balls. He wouldn't flirt. But her friends began to notice him. He was Dee's escort. He absorbed whatever she absorbed. He met Stewart Hines, the junk-bond king. "That female you're with is worth half a billion dollars. She could buy the Chrysler Building if she wants. All it would take is her signature."

"I wouldn't know, Mr. Hines."

The junk-bond king chuckled to himself. "Who's going to be the lucky boy that bags Diana?"

"I guess one of her suitors."

"Have you seen any, son?"

Caroll couldn't say. He was guarding her six or seven times a week. He'd never even kissed her good night. She was Ms. Cassidy and he was Detective Brent. And once, while they were returning to her apartment after some ballet or ball, the slasher appeared from behind a tree with his hunting knife. He was shorter than Caroll. He had the grim face of a poor urban farmer. Caroll recognized him. He was a gardener from the Department of Parks who often cut the shrubbery around Sherwood Forest. His name was Fred.

Caroll stood in front of Diana and moved toward the knife. "Come on, Freddy, you aren't going to use that thing."

"I proposed to her," he said. "She wouldn't have me."

"That's a lie," Diana said. "Detective, I—"

Caroll frowned at her and she shut up.

"Come on, Fred."

The gardener tried to lunge at Diana, and Caroll had to slap him with the butt of his off-duty gun. He handcuffed the gardener and read him his rights. The case never even went to trial. Fred the gardener was still sitting in the psycho ward at Bellevue. Caroll received a five-thousand-dollar check in the mail from Diana Cassidy. And a note. *I miss you.*

He made an appointment with Diana through her social secretary. He returned the check. "I can't take this."

"Why not?"

"It's part of my job. I'm paid to protect you."

"Then call it conscience money, Detective Brent."

"I don't get it."

"You can visit Fred once in a while. Bring him flowers."

"I've already visited him."

"Don't argue," she said. "And why haven't you visited me?"

"Because my tour is over. We found Fred. Or I should say, Fred found us. But tell me one thing. Did you ever talk to him before that night?"

"What do you mean, Detective?"

"He jumped out from behind that tree and said he'd proposed to you but you wouldn't have him."

"I don't recall that piece of conversation."

"But did you talk to him?"

"No, Detective. I didn't talk to him. He's a maniac . . . oh, I might have seen him at the Reservoir. He did work for the park. I might have laughed with him."

"And he might have proposed."

"Detective, things like that happen a thousand times a day."

"But it might not have been a joke to Fred. What if he was serious? He proposed. You rejected him and—"

"He came after me with a knife."

"But you're safe now, Ms. Cassidy. And I have to go."

"What if I wanted you to stay?"

"I'd still go back to my precinct."

"But I could always produce another Fred. I'm spoiled. I'm rich. And I'm rotten . . . take off your clothes."

He made love to Diana while her social secretary sat in the next room. Diana had purple eyes. Her ass didn't have a single flaw. Her body tasted of nectarines ripening on a tree.

He had a visit from her lawyer. The lawyer handed him a document that was seven pages long. It was a prenuptial agreement.

"I don't get it."

"Detective Brent, didn't you ever hear the expression about a 'gift horse'? Just sign the document. Dee wants to marry you."

"She's confusing me with that gardener, Fred. I never proposed."

"Forgive me, sir, but you don't propose to half a billion dollars. She's the only heir to the Cassidy fortune. And she's a hell of a looking lady."

"She's still confusing me with Fred. Good-bye."

Caroll got drunk. He wandered into Sherwood Forest. He didn't have his handcuffs or his gun. His captain sent him home. "Go on, kid. You need a rest." Caroll had a hook at Police Plaza. He was the PC's favorite boy.

Diana was waiting for him when he got home. She sat curled up outside his door, smelling of nectarines. "Do you know how much it cost me to have my lawyer prepare that agreement?"

"You can afford it. You're an heiress. I'm from the Rockaways. I grew up with ten dollars in the bank."

"That's why I need a lawyer. A lot of people want to get into my pants. How could I really tell if a man was in love with me or my father's fortune?"

"Ms. Cassidy, we're not even acquainted."

"We're acquainted enough. You've been seeing me every night for sixteen weeks."

Caroll made love to her again. He signed the prenuptial agreement. His potential sons and daughters would be much richer than Caroll, but he'd get some kind of "dowry" if he stayed with Diana for ten years. They were married in St. Patrick's Cathedral, although Caroll wasn't a Catholic. It was Cardinal Jim who recited the Mass. Caroll's picture was on the society page. He thought the Cassidys wouldn't accept a cop like him, but they were relieved to have a husband for Diana. There was a banquet at the Pierre. Caroll's mom and dad were dead. He came from a line of fishermen. His great-great-grandfather had been very rich, while the Cassidys shoveled pigshit in Sligo or some other Irish county. But the Brents suffered a decline. Each new generation was poorer than the last. Caroll's father was also a fisherman. He died at forty, a shriveled man.

Papa Cassidy was a capitalist. He helped start up companies. He was a bottler, a builder, a grower of grapes and figs. He'd had no sons. And his only daughter couldn't seem to get engaged . . . until she met this cop. He welcomed Caroll into the tribe, wanted to make a venture capitalist out of him, but Caroll was tied to a precinct in Central Park. Papa didn't complain, as long as the boy held to his daughter.

Caroll began to like the Cassidys. They floated with the rich, but they weren't snobs. And he realized he'd been crazy about Diana all the while he guarded her from the slasher. Freddy was the psychopathic Cupid in Caroll's life. He'd never have known Dee without that gardener.

And so he borrowed and borrowed to pay off the vig. He could have gone to one of the Cassidys, but he didn't want them involved in his affairs. He went into the streets and found his own shylock, Fabiano Rice, who was attached to the Rubino "crime family." Fabiano's boss, Sal Rubino, had been murdered in New Orleans. By one of the Rubino captains, Jerry DiAngelis . . . and Isaac Sidel. That was the word out on the street. Isaac was thick with Jerry's father-in-law, Izzy Wasser, the brains behind Jerry's side of the clan. Izzy Wasser had suffered a stroke. And now the Rubinos were in the toilet. But that didn't help Caroll with the vig.

Isaac had gone to jail for being chummy with DiAngelis and his father-in-law. But no jail could hold the Commish. He beat the rap and got rid of Sal Rubino. Only in New York could you have a police commissioner who was also a hitman. Isaac never took a dime, but he was obsessed with the children of Alejo Tomás' schools. He felt that every school board was riddled with thieves. He had to root them out. And Caroll was the gardener he picked. Caroll joined school boards under ficticious names. He chased after the superintendents of several districts. He stopped school boards from lending out pianos. He was shot at, pissed upon, run after with a razor, and all the while he had this vig.

He was in a bad mood. He met with Isaac in a bumpy corner under the Williamsburg Bridge. The sky was black over Caroll's head. There was nothing but walls. Isaac needed a shave. And Caroll had to wonder if Sidel also lived in some fourth dimension. The Commish had a daughter. But she'd disowned her dad. Her name was Marilyn. She'd loved Manfred Coen. Caroll had never seen the lady. But he sympathized with her.

"Montalbán," Isaac said. "I want that motherfucker."

His face was dark blue. He looked like Captain Ahab. But Caroll couldn't tell what kind of whale Isaac had in his ass. He was outside human territory, under the Williamsburg Bridge.

"But you don't have to ruin a poor assistant principal."

"Rosen was on the take. He's going down with Montalbán."

"Come on, Isaac. He's months away from retirement. Jesus, will you leave the little guy alone?"

"He took food from the mouths of second-graders. He robbed fucking pencils. He's part of Montalbán's gang."

Carlos Maria Montalbán was superintendent of School District One B in Manhattan. One B encompassed the Lower East Side. And Montalbán ran the district like a warlord, dispensing favors, hiring, firing, bullying local school-board members. He was a cousin of the chancellor, Alejo Tomás. He'd served in Nam, but no one could find Montalbán's war record. Isaac believed that Montalbán was a pirate left over from the Green Berets. But the PC couldn't prove a thing.

"I'm tired of protecting pianos, Isaac. I want my old nut back."

"Ah, you've been talking to Cardinal Jim," Isaac said, with his policeman's brogue.

"I never talked to Jim. I wouldn't betray you."

"Well, he knows your whereabouts."

"Isaac, the man married Diana and me. He's not blind. He can tell I'm out fishing for you. And he wonders to himself why he can never catch me at my precinct."

"Your precinct is where I say it is."

"I want my old nut."

"I'm not giving you Sherwood Forest, and that is fucking final.
I won't waste my best man. You can talk to horses and trees on
your own time. Montalbán is a thief."

"Then arrest him, Isaac."

"I can't," the PC said in the gloom of all the stones around
him. "No one believes me. The D.A. won't move to indict. He
says I have no case against Montalbán. It's clubhouse politics.
Montalbán and his cousin are Party men. Alejo owns the
Bronx, and Montalbán is captain of the Lower East Side. Let
him steal from the Democrats. But this is my neighborhood,
Caroll. And those are my children he's hurting. I want him
stopped."

"Then oust the fuck. Run for president of the local board."

"I can't," Isaac said. "They'll call it nepotism. The police commissioner sticking his fingers in local school business."

"So I have to be your point man. With illegal searches and
wiretaps. Isaac, I'm the one who could be arrested."

"How else can I grab Montalbán?" Isaac groaned. "And who
would dare arrest you? You work for me."

"Isaac, I was shot in the heel last week."

"You'll survive," the PC said.

"You don't give a shit, do you? As long as you get Montalbán.
But I'm not going to crucify any more little old men."

"Him? Rosen. He's Montalbán's creation. A greedy kike."

"Isaac, he's a member of your own fucking tribe."

"Who says? I'm strictly a Sunday Yid. That's when I light
candles to my dead mama. I have no religion the rest of the
week."

Caroll couldn't wear down this Ahab who worshipped with a
bug up his ass. Education. Isaac wouldn't deal with the Inspector
General's office. He'd send Caroll into some fourth dimension
so Caroll could get killed. And then that merciless man smiled
in the dark. Caroll could see the tips of his teeth.

"Are you short of money, kid? I hear you've been getting close
to Fabiano Rice. He's a bad boy. He belonged to Sal Rubino."

"But Sal's asleep." *You killed him*, Caroll muttered in his head. *He caught some of your buckshot in New Orleans, Mr. Sidel.*

"Caroll, let me help you if you can't make the vig."

"I don't need help."

"It's hard being married to the rich, aint it?"

"I'm doing all right. The son of a fisherman, with a cardinal on his side. I can't complain."

"But I could step on Fabiano's feet."

"It's not your business, Isaac. Fabiano's my affair."

"Does Diana know?"

"It's not your business," Caroll had to say again. And he was close to massacring Sidel, beating him around the ears so that Isaac's blue face would explode with grief. "I'll talk to little Rosen. I'll get him to confess. I'll map all of Montalbán's strategies for you. I'll find the pencils he stole. But stay out of my life."

He walked to Stanton Street, where little Rosen lived, an assistant principal who'd been married and divorced, and returned to the "Cradle," as Isaac liked to call the Lower East Side. The little man was all alone. He had no more wives. He was sixty-two. Like Isaac, he had a daughter who shunned him. Caroll couldn't understand how Rosen had gotten mixed up with Montalbán. Rosen's milieu was Manhattan and Queens, not Vietnam. He didn't snort coke. He wasn't into little boys and girls. Why the fuck had he become a thief?

He let Caroll into his apartment without a squawk. He boiled some tea in a pot, cut slices of strudel from a kosher bakery next to the Harry S. Truman Democratic Club, where Montalbán and his cronies held sway. Little Rosen cried into his tea. He wore a starched shirt. His necktie was royal blue.

"Will I go to jail, Mr. Brent?"

"Not if I can help it," Caroll said. It almost seemed as if little

Rosen was his stoolie. And then Caroll thought, *Fuck. He is my stoolie.*

"What does Montalbán have on you?"

"Nothing," Rosen said.

"Then how did he get you to steal?"

"We didn't see it as stealing," Rosen said. "I was Carlos' bookkeeper. We moved merchandise around . . . from school to school."

"Come on, I have you on tape. You were selling drugs."

"Not to kids," Rosen said.

Little Rosen didn't realize that a lone detective had come to drink tea. He figured Caroll was part of some task force, a labyrinthian team called Isaac Sidel.

"But you sold," Caroll said.

"Yes. So we could have a piano at one school, and . . ."

"Pianos," Caroll said. "It always comes down to pianos. You were the Good Samaritan of drug salesmen."

"No. I'm sure Carlos kept some money for himself. I did. I bought a suit at Barney's. With a fancy label. I paid in cash. But I never wore it, Mr. Brent."

"I'm not after your tail, Rosen. I want Montalbán. Start keeping notes. On all his moves. When he wipes his ass, I want to know about it."

Little Rosen started to cry again. "I believed in Carlos. He stole. I stole. But we helped the children. We gave them—"

"You took money from your own fucking district. You swiped supplies."

"But nothing gets done without Carlos Montalbán. I filed reports. I have a desk full of correspondence on our paper shortages. Mr. Brent, I've been a teacher all my adult life. I married into the system forty years ago. And I suffered until Carlos came along. He's our liquid. He's also our glue. Yes, he steals. But we have our pencils now. The children have their books."

"And Montalbán is a millionaire. You'll help me, won't you, Rosen?"

"Do I have a choice?" little Rosen asked, tugging at his royal blue tie. Caroll felt ill. He drank a glass of water from Rosen's sink and said good-bye. He was shivering on the stairs. He liked little Rosen, who'd have to retire to a hole in the wall on Stanton Street, with his suit from Barney's and boxes of pencils made in Mexico. Caroll hardly knew Rosen, and he loved and hated him like any stoolie. Fucking Isaac Sidel.

3

Caroll had to wear his own blue tie. Diana was giving a party. There were forty guests. They looked like mice on a football field. Diana's living room wrapped around Park Avenue. Caroll couldn't relate to such a long room. He'd always be a guest here, no matter who owned the apartment. He was a WASP bridegroom in a city of Irishers, Italians, Latinos, blacks, White Russians, Chinese, Koreans, Jews . . .

He bumped into Jim. The cardinal archbishop of New York had become his rabbi at One Police Plaza. Jim was drinking a glass of exquisite white wine. The Cassidys had their own fucking grapes and figs.

"Laddie," Jim said, "how's life?" And then he looked into Caroll's eyes. "Pay no mind to me at all. I'm talkative when I get into my cups. A bitter old man."

"What are you bitter about?"

"Isaac Sidel."

Caroll had to hide his own bitter laugh. "I can't discuss police business, Cardinal Jim."

"That's the problem. It aint police business. Isaac's declared himself emperor of Manhattan. He'd like to bring down the whole Board of Ed. I can't allow that. I have sons and daughters in the public schools. I talked to Isaac about you. Did he mention that?"

"Yes, but—"

"I wasn't doing you any favors. Mind, I love Diana. But I don't see why you have to guard pianos for Isaac Sidel. He doesn't have the City seal on his arse."

"Jim, did one of your monsignors track me to Harlem last Saturday night?"

"I have my spies, same as Isaac . . . and you've been worrying your wife. She's not so happy about these midnight treks. Sherwood Forest, that's the place for Caroll Brent."

"Dee said something to you?"

"No, no. I overheard a conversation. I'm a terrible eavesdropper. I have a donkey's ears."

And the cardinal slipped away with his glass of wine into the depths of that living room. Caroll climbed up the stairs of the duplex and entered the vast employ of Diana's kitchen. It could have been the galley on board some monumental ship. Diana had a pair of sous chefs, but *she* did most of the cooking. She'd gone to a cooking school in Paris.

He approached her while she stirred a white chocolate pudding. She had short blond hair and the legs of a gallant pony, this billion-dollar wife of Caroll's. Financiers shuddered when she came into a room, because she was Cassidy's daughter. She had her own full-time accountant, who buried Caroll's income within the book-long pages of Diana's tax returns. He was like a baby inside the household. But he loved her, and Diana's millions only brought him grief.

She had purple eyes. Her nose was perfect. Her mouth was slightly crooked. Her neck was shaped like a bishop's stick. It still excited him to stand near Dee, sniff her perfume in the midst of all her concentration on the pudding. But she could feel Caroll behind her, and she dismissed the sous chefs. "Darling," she said. "We have guests. I have to be down in a minute. I can't leave Cardinal Jim alone. He'll take out his poker deck and make paupers of everybody. So give me one little squeeze."

He kissed her while the pudding bubbled, half his face inside her mouth, but he could sense that something was wrong. She'd been like a sleepwalker in bed during the last month. Some corner of her had turned remote. Caroll wondered if it was family business. He couldn't seem to provide Papa Cassidy with an heir. Dee had gone to the best gynecologists. There was nothing wrong with her . . . or with Caroll's sperm count. But they couldn't make a child.

He wondered about something else. All that pulling away from him. Did she have a lover? He was terrified of losing Dee, not the Park Avenue "mansion" and all the other trappings of their life. He had nightmares of Dee with another man.

"Jim says you've been complaining about my schedule. You shouldn't be talking to him about police affairs."

Her face widened. "Caroll, I didn't."

"I could quit and become a bloodhound for some fancy lawyer."

"Caroll, I wouldn't want you to quit. I married a policeman. But I wish you didn't have to go sneaking up to Harlem in the middle of the night. I worry about you. You don't have a home base . . . I loved to visit you in Central Park."

"It's temporary," he said. "I'm on a case." It was a lie, of course. He was living on Isaac's crazy moon, setting up wiretaps, dogging Maria Montalbán, persecuting little Rosen. He'd become the bloodhound of the local school boards.

He went downstairs together with Dee. Heads turned. The company flowed in her direction, except for Stewart Hines, the junk-bond king, who handed Caroll a piece of blue paper. The blue paper was the signature of Caroll's shylock. It was a cancellation ticket. Caroll was holding the vig, *all* the interest he owed on his debts to Fabiano Rice.

"I can't accept this, Mr. Hines."

"Caroll, I'm doing someone a favor, that's all. I'm the middle-man. I was asked to deliver this note to you."

"Come on, Mr. Hines. How innocent can you be? I've heard you kill half a dozen companies on Diana's upstairs phone . . . moving bonds around. That's your business. But you shouldn't be carrying this paper. It concerns a particular shylock and me."

"Fabiano's a friend of mine. I used to be his broker. And he said, 'If you're seeing Caroll, please tell him there's no more vig.' "

Caroll couldn't punch Hines at Diana's own party.

"I'm sorry, Mr. Hines, but I can't accept this." And he stuffed the blue ticket into Hines' pants.

He couldn't seem to locate the shylock. Fabiano wasn't at any of his usual haunts. Caroll wondered if the Rubinos were having a war party, and the shylock was sitting somewhere in the dark. But Fabiano made his living out on the street. He had to circulate with his own money. He had to collect the vig, or he wouldn't have been much of a moneylender.

And then, while Caroll was chasing his own tail, the shylock suddenly showed. It felt like some abracadabra, a loanshark's trick. Caroll was sitting at his favorite lunch counter, a dive on Clinton Street. Fabiano appeared with his bodyguard. He looked like an art dealer. He was a small, elegant man. Caroll had gone to him in the first place because there was nothing vulgar about Fabiano Rice. And Fabiano wasn't close to the Cassidys.

"Ah, piccolino," he said, "come sta?" as if the whole world were made of good little Italian boys.

And Caroll didn't answer with his usual "bene." He wasn't in the mood to play with this moneylender. "You've insulted me, maestro," he said.

Fabiano sat down away from the window, pinching the pleats of his pants. He ordered an egg sandwich in some melodic lan-guage that only countermen could understand.

"Now tell me why you are so cross?"

"You brought a third party into our agreement. That particular man happens to know my wife."

"But he's discreet, piccolino. I wouldn't harm you in family matters. And I have my honor to protect. It's a third party who has to release you from your vig."

"Why do I deserve such kindness, maestro?"

"Let's say you have an admirer, a friend."

"And that admirer used his influence with Jerry DiAngelis to put the squeeze on my own shylock."

"Foolish boy, consider it a gift from God."

"A god named Isaac Sidel."

"I am not in the habit of bending to Hebrew police commissioners. But you must take the documento. That is the law." And he returned to Caroll the crumpled piece of blue paper. "The debt remains, piccolino. But now it has no attachments."

The egg sandwich he ate could have been a delicacy prepared by Diana's own hands. The shylock's table manners were like a piece of music.

"Good-bye, piccolino, good-bye."

But it depressed Caroll to have his vig erased like that, and not even know who his benefactor was. He couldn't say why, but he thought of little Rosen. Perhaps it was because Rosen was in the neighborhood. Caroll often had premonitions of doom. That was cop country.

He'd lost his appetite. And he was bound by some dumb mafioso law not to destroy Fabiano's ticket. Caroll would have to wear it like a mark of shame.

He rushed to Stanton Street. Little Rosen's door wasn't locked. Caroll had gone back into that fourth dimension. He didn't have to reach very far. Little Rosen was in his bedroom hanging from a light fixture. He'd knotted different neckties to make his hangman's tree. Caroll cut him down from the ceiling with a pocketknife. He heard the beginnings of a cough. He called an ambulance. The dead man wasn't dead.

4

He sat with little Rosen on the way to the hospital. The medic didn't want him in the ambulance. But Caroll had discovered Rosen, and Caroll was a cop.

"Brent," Rosen whispered, coming out of a bloodless sleep. "I'm not a squealer."

"I never said you were."

The medic glared at Caroll. "Are you collecting evidence, you son of a bitch? Is that why you came on the ride? To badger this man?"

Caroll couldn't even get angry. The medic had worked on little Rosen for twenty minutes, massaging him, forcing air into his lungs, connecting him up to a portable machine that served as Rosen's diaphragm. Rosen defended Caroll while the diaphragm breathed in and out. "He's my friend."

"You shut up," the medic told him, and little Rosen returned to his bloodless sleep. He held Caroll's fist, and Caroll felt like some betrayer, as if he'd fashioned that cord of neckties. Isaac's hangman.

The ambulance arrived at Beekman Downtown Hospital on Gold Street. Little Rosen was wheeled through the emergency doors, and Caroll was only one more meddler. He waited outside. He must have been napping on his feet. Suddenly the whole school board materialized, every fucking officer of One B. They stood like dream people—silent, scornful—and Caroll thought of a play he'd seen with Diana at Circle In The Square. Six or seven characters standing like ghosts on the stage, looking for the guy who created them.

The officers wouldn't take their eyes off him. They weren't alone. Maria Montalbán had come to Beekman Downtown. Montalbán wasn't a ghost. He had a little gold star in his left ear. His heels were very high.

"Cabrón," he said. "Isaac's little fairy. You think I don't know how you spy on us? You come to our board meetings and pretend you're a concerned parent. You invent names for children you never had. You call yourself 'Mr. Margolis.' You plant microphones in our office. I could tell the chancellor. But I don't. Mr. Policeman, what's your name?"

"Steven Margolis," Caroll said. He had an alias for every school board in Manhattan.

"Well, Mr. Margolis, fuck yourself. I am Maria Montalbán, superintendent of District One B. You put my best man into the hospital."

"I didn't put him there. I found him trying to hang himself."

"Because you wanted to make him a stoolie, Mr. Margolis, alias Detective Brent. And he wouldn't snitch. Did you tell him we'd all go to jail? Here I am. Arrest me. Go on. I steal supplies. I do drugs. Yes or no?"

"Yeah, you steal, Montalbán."

"And you're Cassidy's son-in-law. Who's the bigger thief, me or him?"

"But he doesn't take from children."

"Mr. Policeman, you have my school board in front of you. They appointed me. Not the chancellor. Ask them what I steal."

Caroll searched that line of faces. He couldn't catch a single bump of sympathy. He decided to leave.

Maria Montalbán shouted at him.

"Keep away from Rosen."

He was sick of playing a submarine. He surfaced at One Police Plaza. Isaac's angel. He had no trouble getting to the commissioners' floor. The First Dep, Carlton Montgomery III, aka Sweets, who'd been the acting commissioner while Isaac was in the can, stopped to say hello. Sweets was a black giant, six foot six. He didn't have a bug in his ass. He would have made a better PC.

"How goes it, Caroll? Isaac have you hopping around?"

"Sort of," Caroll said.

"Folks are beginning to miss you at Sherwood Forest."

The First Dep didn't approve of submariners, but he wouldn't go against Sidel.

"Hey, Caroll, remember me to your wife."

Diana got along with the giant. All the Cassidys did. But Cardinal Jim didn't want a black PC. Jim was patron saint of the Police Department, and he could only maneuver in an Irish universe. He didn't mind a sheenie or two. Sidel was as good as an Irishman. The PC had a brogue. And he had a daughter who was half Irish. Caroll was the lone WASP of One PP. But his wife was a mick, even if she was worth half a billion dollars.

Isaac wasn't happy to see him.

"Caroll, you broke our cover."

"Sorry, chief, but I didn't want to stand under the Williamsburg Bridge. Rosen tried to kill himself. I thought you might be interested."

"It could have waited," Isaac said, with that mad streak in his eye.

"Rosen might not agree. Besides, we're fucked. Montalbán made me."

"So what?"

"Isaac, he knows who I am. He berated me in front of his school board. They were all there . . . at the hospital."

"I'll bet. Like a bloody soccer team."

"Can't you consider for one second that they might have been concerned for Rosen?"

"Hearts and flowers," Sidel said.

"Yeah, hearts and flowers. But I like little Rosen. And I can't be your submarine if Montalbán has my badge number. So send me back to Sherwood Forest, will you please?"

"No."

"Why did you pluck me out of the dark? I was doing time in the Bronx. Why'd you pick me up?"

"It's your name," Isaac said. "I saw it on the promotions list. 'Caroll.' That was Whitey Lockman's real name."

"Who's Whitey Lockman?"

"Christ," Sidel said. "He was the sweetest first baseman the New York Giants ever had."

"Isaac, I was in kindergarten when the Giants left New York. I never saw them play. And I don't even like baseball."

"That's barbaric," Isaac said.

"But you picked me out of a fucking file because my name is Caroll and I reminded you of some schmuck in the grandpa league?"

"Don't say that about Whitey Lockman. I might get mad."

"And will you slap me around? How can I get on your shit list . . . or do I have to resign?"

"You wouldn't resign," Isaac said, a little wounded. "You're a cop."

"I'm not a cop," Caroll said. "I'm a submariner. I spy for you. I save pianos. I threaten little men who try to hang themselves."

"Should I grieve for Rosen? All right, I'll grieve. But he's still Maria Montalbán's private bookkeeper. He still traded drugs. He kept Montalbán's rotten accounts."

"And I cultivated Rosen for you. I groomed him like any

pigeon. But it's too late. I can't go to board meetings. Maria Montalbán will notify every district in town. He'll prepare a rap sheet on me. He'll put my face on the wall."

"Let him," Isaac said. "You'll grow a mustache. You'll dye your hair . . . I can't train another submariner. It's too risky."

"But you're ready to risk my ass. Just because my name is Caroll."

"That's how I found you. In the file. But it's different now. It has nothing to do with names."

"You're not naked, Isaac. You could always rely on your secret service, your fucking Ivanhoes."

"They're disbanded. The Justice Department made me close my shop."

"So I have to walk point for you. I have to take spears in the chest . . . like Manfred Coen."

Blue marks appeared on Isaac's head. "Coen has nothing to do with this caper. He got careless. He was playing ping-pong . . . without his gun."

But the PC had to sit. It was his famous worm. He'd gone underground in the Bronx, turned in his badge to sit in a candy store with the Guzmanns, a gang of Peruvian pimps. The Guzmanns had given Isaac his worm. They'd been friends with Manfred Coen. And Isaac had turned Coen against them. That's how Coen got killed.

"All right," Caroll said. "I'll walk point."

The color had gone out of Sidel. He was a rootless, middle-aged child, the orphan of orphans whose dad was alive. Joel Sidel had left his family to become a portrait painter in Paris.

Isaac's lips moved. "I don't need fucking favors."

"I'll track Montalbán. But I want to know one thing. Did you get near Fabiano Rice? Did you make him release me from my vig?"

"You told me not to step on Fabiano's feet," Isaac said, suddenly interested in Caroll.

"You could have gone to Jerry DiAngelis. Or his father-in-law, the melamed."

"The melamed had a stroke. And Jerry has no clout with Fabiano. The shylock is sworn to Sal Rubino."

"Sal's dead."

"Means nothing. Fabiano is still Sal's man. Everybody thinks I murdered Sal."

Caroll couldn't keep quiet. "Didn't you, Isaac?"

"Sure. I went down to New Orleans with a Mossberg Persuader and shot Sal's head off. Are you satisfied? I'm the PC. I dance wherever I like."

He made an appointment with Stewart Hines at Hines & Neuberger of Nassau Street. Hines was reluctant to see him. But Caroll pushed. And so the junk-bond king squeezed him in between two other appointments, perhaps because of the Cassidy connection. Caroll couldn't say. But everybody at the brokerage house pampered him. People figured he was one more billionaire walking loose at Hines & Neuberger. He didn't look like a detective.

Hines' office had no view of the Brooklyn Bridge. It was locked within a world of towers. Hines must have liked that claustrophobic grid of stone upon stone. There was a constant shadow behind his desk.

"I need to know your source," Caroll said.

"Always the policeman, aren't you, Caroll?"

"Papa Cassidy wouldn't go to a shylock. It's someone else. Who's my admirer? Who's my friend?"

"Admirer?" said the junk-bond king. "You married a billionairess. That's all the admiration you need."

"Hines, don't fuck with me. Fabiano isn't important enough. When you took that blue ticket from him, you were doing someone else a favor."

"That's not illegal, you know. And I'd think twice before you start threatening me. Borrowing from a shylock might not look so good on your dossier."

"But I've got magic. Isaac Sidel."

"That man's been in jail."

"He was acquitted, Mr. Hines, or doesn't that mean something?"

"I could still go to Internal Affairs."

"Papa Cassidy supports the Police Athletic League. He has lawyers who've never lost a case. And I have wings. So start talking."

"I have nothing to say."

"You were carrying for a shylock. Why?"

"Please get out of my office," said the junk-bond king.

"Make me," Caroll said. "Call the janitor. Tell him I'm a vagrant, or whatever you like. I'm not moving, Mr. Hines, until you reveal who your source is."

"Go to hell."

"That's not nice. I'll ask Diana to poison her next pie."

"You're the one who's eating poisoned pies. Dee's not in love with you. You're her pet monkey, the cop she married."

And Caroll saw blood. He couldn't concentrate on a disappearing vig. Or School Board One B. Or Carlos Maria Montalbán. Or Isaac Sidel, the Pink Commish, who was in love with Joseph Stalin. He saw blood. He traveled around Hines' desk and began to throttle the junk-bond king.

"Have you been sleeping with my wife?"

Spittle appeared on Hines' mouth. His tongue waggled like a crazy fish. His eyes grew sleepy. Caroll let him go. He could have killed the junk-bond king. Anything about Diana seemed to conjure up an amazing jealousy. He left the brokerage house.

He stood on Nassau Street. He could see the Stock Exchange at the bottom of the hill. He remembered all the lions' heads near the roof and the stone figures in the front wall, toiling in some strange manner, men with their testicles sticking out. He'd visited the Exchange when he was a boy, arriving with his junior-high-school class from the Rockaways. His teacher, Mr. Frost, had crumpled pants. Frost was an old-time anarchist. He called the Exchange "God's house of gold." Caroll went up to the visitors' gallery with his class. He couldn't keep his eyes off the trading pit. He'd never seen so much activity in one enormous room. It was more compressed than the beach at Coney Island. Frost ranted, but Caroll didn't care. He loved the mad motion and music coming from that cave.

They went to the Woolworth Building. Caroll adored the blue-green glass in the barreled ceiling of the lobby. Frost babbled about robber barons and pirates. But Caroll couldn't complain about a pirate who provided so much glass.

They went to the old Police Headquarters on Centre Street. It had its own lions and glass chandeliers. Frost muttered about the hostages who were held in the basement, the beatings that had occurred in the halls. But Caroll only saw the cops who took his classmates around. A young deputy inspector was kind to him. All the kids called him "chief." The deputy inspector had sideburns and a balding head. It was Sidel, who was taking time off from undercover work to brief some schoolchildren. Sidel was a sucker for kids. That's how Caroll had met the Pink Commish.

But Sidel stopped giving tours. He had his own team at the Police Athletic League. He was married to the worm in his gut. He made Caroll pick on little Rosen. And Rosen was lying in a cubby at Beekman Downtown, an assistant principal who moonlighted for Maria Montalbán.

Caroll went to his diner on Clinton Street. He had three cups of coffee that tasted like sweet tar. Caroll had no worm to feed. The counterman winked at Caroll and pointed to the telephone. "Kiddo, it's for you."

No one had ever called him at the diner. Caroll picked up the phone.

"Who is it?" he asked, like a kid from junior high who'd never finished that tour.

"An admirer."

Caroll felt like a bride. "When can we meet?"

"Right now."

"What should I do?"

"Sit. Drink another cup of coffee. I'll be there, Caroll. Goodbye."

5

The bride drank more coffee. He watched the counterman's clock. He waited an hour. His "date" didn't show. He wondered if Maria Montalbán were setting him up. He didn't trust school superintendents with gold stars in their ears.

"Fuck you, Mr. Benefactor, whoever you are."

He paid the counterman and stepped outside. A white stretch limo was waiting for him. It looked like a long sculpted beetle with antennas and wheels. Caroll didn't knock. He climbed into the back seat. There was a whole world of glass between him and the driver. There was a monstrous TV, a sink, and a sofa. Caroll was alone. He could have been inside the belly of a whale.

The driver headed toward the Brooklyn Bridge. Caroll could see all the wires from his window. He had a curious kind of weightlessness. He was a hillbilly from the Rockaway peninsula. And the bridge seemed to mark a freedom for Caroll, a passage outside Manhattan's stone walls. He could have called his wife on the car's cellular phone, but he'd have talked to Diana's social secretary. Dee was seldom at home.

So he sat inside the white whale. He had several glasses of Scotch and soda. He listened to Mozart, and his policeman's life began to bleed off him. He dialed Beekman Downtown Hospital, and after screaming at a few nurses he got little Rosen on the line. Caroll was very drunk. For some reason he started to cry.

"I'll protect you, Rosen. You don't have to be a fucking rat fink bastard. I don't want you planning any more suicide parties, you hear?"

Little Rosen was also crying. "You shouldn't have saved me," he said.

"Come on, you'll be all right."

"I betrayed my own charges, Mr. Brent. I lied to children. You shouldn't have saved me."

"It's Montalbán. He fucked your head. He's an evil magician."

"No. You could never understand our budgeting. It's medieval. He stole to keep us alive."

"I'll break his balls," Caroll said. "He took advantage of you. He pressured you to sell his drugs."

"There was no pressure."

Suddenly a nurse got back on the line. "Who is this?"

"Detective Caroll Brent . . . of Sherwood Forest. I mean, Central Park."

"I know what you mean," the nurse said. And she hung up on Caroll.

He drank another Scotch and soda. He looked outside the window. "I can't believe it," he said. The white whale had taken him back to the Rockaways. He was in his home country. Beach 101st Street, where he'd looked across the channel as a kid, across the marshes, and seen the lights of Manhattan like a spectacular electric bell.

"I can't fucking believe it."

They drove across the Atlantic Beach Bridge, into Nassau County, where his dad had liked to fish. Caroll should have been born in a whalers' town. Then he might have struggled with his forebears. A Brent among Brents. Not a cop with a gold shield, a refugee from Sherwood Forest, assigned as a submarine to Isaac Sidel. But he wouldn't have met Diana in some fisherman's bog.

They got to Long Beach, among all the retirement hotels,

kosher and nonkosher homes for the rich and the poor, Medicaid factories and mills. It saddened Caroll to think of these endless colonies.

The limo stopped on West Broadway, in the heart of some retirement lane. Caroll got out, and it felt as if the car had disgorged him, vomited him out onto a little sea of grass. Caroll was in front of the Oceancrest Manor, a dump that was decorated with porches. One more Medicaid mill. He climbed the front porch, said "Hello?"

No one answered him, and Caroll figured the driver had parked near the wrong house. The Oceancrest Manor seemed deserted enough. The walls hadn't been painted in years. The windows were chipped. The porches were treacherous. They sagged and sank in the middle. And Caroll had to laugh. He wondered if the Oceancrest were a whaling boat that had been bumped onto land and forgotten in some fisherman's dream. He was about to retreat when the front door opened.

Caroll ducked inside. The Oceancrest was dark and dusty. Two men with shoulder holsters greeted him. They didn't have the stink of cops. They were simple soldiers of some mob that had decided to take a sea cure. They weren't native to Nassau County. Caroll could tell. They didn't ask him about the Smith & Wesson he was carrying. They didn't search Caroll. They excused themselves and wheeled a man into the front room. The man wore a blanket. He had enormous pits in his face. His scalp was practically gone. His head looked like a blue ball. But he wasn't that much older than Caroll. He must have survived some terrible firestorm. Caroll had pity for him, whoever he was. Only one of his eyes worked. The other seemed to wander off into phantom space.

He held out his hand. It was as pocked as the rest of him. Caroll shook the hand. He liked this curious invalid.

"I'm sorry if I caused you trouble with that blue ticket. But it was my way of introducing myself . . . from a distance. I'm Sal Rubino."

Rubino's dead, Rubino's dead, Caroll muttered. "You didn't die in New Orleans, did you?"

"But your sweet boss left me for dead . . . him and Jerry DiAngelis. They killed my cousins, the Leonardo brothers."

"Pimps from Royal Street."

"Ah, you know the Quarter," Sal said.

"A little. I've been there. To a couple of charity balls."

"With the wife?"

"Yes," Caroll said. "She loves Mardi Gras. She went to school in New Orleans. Sophie Newcomb College."

"Never heard of the place."

"It's part of Tulane," Caroll said. *I have to talk. I have to talk. Or the son of a bitch will shoot my eyes out.*

"Tulane, yes. They have their own fucking float during Mardi Gras."

"My wife endowed a couple of chairs at Tulane."

"Chairs?" Sal Rubino said, while his soldiers stared at Caroll as if he were a moon-crazed child.

"Yes. Academic chairs."

"You mean fucking professorships."

"Exactly. One in the sciences and one in the liberal arts. And her dad is helping them to build a high-powered telescope."

"Patrons, your wife's people. Like the Medicis."

"Sal, what's a Med-itch-ee?" the shorter soldier asked.

"Shaddap," Sal said.

"Yeah, like the Medicis," Caroll said. "But they're not Italian."

"Been to Rome?"

"Yes. At the last Jubilee."

"The wife's religious, eh? A good Catholic girl. Well, the Leonardos weren't pimps. They were good boys."

"If you say so," Caroll said.

"Don't mock me. I'm a fucking zombie with a brain stem. I can't walk. I can barely shit. Sometimes I have half an erection. My joint looks like it's covered with chicken pox."

The soldiers started to laugh.

"Shaddap," Sal said. "And take a walk, will ya, Angelo? With the kid."

"And leave you alone with him?" the shorter soldier said.

"He can't hurt me where I aint been hurt. He's a good boy."

"I don't like him," Angelo said.

"You don't get paid to like. Now get the fuck out of here before I lose my temper. I'm worse than a snake. My spit has enough acid in it to bite through your head."

"But who's going to wheel ya?" the tall soldier asked.

"He'll wheel me. Isaac's boy. Now blow."

And the soldiers withdrew deeper into the house.

"You can't hire talent these days," Sal Rubino said. "They're either stupid or greedy. Or both. And if you slap them, they rat on you and run into the witness-protection program. It's a hard time for employers."

And Caroll almost smiled. He still liked Sal. "If they're your soldiers, give them some kind of sergeant's test."

"They'd never pass, no matter who the fuck administered it. They're mental dwarfs. Wheel me into the light, will ya?"

Caroll took the grips of the wheelchair and placed Sal near the window.

"The Leonardos died for nothing. Did you know that? They were in love with Isaac's girlfriend, Margaret Tolstoy. Ever meet the lady?"

"No."

"She's a witch. Born in Roumania. She worked for the KGB, the FBI, you name it. A slut. I was crazy about her. That's my weakness. I'll do anything for a woman. Even now when I can't get it up. Well, this Margaret kills a man of mine. My captain, Eddie Stafano. Then she runs down to New Orleans, seduces the Leonardo brothers for some Justice Department hotshot. Both dummies wanted to marry Margaret . . . and that's where I come in. I mean, Margaret's in her fifties. She's not right for these boys. And we were preparing to ice the lady, give her some permanent grief, even though the boys didn't have their hearts in it. They stall and stall. Isaac catches us in a sausage factory where we intended to finish the job. His backup is that fuck, Jerry DiAngelis. They shoot the goddamn shit out of us. The boys don't survive. But I'm lyin' still like an angel. I can't move. A fucking farmer finds me. Comes right in off the bayou. So I whisper in his ear, because I'm a thinking man. The farmer makes a call. My friends arrive. They whack a bum who's sleeping outside the factory. They substitute him for me, the new, dead Sal Rubino, who's really dead, and they hide me in a little hospital outside Baton Rouge. It took five fucking surgeons to take all that poisoned lead out of me and sew me together, if you can call this 'together.' Because I'm a corpse, Mr. Caroll Brent."

"Corpses can't tell stories," Caroll said.

"You're humoring me."

"I'm not. I just didn't know you were alive."

"That's privileged information. Swear to me you won't tell Isaac."

"How can I do that, Sal? I'm a fucking cop."

"I took care of your vig."

"I'm a cop."

"What if I told you you'll never leave this house."

"I still couldn't swear. Or if I did, it would only be a lie."

"Now I trust you. I don't give a shit what Isaac learns. Tell him what you want."

"Sal, why did you interfere with my vig?"

"I want to hire you."

"How? To spy on Isaac?"

"No. To kill him. I could hire plenty of hitters. But it's no revenge unless you do it. I want him to feel it in his fucking gut. I want him to get it up close, from his own boy."

"It's a pretty plan," Caroll said, shivering in the dark. "But why should I kill Isaac?"

"For money maybe. Because I'll cancel your whole fucking debt and I'll make it so you'll never have to borrow another dime. But that's not the main reason. The man's been using you, kid."

"He uses everybody. That's his nature. He's the PC."

"He sent you after Montalbán, right? As a solo, a submarine. But what if I tell you now that you were only a decoy, a duck, that the man is using you to hide a full-scale operation. You were put there to soothe Maria Montalbán, to calm him into fucking tranquility."

"I'd say you're full of shit."

"Do I have to give you the names of Isaac's task force? Let's start with your old boyfriend, Joey Barbarossa."

"Barbarossa? Isaac hates his guts."

"It's a scam, kid. Isaac's been grooming him for months. Who would ever believe it? His personal commandos, a little squad of submarines."

"How do you know all this?"

"I have my squeal in the Department. I always did. It's not corruption, Caroll. You buy a little. You sell a little. And then I piece it together."

"But you're sitting in a wheelchair."

"So what? I haven't lost my tubes. I've always been a thinker."

"I don't care how many commandos Isaac has. I wouldn't kill him."

"I'll wait," Sal said.

"Dream, Sal, because that's all it is."

"I promise you, Caroll. I won't make my move without ya. You're my man."

"I'm going to start paying Fabiano his vig."

"You took the blue ticket. You can't give it back."

"Then call your soldiers, Sal. Tell them to whack me."

"What for? You've been a kosher kid. I'll wait. When the time comes I'll give you the gun."

"It's going to be a long, long wait, Sal. They'll have to build you another wheelchair."

"What's a wheelchair? Nothin' but sticks. I'll wait."

6

He took the same route back, in the white limousine. He could have gone to One Police Plaza. But he believed that crazy man in the wheelchair. Sal wouldn't kill Isaac without Caroll. Still, he should have confronted Isaac about those other commandos. He didn't. He went home to his wife. Dee had returned from some party or board meeting. She had cold cream on her face. There was that distance between them he couldn't define, as if she'd gone into her own fourth dimension. He didn't tell her about that man in the wheelchair, Rubino, who'd risen like Christ. They made love. It was like some brutal exercise. He tied her arms to the bed because she liked it. He went deep inside her, held her bound wrists, and came like a hippopotamus. She could always draw noises out of Caroll. But he heard no noises from her.

He untied her arms. She laughed once, like a pony, and he wanted to ask her what the hell was wrong. If she did have a lover, Caroll would have to waste the son of a bitch. He smiled. Perhaps he ought to borrow a gun from Sal.

"Sweetheart," he said. "Couldn't we have a holiday tomorrow?"

"Holiday?" Her eyes were closed. He'd never survive with-

—38—

out Dee. He was her child husband, the submariner, Caroll
Brent.

"You're never here, and now you want to play. We're giving
a party tomorrow for the PAL. You know that."

Diana was grand duchess of the Police Athletic League. The
Cassidys supplied baseball uniforms, gloves, and bats. Cardinal
Jim and the Pink Commish both managed teams for the PAL. It
was a world of Whitey Lockmans, but Caroll was the odd man
out. He'd never even been to a baseball game.

"Couldn't you have Susan prepare your agenda . . . and buy
the hors d'oeuvres?" Susan was her social secretary. And she
was much more vital to Diana than the submariner himself.

"I wouldn't cater a party like that," Dee said. "I'm doing the
hors d'oeuvres."

He'd forgotten for a moment that his wife was a world-class
chef.

"We played a lot when you were in Central Park. You could
always come home for a quickie . . . or take my panties off in
the police garage."

"Behind the motor scooters," Caroll said. "On one of the late
tours . . . when half the precinct was asleep. But I'm not at
Sherwood Forest anymore."

"Is that my fault?"

The lovemaking had accomplished very little. Caroll couldn't
seem to crawl back inside Diana's nest. He was a boarder at
the "mansion." It was where he kept his socks and service revolver . . .

He was afraid to fall asleep. He would dream of her with
another man. And he couldn't tell the man's face in his dreams.
It was some half stranger, indistinct. He dozed through the night
with Diana beside him.

He went to Sherwood Forest in the morning, walked into his
old precinct, a two-story converted brick-and-stone stable that

was like no other precinct on the planet. There were no loiterers around, no bombed-out buildings. The traditional green lamps were tinier at Sherwood Forest and had a much softer glow. The attic was right over your head. There were no horses at the stable, only scooters and cars and ALTs, all-terrain vehicles that could follow any bandit across the veldt of Central Park. Caroll had loved this place, his own curiosity shop, a relic from another century. There was violence in all its five sectors, Adam, Boy, Charlie, David, and Eddie, and its forty foot patrols, but it didn't seem to damage the fabric of Sherwood Forest. The precinct itself was in David, Sector D, at the Eighty-sixth Street Transverse.

The desk sergeant barely said hello. Two patrolmen were playing chess, and ignored Caroll. The detectives' door was shut. His old commander, Captain Lucas White, couldn't afford to be too unfriendly. He was looking at Isaac's angel. White's office was near the women's locker room. He was the one man at Sherwood Forest who had his own toilet. He would watch the female officers parade in and out of their lockers, or hide in the can and read for hours. But he had a crazy intuition about crime in the park. And he'd once been very fond of Caroll.

"How's life at One PP?"

"Come on, Cap. I'm a submariner. I surface from time to time. East Harlem one day, Crown Heights the next."

"And you just happened to float in here."

"No. I was looking for Barbarossa."

"Barbarossa's doing his ping-pong . . . like Manfred Coen. And Caroll, do me a favor. Don't come around again. You leave a shadow. And it might cover us all in shit."

"I get ya, Cap," Caroll said. He went out the precinct door, crossed to the other side of the stable, and walked into the old muster room, which had been turned into a lounge. The lounge had several upholstered chairs and a ping-pong table. Barbarossa, a thirty-six-year-old detective from Sherwood Forest, was playing ping-pong with an auxiliary policewoman. It was like foreplay, Caroll figured. Barbarossa never even had his eye on the ball. Ping-pong had become a sacrificial game under Sidel. There were no tournaments or championships in the Department. Manfred Coen had died in the middle of a game. Coen had left his curse. No one wanted to be another Blue Eyes.

"Joe, can I talk to you for a minute?"

"Talk," Barbarossa said.

"Not at the table."

Caroll knew that Barbarossa was a thief. Barbarossa sold drugs. He was also the most decorated cop in the City. He'd done two tours in Nam. He was the second- or third-last Marine to get out of Nam alive. He was in-country during the whole fucking fall of Saigon. That's where he'd learned to play ping-pong. He was champ of the Embassy compound. But ping-pong couldn't get him a promotion in Isaac's Department. He'd busted too many heads. And Isaac had banished him to the veldt.

"Excuse me, darling," Barbarossa said to the auxiliary policewoman. He wore a white glove when he played. That was Barbarossa. He would beat your brains out with that same glove. He'd rescued old women from hatchet-bearing husbands. And he'd probably killed some pushers during a big score. He was corrupt and crazy. And he was festering in Sherwood Forest. He only had the woods . . . and a ping-pong table. He'd been Caroll's partner. But that was a long time ago.

"Joey, are you freelancing for Isaac?"

Barbarossa laughed. The scars along his mouth behaved like inchworms.

"Isaac's been trying to hump me for years. He put me in this morgue."

"But I've seen him turn a feud around for his own benefit. Joey, are you chasing Maria Montalbán?"

"Montalbán's my hero."

"But are you chasing him?"

"No."

"I don't believe you," Caroll said.

"Buddy, kiss my ass."

Caroll had to go sleuthing on his own. He took a train to the Lower East Side. He looked for suspicious panel trucks where Isaac could have placed a soundman. But he couldn't find any more submariners. He looked for undercover cops. He crossed Montalbán's district, picked it clean. There weren't any floaters. He returned uptown and dressed for Diana's party. The cardinal had brought kids from his baseball team. The kids wore cleats. Caroll bumped into Lieutenant Sarah Potts, police liaison to the PAL, which had its own civilian director. But there was always some kind of police presence in the PAL shop.

He'd been seeing Lieutenant Potts until Diana came along. Sarah was only a sergeant then.

"What's it like," she asked, "fucking a billion dollars?"

"I'm not sure," Caroll said.

"We would have gotten engaged without that bitch. Does she suck you better that I did?"

Then Jim arrived, and Lieutenant Potts, who was Catholic, kissed his ring. "My two soldiers," the cardinal said. "Sarah darling, you aren't letting them shove you around at PAL, are you?"

"I kick ass, Jim. I always do," she said, looking at Caroll.

"My own little daughter in Christ . . . I have to question this thug. Will you forgive us, dear?"

And the cardinal drew Caroll away. "Can't you make some peace with Lieutenant Potts?"

"What can I do?" Caroll said. "I ditched her for Dee."

"Then take her to lunch. Flirt with her for five minutes."

"Forgive me, Cardinal Jim. But she'd want to go under the table."

"She can't force you, Caroll. You're a free agent. God did give you a soul . . . you wounded the woman, for Christ's sake."

"I try, Jim. But I only make it worse."

"Because your heart's not in it. You've gone wild in the streets. You're creating havoc."

"I haven't done a thing."

"Don't argue with a prince of the Church. If Isaac won't pull you, I will."

And the cardinal went off to chat with his team, the Manhattan Knights. The kids adored him. He was the most powerful manager in the PAL. He didn't look to the Cassidys. He provided his team with a bus, a travel allowance, and a variety of catcher's masks and mitts. He was ruthless in his search for talent. He raided whatever school he could, public or private. The Knights sat at the top of their division the last seven years. Caroll couldn't understand the mumbo jumbo of baseball, but he got a kick out of this cardinal who could dominate an entire league.

Jim basked in the luxury of his Knights, with their red stockings and their blue-billed caps, until another man walked into the party. He looked like a circus bear in boy's clothes. He had his own billed cap and gray socks. It was Isaac Sidel in the uniform of the Delancey Street Giants. The Pink Commish had come to advertise his own team. He'd outmaneuvered Jim. He was grabbing all the attention. What other PC would wear knickers in front of fifty guests?

Caroll started to smile. Then he saw Diana whirl around the bear. He noticed a curious delight in her eyes. The bear had touched her in places Caroll no longer could. Now he was able to read those nightmares of his. The stranger who'd been caressing Diana in his dreams had also worn a uniform. That's why Caroll couldn't recognize him. It wasn't the uniform of a soldier or a cop. It was a ballplayer. And while Diana laughed, here in her living room, Caroll thought of homicide.

He could have warned Isaac about Sal Rubino. He didn't say a word.

It was the cardinal who danced toward Isaac with a purple face.

"You're a villain, you are, Isaac Sidel. Competing with my lads. They got all dressed up, and you had to steal their thunder with this charade."

"I also have a team, Your Eminence. The Delancey Street Giants."

"I'm aware of that."

"And they don't have a chance. You threaten the umpires with damnation if they make a call for my men. I have to put on their colors, or they might disappear."

"I didn't threaten," the cardinal said. "I argued a couple of calls. That's my privilege. I am manager of the Knights."

"And cardinal archbishop," Isaac said. "I'm only a commissioner, Your Eminence."

"Formal with me, aint you, Isaac? I'm the bad bishop of baseball. Don't make a spectacle of yourself. Or I'll slap you in front of the boys."

The big bear smiled like a baby. Cardinal Jim was his rival *and* his friend. But he turned gloomy when he glanced at Caroll.

"What were you doing up at Sherwood Forest?" he whispered in Caroll's ear. His baseball cap was a size too small. It hugged his crown like an idiot's hat.

"Looking for submariners like myself."

"What submariners?"

"Come on, Isaac. You have a whole other detail covering Maria Montalbán."

"Who told you that?"

"Donald Duck."

"I don't have a detail . . . Montalbán's dangerous. I asked Barbarossa to look after you a little."

"Your favorite detective."

"He's still a good cop out on the street. And he was your partner. He broke you in."

"And you're mounting an invasion against Montalbán and his school board."

Isaac grinded his teeth. "Caroll, not here . . . we can have a long powwow under the bridge."

"Afraid of Jim?"

"Shhh," Isaac said, a bear in a baseball beanie.

"Rubino's alive," Caroll said.

Nothing moved on the bear's face. There wasn't a twitch or a blink.

"Did you hear me, Isaac? Sal Rubino crawled out of that grave you prepared for him in New Orleans. The shotgun party didn't work."

"How do you know?" Isaac asked, like some bored attorney.

"I met with Sal. Yesterday. At a Medicaid mill in Long Beach. The Oceancrest Manor. It's a blind for Sal Rubino. He sits in a wheelchair. He dreams of you dead."

Isaac covered his eyes with a paw. "I am dumb. It's business as usual with the Rubinos. And I can't tell why. Jerry DiAngelis is pushed into a corner. And Rubino's captains are thriving."

"He asked me to kill you," Caroll said.

"And what did you say?"

"I told him I'd think about it."

And the bear was smiling again.

"Isaac, maybe we should continue this talk in the toilet."

"There's nothing to talk about."

"But Sal could have contracts out all over the place for your fucking head."

"Then why advertise himself to you? No, kid. I'm a public character. Rubino had plenty of chances. He could have popped me a month ago. He was sending up a kite. *Dear Isaac, I'm alive. Love from Sal.* And you were the string."

"And Margaret Tolstoy?"

The bear lost his jovial mood. "Who told you about Margaret?"

"Come on, Isaac. Half the Department knows she's your sweetheart."

"She's a fucking FBI informant," Isaac said.

"Who isn't?"

"Margaret's safe. For now."

"And yourself?"

"Sal will go to his guns. But first he wants to eat my fucking heart out."

And Isaac returned to the party, with his knickers and his shirt from the Delancey Street Giants.

7

He couldn't get that image out of his mind. The big bear making love to his wife. It was absurd, the idea of Dee and the Pink Commish. But then Caroll had to wonder. Isaac had stolen him from Sherwood Forest and sent him on some phantom patrol. And now Caroll was reduced to this mean fucking business of following his wife. He didn't care about Carlos Maria Montalbán. School Board One B could take and take. The children would have to fend for themselves. Caroll wasn't their keeper. He was a husband with a marriage that was about to sink.

He could have borrowed Dee's calendar, marked down whatever appointments her social secretary had made, but he wouldn't do it. He wasn't a thief. He was only a submariner and a spy. He tracked her for two days, slinking into bed at night, his body beside her. He would listen to her breathe. He despised himself. But he didn't stop tracking. And on the third day, when Dee was in SoHo, touring art galleries, he got a little careless. She caught him outside Leo Castelli.

"You've been following me. How many days has it been?"

"Three."

"What's it about, Caroll?"

"We haven't been getting along, and . . ."

"How can I get along with a stranger?"

"But we were always tight in bed."

"Should I close my eyes and fake it? Who should I pretend I'm fucking? Cardinal Jim? My dad? One of my sous chefs? Or my social secretary? Tell me."

"Sidel," he said.

"So that's it. You think I'm fucking Isaac. Just ask."

She slapped him while they were on the sidewalk, outside Leo Castelli.

"*Ask.*"

"Are you sleeping with Sidel?"

"Talk like a detective, darling. '*Are you fucking the PC?*' God, you're lost outside Sherwood Forest. That's why Isaac put you there. He wanted a detective with handsome teeth, some guy who could parade for the media or stroke a rich bitch. Imbecile, he was our marriage broker. If he hadn't put you in the park, how would we have met?"

"I can't tell. You were an heiress and I was a cop."

"Don't play that trick. I'm not up to it, Caroll. You're the patrician. My family is black Irish."

She started to cry. "I love you. Isn't that enough?"

She ran down the street, away from Caroll. He couldn't follow her. He was one more tracker gone awry. He'd been no more successful dogging Maria Montalbán. Perhaps he did belong in Sherwood Forest, with the squirrel patrol. All a cop needed was a bag of nuts. That was the old saying about Central Park Precinct, CPP.

He drove out to Long Beach in the silver Porsche the Cassidys had given him for his birthday. A fifth of his salary went into that car. It was eating up mechanics every six months. And Caroll was a beggar who had to borrow from Fabiano Rice. Dinners at Caravelle had put him into debt. Diana would have paid. But she was unconscious about anything to do with cash. And Caroll didn't want some kind of meal allowance. He wasn't Papa Cassidy's pet. He was a detective on loan from squirrel land.

He arrived at the Oceancrest Manor. He looked at the sagging porches, the chipped paint, the television wires on the roof that reminded him of a witch's hairdo, and he thought of Sal Rubino in his wheelchair. Sal was only one more disabled don, but why did Caroll pity him? It wasn't the wheelchair or the marks on his face. Caroll had seen worse casualties of war. Was it because Sal's life, like Caroll's, was bound to Isaac Sidel?

He had to meet with Rubino one more time, make it clear that no vigorish was going to put a gun in Caroll's hand. But he also wanted to chat with the invalid, wheel him around the hotel's front room, not as a cop, but as a fellow prisoner of Isaac's. Because no force was big enough to defeat the Pink Commish. Neither a school district nor a Mafia clan.

Caroll entered the hotel. It was as dark as the last time. "Mr. Rubino," he said, "it's me, Caroll Brent." But there were no simple soldiers to greet him. Just two men with shotguns. Caroll recognized their faces in the dark. They were commandos from the NYPD who'd strayed into Nassau County.

They laughed at Caroll. "Look, it's the little sister."

These two were called Jimson and Jakes. The PC's commandos were all alike. They wore leather jackets and dark brown boots. They modeled themselves after Isaac, who was also fond of leather, and loved to consider themselves as some "Good Gestapo." Caroll hated their guts.

"What are you doing here?" he asked.

"Waiting for Sal," Jakes said. "But we'll ask the questions, little sister."

They dug their shotguns into Caroll's belly. But they wouldn't have been so talkative if they'd meant to kill. The whole fucking scenario surrounding Isaac had begun to piss him off. They shouldn't have pointed shotguns at him on the afternoon his wife had slapped him in the face.

"Now tell us, sister, how come you're visiting Sal."

"Fuck you, Jimson. Fuck you, Jakes."

Jimson whacked Caroll's forehead with the butt of his gun. Caroll fell to the floor. He was already floating into a warmer world. His eye was wet. It was like a toke of Thai stick. Caroll was in Buddha heaven. He'd had his best tours at Sherwood Forest smoking grass with Barbarossa.

"You have a lovely car out there." That was Jakes. Caroll heard him like a horn.

"Did your wife give it to you?"

"Ah, leave the little sister alone. He likes to play with the squirrels."

"But he has to tell us why he's visiting Sal."

"Because," Caroll said, "I'm Sal's little sister," and he tackled Jakes, knocking his kneecaps out from under him. Jakes banged into Jimson. And Caroll rose out of Buddha heaven to bite Jimson's ear and dig a finger into his throat. He'd captured their shotguns. He handcuffed them back to back, with their own cuffs. They sat on their asses like silly Buddhas in black leather coats. He left the Oceancrest without wiping the blood from his eye.

His beeper sang to him as soon as he hit the Rockaways. He stopped on Channel Drive and called One PP from a phone booth.

"Nice," Isaac said. "Are you proud of yourself?"

"I thought you didn't like me to call Headquarters."

"This is an emergency. You handcuffed two of my men."

"That's because they tried to knock my brains out."

"They were interrogating you, that's all. I told them to interrogate whoever walked in."

"Isaac, since when are you a Nassau County sheriff? You can't interrogate shit."

"Watch your language. Why were you out there?"

"I was getting lonely for Sal."

"I'm beginning to believe you," Isaac said, and he hung up on his protégé, whom he'd plucked out of Central Park and sent on a crusade against the school boards. It was one more mission without an end.

He visited little Rosen at Beekman Downtown. The assistant principal was out of danger. He was all alone in a semiprivate room. Caroll had brought him some strudel from the kosher bakery on East Broadway. He supplied Rosen with a napkin, and the two of them ate like pigs, while nurses who passed the doorway stared at the blood in Caroll's eye.

"I have blackouts, Mr. Brent."

"Rosen, that's what happens when you try to hang yourself . . . has Montalbán visited you yet?"

"Every day."

And Caroll saw the bounty of those visits: a basket of fruit, a radio, a VCR.

"He's loyal," little Rosen said.

"I'm sure he is. But do me a favor, Rosen. Ask him to find a new bookkeeper, so I won't have to follow you around."

"I belong with him," little Rosen said. "I'm part of his team."

"You sound like a fucking baseball player. And I hate baseball, Rosen. People dress up in long stockings. Some of them wear fucking masks. They fight. They argue. They beat the shit out of a little ball."

"I don't play baseball, Mr. Brent. I steal."

"You shouldn't say that. You're convalescing."

"I steal from A to give to B. It's simple arithmetic. Supply and demand. We sell drugs so that some of the children can eat."

"This is a social call. I'm not hassling you."

Rosen bit into the strudel. "Detective, I appreciate your concern. But don't come again. I wouldn't want Carlos to think I was your personal stooge."

"You're not a stooge. But Carlos Montalbán is feeding himself, not any fucking kids. I've been to your school, Rosen. I've seen the kids. They look awful hungry to me."

"But did you see them before Carlos was appointed to the district? Some of them didn't have a shirt. They suffered from pellagra. They had black teeth and red skin . . . what happened to your head?"

"A squirrel bit me."

Caroll went home to the "mansion." He dreaded meeting Diana. But she was at some important tea. So he hid out in his study until he was summoned to dinner like a little boy. Caroll sat alone with his wife at a table that could seat sixteen. Diana was remorseful. "I'm sorry I slapped you. I was upset. You shouldn't follow me . . . Caroll, you have a bump, a great big bump."

"It's nothing," Caroll said.

"Are you sure? I could ring Dr. Patterson."

"I'm fine," Caroll said.

"I have been seeing Isaac. I'm worried about you. So we talk."

"About what?" Caroll asked, playing with his salad.

"About your career. I can feel your absence, Caroll . . ."

"I'm not absent," Caroll said. "What did Isaac say?"

"That you were on special assignment. It's all hush-hush. But it would be over soon."

"What else did he say?"

"That you were having some kind of money problems."

I'll kill that fuck, Caroll said to himself. Isaac must have mentioned the vig.

"Have you been gambling, Caroll? Isaac wouldn't tell me much. He's like you—so secretive."

"I'm not secretive."

"I don't care if you gamble. I'll write you a check."

"I don't want a check. And I'm not a gambler. I never was."

"We'll economize, dear. I'll fire one of the maids. And I'll contribute to your kitty."

"I don't need a kitty. I'm all right."

Should he tell Dee not to order an appetizer at Caravelle? Or else line his pockets with hundred-dollar bills? She raised money for the Metropolitan Museum of Art. She sponsored obscure Czech orchestras. She cooked for an army. She loved Caroll. But she was careless about her own money, and part of that carelessness spilled into his lap.

They didn't make love that night. Caroll was still brooding over the Pink Commish. Isaac shouldn't have seen Dee behind his back. All Caroll could do was float further and further away. He was in his own fucking latitude, where baseball or a detective's shield didn't count. He was a fisherman's boy who loved to sit on a rock with his dad and watch the whales blow. But there were no whales in Central Park.

He floated into East Harlem. He followed Montalbán's mules. School District Eleven A was Montalbán's favorite "cousin." It bordered on Central Park, overlooked the Harlem Meer and its burnt-out boathouse. The Meer had become a desolate pool, filled with junk and black water. Montalbán's men would often meet in the boathouse. One or two were teachers Montalbán had brought into his own district. They would have their breakfast in the boathouse and wander from school to school. They were bartering crayons and brooms. It bothered Caroll. All this monkey business. Montalbán had his own duchy in Manhattan. He was lord of school supplies.

Caroll took notes. He always did. And then he'd have his meets with Isaac under the Williamsburg Bridge. He was getting out. He'd give Isaac back the gold shield. He'd go to work for Papa Cassidy. Or sell Thai stick in the street. Or he'd sign on with Sal Rubino, become the guardian of Sal's wheelchair. He fashioned a conversation in his head. *Isaac, fuck you.*

He arrived in that dark, damp corner under the bridge. Isaac was late. Caroll continued to rehearse his spiel. *Are you Dee's confessor now, you son of a bitch? Leave that to Cardinal Jim.* He heard a rustling in one of the territories where the winos lived. Isaac often fed them cigarettes, got them meals at Katz's delicatessen or Ratner's on Delancey Street. When Caroll couldn't find the Pink Commish, he'd go to Ratner's and discover him at a corner table with a clutch of broken men, discussing the fate of New York City. Isaac always blended in. He looked like a bum, and the proprietor wouldn't dare throw him out. It was Caroll who ended up paying the bill, because Isaac didn't believe in cash.

But this rustling bothered him. There were no winos tonight. Caroll would have heard the crash of bottles by now, would have sniffed them, seen their outline under the bridge. He'd make a run to Ratner's, but first he stepped deeper into the dark.

He looked down at the figure of Isaac Sidel. There was a beard of blood under his mouth, and his whole chest was like a big black well. Caroll couldn't say how many times Isaac had been shot. He looked almost as dead as the Harlem Meer.

Part Two

8

The newspapers already had editions mourning Isaac Sidel. The flags at City Hall were flying low. The chief inspector was preparing the funeral. There would be a parade. Isaac would have cannons and magnificent black horses. No other Commish had been gunned down like that. Her Honor, Rebecca Karp, bawled into her handkerchief on the six o'clock news. Isaac had been on the table ten hours. Three surgeons attended to him. There was talk of a massive blood clot, damage to the brain. He was supposed to die but he didn't.

He lingered on some crazy thread. He lay in a coma at Beekman Downtown, wrapped in bandages like a mummy. He sang nonsense, like Dutch Schultz had done before *he* died. "Harry on the handle . . . one two three. Harry on the handle."

It took a retired sports writer from the *Daily News*, ninety years old, to find the key. "That's not gibberish, my friends. Isaac's appealing to the Bomber, old Harry Lieberman of the New York Giants. That's how Harry's fans would serenade him at the Polo Grounds in 'forty-three. Whenever he'd pick up a bat, the crowd would cry, 'Harry on the handle, Harry on the handle.' We'd beg him to hit one out of the park."

The whole town grew excited. Journalists sought out this forgotten Bomber as Isaac lay dying. They recalled his batting averages, his jump to the Mexican League in 'forty-six. Suddenly he was another Joe DiMaggio. Photographs appeared of Harry swinging his bat. There were remembrances from other retired reporters and old fans of Harry's. The City had a new star, a ballplayer whose life was mostly a blank. The Bomber had come out of obscurity, because a mortally wounded Commish had recited the magic formula: "Harry on the handle, one two three."

He lived in Washington Heights. He had no wife or children that anyone could see. He was all grizzled. He had huge hands. It was hard to imagine him as anyone's hero. But he'd haunted Isaac's head.

He wouldn't talk to the press. He was a member of the Christy Mathewsons, a club devoted to antiquarian baseball. The Christys wouldn't give any interviews about their silent star. And the town mourned the Polo Grounds and the New York Giants, who'd run to San Francisco in the fall of 'fifty-seven. Only a dead man like Isaac could evoke a kinder past when the Bomber patrolled center field in a ballpark that had become a Harlem housing project. But the dead man still wouldn't die.

Isaac didn't call out to Harry anymore. He had metal pins in one shoulder. He slept like a great big wounded bear.

And then Isaac opened his eyes. He couldn't talk. There was a tube in his mouth, like a curled-up cuspidor. He started to cry. He remembered who he was. He didn't want to be Sidel. He wanted to be a center fielder.

"Harry on the handle."

It took weeks for the doctors to go away. They examined all his fluids. He was in some isolation ward where he could have no guests.

"I have to see my people," Isaac said.

"Do you realize how close you were to dying?" the chief cardiologist said.

"I've been there," Isaac told him. "It's no big deal. Now can I talk to my people?"

They wheeled him into another room. Nurses shaved him and sponged his chest and back. He had bluish marks where the bullets had entered his body. They looked like the marks an arrow might make. He was like some illustrated man, with signs and symbols all over him, signs no one but Isaac could read. He saw his face in the mirror. He'd bloomed on the operating table. He was all pink.

"Sir," the chief cardiologist whispered in Isaac's ear. "I don't give a fuck about your people. You can have one guest."

"I'm not your prisoner," Isaac muttered.

"Yes you are, Mr. Sidel."

The mayor wanted to see him. She'd had roses delivered to his room every day of his long sleep. She'd offered a hundred thousand dollars of the City's cash to anyone who could identify Isaac's phantom hitter. "I'll kill the cocksucker, whoever he is." She presented herself as some sort of grieving widow. But Isaac wasn't buying the package of Becky Karp. He wanted Sweets. Not his daughter, Marilyn the Wild. Not his estranged wife Kathleen, the Florida real-estate goddess. Not his dad Joel, the portrait painter who was hiding in Paris. Not his baby brother Leo, who was in and out of alimony court. Not his sweetheart, Margaret Tolstoy, who broke up gangs for the FBI. Not Cardinal Jim, who was one of the few friends Isaac had. Not the Bomber himself. But Sweets.

Isaac's First Deputy arrived in his shirtsleeves. He had a whole Department to run without this crazy Commish. Isaac was on extended sick leave. And for the second time in two years, Carlton Montgomery III was acting police commissioner. He was much more patrician than Isaac Sidel. He'd finished college. He'd gone to law school. He could talk about Malcolm and Martin Luther King and Oliver Wendell Holmes. He could have resigned from the Department and run the Ford Foundation. He could have been the first black professor at Harvard Law.

But he wouldn't desert One PP. He was devoted to the Commish. He'd heard Isaac lecture years ago and that had galvanized him, made him fall in love with the cops. He liked the outlaw in Isaac, the curious chivalry that left him a pauper with a paycheck. But he couldn't always cover for the Commish.

Seeing him in a hospital gown, with a shaved skull, Sweets felt some remorse: he would have done anything for the outlaw, but he wouldn't ruin the Department.

"How are you, boss?"

"I'm not your boss," Isaac said. "I'm just a man in a long shirt. I have no status here."

"But you have a family. How come I get to see you first?"

"Because I don't have time for family. Talk to me, Sweets. What did the Crime Scene boys come up with?"

"Very little. Whoever hit you, Isaac, was a cool customer. He cleaned up after him. He swept the place, picked up all the shells."

"But he wasn't a magician, Sweets. He couldn't have walked around with a flashlight on his head and gathered all the spent bullets, every fucking fragment."

Isaac was pissed off. He didn't have much to do with the Crime Scene Unit. CSU occupied an office building on Fordham Road and Webster Avenue, near the bombed-out barrios of the Bronx. No one else wanted to rent the space. The lads from Crime Scene covered all five boroughs. They would arrive in their white gloves and white coats like miraculous bloodhounds. Isaac could imagine how his own crime scene must have gone. There would have been a furor at One PP. "The Commish is down, the Commish is down." And the bloodhounds would have borrowed powerful lights from Emergency Service and turned that crime scene into a movie set.

"Sweets, can't our lads even get a make on the gun?"

"I'd say you were stopped with a nine-millimeter cannon. That's only an educated guess. The impact was terrific. Crime Scene says you fell like a moose. You left little craters in the ground. You had five holes in you, Isaac. The bullets went in and out like a whistle. You shouldn't be alive."

"Our people didn't search hard enough," Isaac said. "There had to be something in the grass."

"Come on, Isaac. You can't blame CSU. The fragments they found had no fucking value. Ballistics confirmed that. Here, have a look."

Sweets handed Isaac a copper slug that resembled a slightly thickened penny. "The bullet struck a wall, and that's what's left. There are no grooves, Isaac. How's Ballistics supposed to read a sweetheart like this?"

Isaac clutched the penny. "Can I keep it?"

"Why not? . . . the bullets had a copper jacket. That's all we know."

"You think I could have been glocked?"

"Yes," Sweets said.

"With my own gun?"

"No. Your gun was clean. It hadn't been touched."

The Glock was a 9 mm semiautomatic. The Austrians had introduced it. Most of it was made of plastic. The Glock wouldn't rust. It looked like a space gun out of *Star Wars*. Skyjackers were fond of the Glock, because they could smuggle most of it through a metal detector. Drug lords liked to use it. The Glock had incredible firepower for such a light gun. It had been given to elite squads at the NYPD. And sometimes, during a firefight, a cop might get glocked with his own gun.

Both Isaac and the First Dep had Glocks, which were housed in special holsters. They would go to the shooting range three times a year to fire their Glocks.

"Now will you tell me what happened to you, Isaac? How come your new favorite, Caroll Brent, finds you under the Williamsburg Bridge?"

"I have no favorites," Isaac said. "Caroll's a good detective."

"So good, you take him off the chart. He's our phantom. He's the one who could have glocked you."

"No, no. Not Caroll. Where'd you put him?"

"Back in Sherwood Forest, where he belongs."

Isaac groaned. "He's on special assignment."

"Not anymore. Isaac, I could bust him right now. He's been borrowing from a shylock. The shylock belongs to the Rubinos. Fabiano Rice."

"He's harmless."

"So harmless he had one of his clients kicked to death a year ago."

"Fabiano laughed his way out of court."

"I don't care. No more witch hunts, Isaac. You want to build a case against Maria Montalbán, you build it through the Department."

"Come on, Sweets. Montalbán's a protected man. He has the Democratic machine behind him. He goes to banquets with the district attorney. Judges like to kiss his ass. He's stealing from kids."

"Then talk to Alejo Tómas and his inspector general."

"Alejo and Maria Montalbán are cousins, for Christ's sake."

"That's tough, Isaac. Now tell me what happened."

"I was waiting for Caroll . . . I don't remember the rest. I heard a noise. And then I was on my ass. I thought a hurricane had come to Manhattan. My ears wouldn't stop ringing."

"Any idea who the hitter was?"

"One of Sal Rubino's soldiers."

"Sal can't have much of a crew," Sweets said.

"Of course not. I killed him."

"Jesus Christ, do you have to tell me that? I'm the Acting Commish."

"Everybody knows I iced Sal. Why pretend? But it seems I didn't ice him enough. Rubino's alive. Caroll talked to him. Rubino offered him money to whack me out."

"Then it could have been Caroll . . . with the Glock."

"Can't you listen? Caroll's on my side. And he's not a gun buff. He never used a Glock."

"He could learn. Sal might be a terrific teacher."

"Sal's in a wheelchair. He's a vegetable . . . like me. Don't you get it, Sweets? He only wanted me half dead, so I could suffer and be another Sal."

"He's not that much of a poet," Sweets said.

"Yeah, he's a regular Euripides."

"So are you. Isaac, Isaac, it's deserted under the bridge. If you knew Sal was alive, why did you pick such a dumb spot?"

"For sentimental reasons," Isaac said. "It's the only part of Sheriff Street that still exists. The rest has been lost inside housing projects."

"What's so special about Sheriff Street?"

"It was my favorite block. I used to go there when I was a boy. It was dark because of the bridge. I had my own cave, like Ali Baba."

"Sheriff Street," Sweets said. And he felt impulsive. He swooped over Isaac and kissed him on the forehead, because he couldn't imagine a world without Sidel. Sweets could run the Department, but he needed that crazy man with his crazy desires. He left Isaac in peace and walked out of the hospital. Who else but Sidel would have used his boyhood hideout as a meeting hall?

Reporters descended upon Sweets.

"How is he, sir? Does he have all his faculties?"

"He's fine."

"Can he speak sentences, or does he have to signal with his hands?"

"He does both," Sweets said. "Now stop haunting this hospital."

"Sir, sir, who shot Isaac?"

"No comment."

"Do you have a possible perpetrator?"

"We have several. Starting with Santa Claus . . . I'm not holding a press conference here, while you wait for Isaac to die."

"Sir, sir, what did you talk about with Sidel?"

And Sweets had to smile. "About the Bomber, who else?"

"What did Isaac say?"

"Harry on the handle, one two three."

Isaac was dreaming of center field. He'd had only one hero. Awkward Harry. He liked to play his little game of "Faust." Isaac would meet with the Devil, who looked a little like Sal. "Just give me one summer. Nineteen forty-three. Center field at the Polo Grounds. I want to be Harry. You can have my soul . . . and my police career."

"Including your Glock?" the Devil told him.

"My badge and my Glock."

The Devil played with Isaac's gun. "How many bullets does it hold?"

"Fourteen in the clip and one in the chamber."

"Sidel, are you trying to stiff me with some toy?"

You could always pull the trigger, Isaac started to say, but before he could finish he was in center field, wearing the Giants' whites. He wanted to cry. But a fucking nurse had spoiled it for him. She'd come into his room with a tray . . . and Isaac lost the whole sensation of center field.

"Nursey, I don't want my chicken broth. Can you please knock next time? And where's my lime jello?"

"Up your ass," the nurse said, and Isaac took a closer look under her cap. He should have recognized her figure, the fall of her hands. But he'd grown a little stupid in bed.

"Margaret, how the hell did you get in here? The security's supposed to be tight as a tit."

"I sapped a nurse and borrowed her uniform. Don't worry. She'll recover. She's sitting in a closet somewhere."

"Well, take off that hat. You look like my Aunt Bea. She was a mother superior at a Hebrew convent."

"I never heard of a Hebrew convent, Isaac."

"This is America. You can find anything you want."

"Aren't you going to say hello?"

She removed the cap. Her hair was dark this week. She'd become a brunette for the FBI. She was on the far side of fifty, like the Commish. But her eyes were a constant almond color. He'd been in love with Margaret Tolstoy forty years. She was a Roumanian refugee, a dirt-poor princess who'd invaded Isaac's junior-high-school class during the war, when searchlights cluttered the Manhattan sky and Isaac was a little pest who lived at the Polo Grounds.

"I tried to get in touch. I kept calling the Justice Department, but Justice wouldn't return my calls. I couldn't tell if you were in Kansas or Ohio, or what gang you were sleeping with . . . Margaret, Sal is alive."

"Tell me about it. He's been sending out his soldiers, and I've been punishing them."

"But you can't keep hopping from gang to gang. Sal has his own grapevine. He'll get to you, like he did in New Orleans. And I might not be able to deliver."

"You'll manage."

"Margaret, I can't even go to the toilet by myself. I live on lime jello and castor oil. I have metal pins in my shoulder. I wake up in the middle of the night and I don't know who I am."

"That's a good sign," Margaret said. "It means you'll recover."

"Margaret, get out of circulation. Disappear."

"And what should I do about my Isaac?"

"We'll meet someplace in Alaska . . . or Singapore."

"You'll die of malnutrition. You're just a brat from the Lower East Side."

"And what are you?"

"A homicidal lady. I have no home, Isaac."

"Tell LeComte to hire a new gangbuster."

Frederic LeComte was cultural commissar at Justice. He'd appointed Isaac as the first Alexander Hamilton Fellow. Isaac had gone around the country talking to police chiefs. But his tour was over. Isaac had embarrassed LeComte. He'd hid behind his travels to follow Margaret to New Orleans and shoot Sal in an old sausage factory. Margaret had lived with Sal and spied on him, she'd lived with LeComte for a week, but she'd never lived with Isaac. Sick as he was, the big bear wouldn't have let her breathe.

"LeComte wants me to retire so I can become his number-one mistress. I'd rather be out in the field."

"You could stay with me," Isaac said, with all the sadness of a police commissioner.

"Should I ask the hospital to wheel another bed into your room?"

"Not now . . . after I heal."

"Ah, you mean your little palace on Rivington Street, with that cosy tub in the kitchen. I'd get antsy, Isaac."

"I could move . . . to Sutton Place."

"I'd start flirting with all the millionaires. You wouldn't like it."

"But I can't look after you when you're in Milwaukee, romancing some hood on LeComte's hit list. Justice cut off my stipend. And who knows when I can travel?"

She pulled gently, gently on his ears, because she didn't want to create some new trauma for Isaac Sidel. "I'll be all right. I'm always careful."

"You weren't so careful in New Orleans," Isaac said, and he started to blubber. "Rubino would have bumped you if I'd been five minutes late."

"That's because he was jealous. He couldn't bear it that I liked you better than him."

"I didn't know you liked Sal. I thought he was only a trick."

"I lived with him, didn't I? It was almost like a marriage."

"You'd live with him, but not with me."

"Come on, Isaac, you'd ask me to wear an apron and you'd start feeding me fertility pills. I can't be a mama. I'm fifty-three."

There was a sound at the door, and Margaret poked a gun out of her skirt. It was a plastic 9 mm piece.

"Since when are you carrying a Glock?" Isaac asked. "I didn't know it was a Justice Department gun."

"It isn't," she said. "Isaac, I'd better blow. Someone might have found that nurse. And I can't afford to lose my cover. LeComte will get mad. He'll think I've been playing hardball with the Hamilton Fellow."

"Where can I find you?"

"I'm in the phonebook, Isaac. Just look up the Roumanian Relief Society."

"It doesn't exist."

"It will. In a little while."

And she went out the door with Isaac's jello.

9

The bear was sleeping twelve hours a day. After he woke he was given a halter and lowered into a little pool. The halter held him tight, and Sidel swam without moving. His legs wouldn't kick. His arms began to tire after a hundred strokes. He would rather have swung a bat. But the nurses wouldn't let him play Harry on the handle. He had to swim in his corset.

Now he understood the psychology of an invalid. He lived from meal to meal. Lime jello was his greatest priority. He had to flatter the dietician, or the green jello would disappear. He didn't like lemon or cherry or peach. And he'd bay like a wounded animal if the nurses switched colors on him. He despised his own pettiness. But he couldn't help himself. It was lime, and lime alone, that could soothe his tongue and satisfy the Commish.

His daughter called from Seattle.

"Daddy, I could come . . . whenever you like. The hospital said you weren't supposed to have any visitors."

She'd arrived in New York hours after the big bear had been shot, when the bear was dreaming of old Harry. She'd stayed for a month, until he opened his eyes. Isaac couldn't remember now. He must have mistaken her for a nurse. She could chill his blood. And perhaps he didn't want to wake out of his sleep to the image of Marilyn the Wild. He hadn't been much of a daddy. He was jealous of all her old boyfriends, including Manfred Coen. Marilyn thought her daddy had plotted to kill Blue Eyes. It wasn't so. He'd tossed Coen at the Guzmanns. That was his job. But he didn't mean for Manfred to die. The Guzmanns had given him his worm. The worm mourned Manfred as much as Marilyn did. But whoever had shot Isaac must have also shot the worm. Isaac had an instinct about his guts. The worm wasn't there.

"Ah," he said. "Marilyn, I have work to do. I have to catch the phantom who clipped me . . . he killed my worm."

"Daddy, are you delirious?"

"No. I'm grieving for the worm . . . maybe you could come next month."

"Who knows where you'll be? You have a habit of disappearing on people."

"You can always catch me at the office."

"Wanna bet?"

She was crying. The big bear could tell. His baby was crying. He felt like shit. They could never be civil to one another. All their encounters were a kind of incest. He couldn't deal with Marilyn right now. One day he'd die of his daughter. He knew that. The longing was too great.

"I'll see you next month," he said. "I promise. The minute I get out of this joint."

He wanted to tell Marilyn that he loved her, but he couldn't. He would have called her *baby*, like he did when she was young enough to sit on his lap. But he had to be careful with the daughter.

"Good-bye, sweetheart," he said.

And when he hung up the phone his shoulders started to heave. He was bawling like that when the cardinal came in unannounced. Jim was dressed like a simple priest. He didn't wear the colors of his station . . . or his pectoral cross.

"Jesus, should I call the surgeon?"

"I don't need a surgeon," Isaac said. "I was thinking of my girl."

"Madame Tolstoya?"

"No. Not Madame Tolstoya. Who let you in?"

"It's hard to keep out a cardinal. I'd cause a big stink."

"Always conniving, aint you, Jim? You ought to be glad. The Delancey Street Giants are in last place without me. And you're at the top of the division."

"Didn't realize you were following our league, Isaac. I'm flattered."

"You shouldn't be. You're a scoundrel. You raid all the schools. You steal the best players . . . and you leave me with shit."

"Shhh, I'm a cardinal . . . who's coaching your lads these days?"

"I'm not sure."

"Well then, I have a bit of news. The Bomber agreed to take the position . . . until you return to the fold."

"You talked to Harry?"

"Indeed I did."

"But he hates me. He thinks I tried to sabotage the Christy Mathewsons."

"He has a forgiving nature. Besides, he wouldn't leave the Delancey Giants in the lurch. I cleared it with the PAL commissioners. Harry having been a professional and all. But the commissioners were delighted to have him. So you see, Isaac, I do look after your lads."

"As long as they're in last place."

"Well, I'm not the village idiot. Are you comfortable, love? I could harangue the nurses. I could make the hospital shit a couple of bricks."

"Watch your language," Isaac said. And he started to smile.

"That's better. I thought I could get you to grin if I worked hard enough . . . boyo, any word about the blackguard who shot you? Or is it much too secret for a cardinal's ears?"

"I have no secrets," Isaac said, still smiling.

"Bloody hell you don't. You'd sabotage my team if you had half the chance. Have to watch you like a hawk."

"Shhh, Jim. Your blood pressure will go up."

"Never mind my blood pressure. But who'd be dumb enough to shoot a police commissioner? That's like asking for a holy war."

"Maybe it is a holy war," Isaac said.

"Boyo, you'd better go back to sleep."

And Cardinal Jim left the big bear to hibernate. But the bear wouldn't sleep. He was ambivalent about having Harry manage his Giants. What if the kids fell in love with the Bomber? Isaac would have to remain on the sidelines, an assistant coach. He couldn't lead his Giants onto the field.

Isaac was in the middle of an anxiety attack. He called to the police sergeant who was outside his door.

"Adam, be a good boy and get Caroll Brent on the horn. Tell him I'm lonely for my card collection. I'd like him to fetch the cards for me. I wouldn't want any burglars to get at my collection."

His flat on Rivington Street was a firetrap. He worried that the cards might burn. Or squatters might break into the flat and consider the cards as fancy toilet paper.

So he waited for Caroll Brent. He drank his lime jello. He had his swimming lessons in that idiotic pool. He had more jello, sucking at the lime with his teeth. Lime jello had become the focus of his life. Forget assassins. Forget Sal. Forget Harry Lieberman and the Delancey Street Giants.

And just as he'd given up waiting for Caroll, Caroll arrived with the cards in a manila envelope. The Commish turned white. *Jesus, he does look like Coen.* The boy had that same kind of sad and savage stare. But he didn't play ping-pong. And his eyes weren't blue. The big bear needed an adjutant. And if it hadn't been for Whitey Lockman, Isaac might never have found Caroll. It wasn't his fault that both of them had such an odd Christian name. *Caroll.* Like a boy king. This Caroll had a wife. He wouldn't fall in love with Marilyn the Wild. And then the bear remembered that Blue Eyes had also had a wife. Her name was Stephanie. And she broke with Manfred because Isaac was always there. He was like a marriage on top of their marriage. Isaac wouldn't leave Blue Eyes alone.

"I brought your cards," this Blue Eyes said.

"Thanks, kid."

"But I had to pick a couple of locks."

"It's nothing. I do it all the time. I'm a habitual lock-picker . . . kid, you probably think something is going down between your Diana and me. It's not true. I like Dee, but I'm in love with Anastasia."

"Who's Anastasia?"

"Margaret Tolstoy. That's what she called herself in junior high . . . I'm sorry I was so secretive about the wife. I asked her not to tell you anything. I didn't want you to get involved. You're a cop. You're attached to me. I'm trying to mount a campaign to cure the libraries. I call it the Monday Morning Club. Because the libraries are closed on Monday mornings. It's a scandal. Little kids can't even find a fucking book. But I don't dare complain. I'm the PC. So I asked Diana to be my stalking horse and start the Monday Morning Club."

"And she agreed?"

"Not yet. I've been wooing her . . . you know what I mean. We had lunch in Chinatown before I got zapped. I showed her the reports I'd been preparing."

"Who was helping you, Isaac? Your Intelligence Division?"

"Don't be crazy. I can't involve the police. A couple of retired detectives are freelancing for me. But it's innocent, Caroll. It's nothing at all."

"As innocent as my going after Maria Montalbán?"

"Montalbán's a thief . . . how's life?"

"I'm back in Sherwood Forest, thanks to Sweets."

"Don't be so quick to thank him. Did he bother you a lot?"

"About what?"

"About finding me under the Williamsburg Bridge. Sweets thinks you might have staged the whole affair."

Caroll was silent. His brown eyes were as fierce as Coen's.

"Not to worry," Isaac said. "I told him to stuff his theories."

The brown eyes didn't go off Isaac. "Why didn't Sweets haul my ass in? He's the Acting Commish."

"Forget Sweets. Just tell me what happened."

"Happened? I went to a meet. It was dark. I looked down. There you were, Isaac."

"But did you notice anything? . . . come on, kid. Give me a fucking detail."

"There were no details, Isaac. It was dark."

"Caroll, I may be romantic, but I'm not a stupid pig. You held the only key to our meeting ground. I never talked to another person under that bridge . . . could someone have been tailing you?"

"Someone like Sal's soldiers? Is that what you're saying?"

"For starters. But it didn't have to be Sal. It could have been Maria Montalbán. He must wish me dead a couple thousand times a day."

"I've wished you dead, Isaac."

"But you're not Montalbán. You don't steal from school-children."

Jesus, Isaac thought, it was like a goddamn marriage. Love and hate, love and hate.

"Isaac, suppose someone followed *you* under the bridge."

"I'm not that easy to tail, kid."

Isaac took his thickened penny and dropped it into Caroll's hand.

"What's that?"

"A souvenir. All that's left of a bullet that went through me."

"A copper jacket," Caroll said.

"Exactly. Sweets figures I might have been glocked. So do I."

"Sal's soldiers wouldn't play around with a plastic gun. People might laugh at them."

"Not unless Sal wanted to make it look like the phantom hitter was a cop."

Caroll returned the penny. "I don't have a plastic gun."

"But you're a cop. Don't you get it? Sal makes his debut as a fucking live man in front of Caroll Brent. He cancels your vig. He asks you to whack me out as a family favor. The next thing that happens is I get hit . . . Sal's been pulling your chain. Or else someone's making a monkey out of me, you, and Sal."

"That leaves Montalbán."

"Ah, there's others. I've got enemies all over the place."

"That leaves Montalbán. So stop fucking with me, Isaac. Tell me about your plan to close Montalbán's shop. How many cops are in the picture? Barbarossa and who else?"

"Five or six."

"And where's your command post?"

"Sherwood Forest."

The brown eyes seemed to shove into some pale country. "Holy shit."

"I had to pick a quiet precinct," Isaac said. "That's why I got you out of there. So people wouldn't get suspicious."

"Holy shit."

Ah, it was Blue Eyes all over again, because Isaac could sniff that anger in Caroll, the anger of a disappointed bride.

"Come on, kid. I wouldn't let you down."

"I almost got my ass shot off, you son of a bitch."

"Barbarossa was right behind you . . . you couldn't see him, but you always had Joe. He's the best we have in a firefight. The man has two combat crosses and the medal of honor."

"That's why you banished him to Sherwood Forest. He was another submariner, a cop you were holding in reserve."

"No. I busted his ass for good reason. He was ripping off drug dealers in Manhattan North. He was freelancing a lot. I didn't want Internal Affairs to sink him. So I lent Joey to the squirrels in Central Park. But I never forgot about Joe."

"And who are your other commandos at Sherwood Forest? Is Captain White involved in your caper?"

"A little. I'd never sneak around the Cap in his own yard."

"Who else?"

"Wilson and McSwain."

"They're auxiliary policewomen. Joe is banging them left and right."

"That's his business. But they're not auxies. They're regular cops. I borrowed them from One PP. Wilson was with Public Information. McSwain was with Community Affairs."

"Who else?"

"Sergeant Weiss."

"He's a grandpa," Caroll said. "Been in Central Park so long, the squirrels gave him his own tree."

"Perfect camouflage. No one would believe Weiss was involved in any intrigue."

"Who else?"

"That's my team. Barbarossa. White. Wilson. McSwain. And Weiss. I don't have subpoena powers. I have to go with what I can get."

"And walk a shaky line between legal and illegal."

"That's the kind of PC I am," Isaac said. "If the law protects Montalbán, then I have to bend it a little."

"And use me as your bait. I was the screen for your fucking commandos."

"That's all over now."

"Yeah, Isaac. I have to live around your conspirators at Sherwood Forest."

"I could move you to a different precinct."

"You can't do shit. You're a civilian in a hospital bed. It's Sweets' show. I'll do my tours at Sherwood Forest while you convalesce. But the day you're back in harness, that's the day I resign."

Caroll walked out of the room, and the big bear was left with his thickened penny and all the cards in his baseball collection.

10

It should have been a lazy day at Sherwood Forest. The wind howled through the old horse stable. Caroll could have napped in the detectives' squad room. No one interfered with him. He'd found the PC in the ruins of Sheriff Street. Only the phantom hitter or Caroll could have gotten that close to Isaac. Sweets had put him back on the chart. But he was like a goodwill ambassador who talked to movie stars or the mayor's people. Caroll didn't feel like climbing up a tree to return the lost cat of some deputy mayor. He wasn't Blue Eyes, who was always on loan to the Bureau of Special Services . . . until he got killed. Caroll was still a submariner, no matter whose chart he was on.

He knocked on the CO's door. Captain White had been taking a leak in his private toilet. White had a mournful, yellow face. His eyes were a little crazy. He was cautious around Caroll. He zipped his pants and invited him into the office.

"What can I do for you?"

"I had a powwow with the chief."

"I don't understand."

"Yes, you do," Caroll said. "Isaac told me about his little command post in Central Park."

"I'm forty-six. I'm a police captain. What the fuck do you want?"

"You've been monitoring Maria Montalbán for the PC. You're his new secret service."

"I could toss you out of this precinct. I don't have to tell you shit . . . I'm sorry. Yeah, Isaac recruited me. He's an eloquent man. But Internal Affairs might be looking up my ass. We have a Commish who writes his own book of rules. Sit down, Caroll, and close the door."

The captain came out from behind his desk to pat Caroll's clothes.

"I'm not wearing," Caroll said.

"Who says? You could work for Isaac and still be a rat."

"Believe me, I'm not wearing a wire."

"I have three kids. I have a mortgage. And I'm catching for Isaac the Brave."

"You should have declined his offer, Cap."

"Fat chance. He's a vindictive son of a bitch. He'd start flying me to other precincts. I'd be a permanent relief man. You know what happens when you're a flier? Everybody pisses on you. They call you Captain Midnight. No, Caroll, I'm staying here."

"With Isaac's team? Old man Weiss, the two babes, and Vietnam Joe Barbarossa . . . relax, Cap. I'm not the head ghee. You are. What do you have on Montalbán?"

"Plenty if you count all the illegal wiretaps. But if we move on the cocksucker, he could laugh us out of court."

"So you're in Zeroville, right where I began. Some commandos you are."

And Caroll walked out of the captain's office. Weiss was behind the sergeant's desk. He looked like a lost cavalry man. He was sixty years old and would have earned almost as much by sitting home with his pension. But Weiss couldn't retire. He was the precinct's own historian.

"We're carrying a dead man on our roster," he said. "Mulrooney died a year ago, but he's still collecting his paycheck. That's the kind of Department we have," he said, winking at Caroll.

"You're right, Sarge. Aint it a bitch."

Caroll couldn't remember this Mulrooney, but the sergeant was never wrong. There had to be a dead man on the roster. He didn't say a word to Weiss about Isaac's commandos. What was the point? Half of Sherwood Forest believed Caroll was the particular phantom who had shot the Pink Commish. And Caroll liked the old sergeant, who knew every detail about the Park's first hundred and twenty years. A camel from the Menagerie had mowed the grass in 1861, according to Weiss. Red deer roamed the North End in the 1920s. So did enormous schools of bats. These bats had colonized the Park, knocking birds off trees with their incredible radar, tangling themselves in the scalps of little girls and boys, until they were declared a menace and their caves were sealed off. Every single school died within the caves. But now there was a new menace. The Norway rat.

There were at least a million "Norways" in Central Park. They bit into the sewer pipes under Sherwood Forest and caused a terrific flood. They would jump into baby carriages like a new breed of flying fish. They had sheet-metal stomachs that could tolerate whatever poison the Parks Department prepared for them. They were supposed to die of internal bleeding after seven days. Blood would drip from their entrails, but the rats didn't die. They continued to eat the sewer pipes. And Sherwood Forest had to endure the periodic storms they produced.

But Caroll learned to admire these Norway rats. They were the healthiest population in the Park. He wondered about the very first rat who had arrived from Norway on a tall ship hundreds of years ago. This rat must have been older than the United States. Caroll considered him as some kind of pilgrim.

He could have sought out Joe Barbarossa at the other end of the stable. But what could Joe tell him about Isaac's commandos? Joe was a maverick with lots of medals. He had to do whatever

Isaac wanted or he would have lost his pension *and* his perch as the robber policeman. Joe was probably wearing his white glove and fondling Wilson and McSwain, Isaac's undercover girls who were posing as auxiliaries. Caroll was willing to bet that their crush on Barbarossa was part of Isaac's game plan. Wilson and McSwain were more interested in each other than in Vietnam Joe.

They didn't curse or spit like the other lady cops at CPP. They were a little too refined to live around a locker room. Isaac had a fondness for soft-spoken dykes who could eat his heart out with their handsomeness. He seemed to trust their minds and their sensibilities. But Caroll was a bit more guarded. Perhaps it was because he had a residual attraction for McSwain, with her high bosoms and short, curly hair, her dark little hands that burrowed out of her sleeves. McSwain bothered Caroll.

He walked around the bow of the Reservoir, crossed the bridle path near Mariners Gate, and stopped at a secluded lawn. A man was sitting in a wheelchair, with a blanket around his middle. Caroll recognized his injured face, his pocked hands, and the one eye that wandered off the landscape. It was Sal Rubino. None of his soldiers were in the neighborhood. A Norway rat scurried under the footrest of the chair.

Caroll started to chase the rat.

"Leave the little guy," Sal Rubino said. "He's my friend. He keeps all his brothers and sisters from biting my toes."

"You shouldn't be here all by yourself. You could get clobbered. The Park's not a nursing home."

"Sure it is. It's my own winter garden. I like to hear the leaves. Caroll, when I was a kid the cops wouldn't let a downtown macaroni like me near the nurses and their baby carriages. I didn't have the stink of Manhattan. I didn't dress like Park Avenue."

"Neither did I."

"But you're a cop. You can go anywhere. And I'm a haunted man. I gave up my ghost in New Orleans."

"You got it back."

"It aint that easy, kid. I'm in some fucking purgatory, waiting for Isaac to clean all my wounds."

"You tried to have him killed."

"Under the bridge? That wasn't Sal."

"But someone in your Family pulled the trigger."

"I'm not a two-timer. I have a contract with you. I wouldn't ruin your gig."

Caroll almost believed him. But it couldn't have been an accident that Rubino had placed himself in Caroll's favorite corner of the Park. The don was dogging him.

"You're a little crazy, Sal. I don't intend to sock Isaac for you."

"Oh, you'll sock him. Not for me. But for yourself."

"I don't care about Isaac's commandos. He can run his own army againt Maria Montalbán. I'm finished with the schools. I don't chase pianos anymore. I don't chase Montalbán's mules. He can do as much dope as he wants."

"I wasn't thinking of dope. I was thinking of your wife."

And Sal withdrew into his blanket like some pockmarked Buddha. Caroll felt like spilling him onto the bridle path, under a horse's hoof.

"Go on, Sal. Tell me the truth. The Pink Commish is banging Diana."

"I didn't say that. I don't fuck around with bedroom stories. I respect all women, even Margaret Tolstoy, who sort of broke my heart if I ever had a heart. But your Diana, she is some hell of a lady."

"How would you know that, Sal?"

"I talked to her for a minute at a cocktail party."

"Which party was that? The Robbers' Ball?"

"Don't get cute. I'm a big giver to the Police Athletic League. I have my own fucking team, same as Isaac and the cardinal. I mix in a lot of different circles. You ought to know that."

"Fine. You bumped knees with Diana. So what?"

"I didn't bump knees with anybody. Wake up. Isaac is using

your wife. He brought her into his Monday Morning Club. Save the libraries and all that shit. And he has her start a branch in Montalbán's turf. She sits down with the school board. She goes to lunch with Maria Montalbán. And little by little she starts spying for Father Isaac. Aint that how ya recruit a rat? It's always innocent at first."

"Diana's not a rat."

"Add it up or down, kid. Sooner or later you'll have to kill Sidel."

"No. You have it wrong, Sal . . . I'll finish what Isaac started in New Orleans."

"Ah," Sal said, clutching the wheels of his chair. "You don't have the stomach for it. You're a meat and potatoes man. You wouldn't do the dark and the dirty. But you'll have to kill Sidel . . . or let the wife drift into Montalbán's arms. Because I think Maria has taken a shine to her."

"Shut up."

"Hit me, Caroll. I couldn't even feel it. I'm the only friend you got."

Three bodies materialized in the gloom of Central Park. Barbarossa. Wilson. McSwain. They were all carrying Glocks.

"Ah, it's the Central Park circus," Sal Rubino said. There was no alarm in his eyes. It almost thrilled him to see the Glocks.

"How are you, Sally?" Barbarossa asked. He was wearing his single white glove. "I think you have a date with the Commish."

"I'm glad. I'd like the bed next to Isaac's at Beekman Downtown. We could play checkers. I'll steal his pants."

"Nah. Isaac will get out of bed for you . . . Caroll, make the call. We'll be here when you get back."

And that's when Caroll gripped the handles of the chair and drove Sal Rubino between Wilson and McSwain. McSwain's eyes were on him. Wilson held her Glock to Caroll's head. She was younger than McSwain.

"Better stay where you are, Caroll."

He didn't enjoy that touch of plastic on his skin. "Sal," he said, "meet Wilson and McSwain. They have their own brick bungalow. They like to play the part of auxiliary policewomen. But they're detectives on loan from One PP. They're stalking Maria Montalbán."

"Pleased to meet ya," Sal said. But neither Wilson nor McSwain would take Sal's hand. And Caroll wheeled him along the edge of the bridle path, bumping over a layer of dead leaves.

"Caroll."

He stopped, the softness of Barbarossa's voice weaving its own little spell. Joey never shouted. Joey was capable of shooting off Caroll's head. No one was sure of his allegiances. There was room for every kind of murder in that white glove. Joey played ping-pong, romanced Wilson and McSwain, sat in exile at Sherwood Forest, the most decorated cop in New York, who robbed, traded drugs, while he kept anarchy off the streets.

"Caroll."

And Caroll pushed on the chair, wheeling Sal toward Mariners Gate. Sal's soldiers were waiting for him. He grabbed Caroll with his own pocked hand that felt like pumice stone.

"Kid, I wouldn't go back. I've dealt with Joe. I'd trade all my soldiers for him. But he don't believe in brotherhood."

"He was my partner, Sal."

"I know, but it means nothing to him. He would have iced ya if he had to."

"Then why did you sit in the Park?"

"Because I put my faith in Caroll Brent."

And Caroll walked back into the gloom. He searched Sherwood Forest for Barbarossa and the two girls. They weren't in the old mustering room. Barbarossa's white glove was on the ping-pong table. There was no other sign of Joe.

Part Three

11

He began to feel like a boarder at Beekman Downtown. He had terrible chest pains. A whistling would come up from his heart. He was Isaac Sidel, the eater of bullets. He didn't bother about the holes in him. He was like an orphan without his worm. He drank his lime jello, opened the box his driver had brought him, and put on the uniform of the Delancey Street Giants. He wore his cap over the left ear, like Harry Lieberman. But he wasn't trying to imitate the Bomber. Harry's style had wedged so deep into Isaac that it was beyond manners or memory.

He brushed his teeth. He ventured out of the hospital while nurses and residents howled at him. He couldn't even get into a subway. Five patrol cars stopped for him, recognized his bushy hair under the baseball cap. It was Isaac who'd made Harry famous again, and now they were like floating halves of the same self. Isaac got into the fifth police car and rode up to the north playing fields in Central Park.

It was in the middle of a March blow. The trees swayed into the wind. Harry was on the diamond with the Giants. He'd chalked the field himself. He wasn't wearing a uniform. There was no one else out in the north fields except Harry and the boys and Isaac Sidel. The boys were delinquents and orphans and mathematical wizards from Carlos Maria Montalbán's junior-high schools. Isaac had selected them, found them little scholarships, fed them until they'd become a family out on the field. They couldn't compete with Cardinal Jim's Manhattan Knights, who were almost professionals at fourteen, but they were no longer delinquents. Or at least that's how Isaac remembered them before he'd been shot. Now he saw them through the gray hairs at the back of Harry's neck. They had a liquid motion Isaac had never seen before. Harry had given them a melodic line. He hadn't molded them into little Harrys. He'd tested them against their own worth. He'd discovered their playing principle. And Isaac saw a desolate beauty on that frozen field. Harry had willed the Giants into a team.

The boys gathered around him after their practice session. They were glad to see Isaac. But there was a bit of embarrassment in their eyes. Isaac wasn't their mentor now. He was a big brown bear who wore the uniform of the Delancey Giants. They'd given themselves to the Bomber. Isaac was only a puller of strings.

"How are you, Commish?" the Bomber asked, a celebrity in spite of himself. He had gray knots around his ears. His hands were gnarled. But he was still the wonder boy of 1943, who roamed center field for the New York Giants in the middle of a war, bumping into walls, catching line drives between his legs, hitting home runs that sailed into the bleachers like a golden egg. "I'm glad you're out of the hospital."

"I'm not out," Isaac said. "I came for a visit, that's all. But the Delanceys don't need Isaac. They have the Bomber. I never saw them play with so much teeth."

"They're your team," the Bomber said. "You chose them. I'm only substituting for you, Isaac."

"I'm not much of a field manager. I never was. I couldn't lead them out of last place."

"That's because you have that cardinal riding on your tail."

"Ah, don't blame Jim. He's devoted to the boys. Didn't he ask you to mind the Delanceys while I was recuperating?"

"To feather his own lousy nest. He wants to profit from me, Isaac. He's put my picture in all his brochures."

"Well, you're the Bomber. And the cardinal's a businessman. He's always looking for profit. But he's never been mean to our boys. Our whole infield would be in a home for juveniles if it weren't for Jim."

"I don't like him bargaining for any kid's life."

"I think I'll go back to the hospital . . . and look for a bit of lime jello."

"Stay," the Bomber said. "You're our general. You can trade politics with the cardinal. I can't. I was never good at intrigue. He'll start finagling, and he'll finesse me into the ground."

Isaac scrutinized the boys. Perhaps they did need his particular brain trust. Isaac could slug it out with the cardinal, dance with the PAL. Isaac was the Pink Commish. He always had a double motive for anything he did.

"All right, I'll be the general." And the boys returned to the field and one final rally for the Bomber. Isaac was satisfied. From his perch in the northlands of Central Park he could spy on School District Eleven A, which was Maria Montalbán's own private plunder grounds. Montalbán shuffled pianos and school supplies between Eleven A and his own district. He took from Eleven A whatever he lacked downtown. He was like some absentee prince. And Isaac meant to shackle the son of a bitch.

And so he commuted from his hospital bed to the playing fields. He was almost like a landmark in his billed cap, his white jersey with gold borders, his knickers, and his gray socks; the cut of his uniform had nothing to do with any current style. Isaac was dressed like Babe Ruth and the Bomber; he was one more antiquarian, one more relic of a lost tribe.

It was 1984, and the Park had another famous ghost. She called herself Harriet Brown. She had pinched eyebrows and pitiless bangs that hugged her face like a helmet. She'd once been the most beautiful woman in the world. She still was the most beautiful woman to Isaac Sidel. He'd seen her in *Ninotchka* at the Loew's Delancey in 1939, and he couldn't forget the female commissar who is seduced by a playboy and all the guiles and material goods of Paris. Isaac was the only kid in the moviehouse who mourned the commissar's fall from grace. He was a Stalinist at eleven. And Paris was only Babylon with revolving doors and splits of champagne.

He would keep the autograph hounds out of her hair. He never talked of *Ninotchka*, or trespassed upon that anonymous side of herself. She was Harriet Brown, and he was Isaac Sidel, a police commissioner on sick leave. "I'm an aging little boy," she said to Isaac on one of the strolls they took across the playing fields. That's how she liked to think of herself, as a boy lost in a woman's body. She was no hermaphrodite, this Harriet Brown. She was heartlessly female, but an entire planet had fallen in love with her image on the screen, and she resisted that image, chose to be the sexless child.

"How are your wounds?" she asked, holding his hand.

"Healing," he said.

"Will you give a sad boy a cigarette?"

He carried a box of Dunhills for Harriet Brown, who loved to cadge cigarettes like a Central Park waif. She took a sandwich out of her bag and shared it with Isaac: meatless salami on white bread. That was their lunch, half a sandwich and a cigarette. Isaac could imagine her at one of the old automats, dining on a handful of nickels, like some illustrious bag lady.

He bumped into Caroll's wife at the end of his stroll with Harriet Brown, who walked out of the Park at Woodmans Gate.

"Was that Garbo?" Diana asked.

"Not so loud," Isaac said.

"Will you invite her to dinner . . . at my place?"

"I will not. I hardly know her, Dee."

He'd disappointed Diana of the purple eyes.

It bothered him to sneak behind Caroll's back. But the only campaign he could mount against Maria Montalbán was with Cassidy's daughter. His own squad at Sherwood Forest had fallen asleep. It couldn't get near Montalbán. Diana could.

"Well," Isaac had to ask, "did he attend the first meeting of the Monday Morning Club?"

"You couldn't keep him away. His eyes were all over me."

"Be careful, Diana. He could get nasty, our Maria."

"I am careful," Diana said. She wore a red cape from Saks. She looked like a grown-up Little Red Riding Hood who was ready to trap the Wolf. Only the Wolf had been to Nam. He ruled a kingdom of girls and boys on the Lower East Side. He had his own black market in school supplies.

"Diana, have drinks with him . . . in some busy café."

"What am I supposed to do, Isaac, unbutton my blouse?"

"Just get him to talk. He'll start bragging. He'll give himself away. He'll invite you into his little network, show you how he's feeding kids with the money he moves around."

"It's still entrapment," Diana said. "Remember, I'm married to a cop."

Isaac groaned. "You're not gonna lure him into anything. We won't trick the snake. But we'll learn about his apparatus, and then we'll pounce."

"And if he starts pawing me?"

"We'll pull you out of there. I have my best man backing you up. Joe Barbarossa."

"Caroll's old partner," she said. "Vietnam Joe. He might be friendlier with Montalbán than you think."

"He's my best man," Isaac said.

"I thought Caroll was."

"After Caroll," Isaac said. "Pardon me."

"You're a genuine bastard, Isaac dear. That's why I always liked you. You remind me of my dad."

"Not a chance. I'm a little leaguer next to Papa Cassidy."

"No you're not. You're twice as ruthless. And it's not about money. It's all for the general good . . . of Isaac Sidel."

"Then why are you helping me?"

"Because I'm a sucker for lost causes . . . like you. If Montalbán is hurting children, he has to be stopped. And then I want you to get Caroll off the hook. No more crusades, Isaac. Promise."

"I'll give him to the squirrels, I swear to God."

"He already has the squirrels. Just give him to me."

"I promise," Isaac said.

She kissed him on the cheek. "Am I your latest conquest, Isaac? Your little undercover cop?"

"You're not a cop," he said.

She kissed him on the mouth. "Oh, what a liar you are. You'd have made your own mother into a cop."

"My mother was nearly stomped to death. She didn't even like cops."

"I'm sorry . . . I didn't mean . . . I guess it's dangerous for us to be seen together. Maria might be watching."

And she walked away from Isaac, that Little Red Riding Hood who was her own Molotov cocktail, because men couldn't stop loving Diana Cassidy. It made no difference that she was married to Caroll. She'd always be a Cassidy, with her billion-dollar legs.

12

B aby."

She could torture him, give him the blackest headache, with one of her own dark looks. It had always been like that. Her mother had been negligible in Diana's life, an exalted servant who was satisfied to keep within the clan. It was Diana who had ventured out, who'd been her Papa's escort when she was eight years old. She would walk into any restaurant or high-priced bordello and not have to introduce herself. The madams and the maître d's would say, "Cassidy's girl." And she could proceed into the most private corridors. Her father had to practice coitus interruptus, with Diana at the door.

She was all the romance Papa Cassidy required. Her calves hardened when she was twelve. She started to bleed. She developed breasts. Her eyes had that sleepy night color of a cat. A millionaire proposed to her when she was fourteen. That millionaire was removed from Papa Cassidy's boardrooms. Whatever suitors there were fell away from Cassidy's girl. Men would chase her and then disappear, bought off by Papa Cassidy or beaten up. Until Papa realized she might become an old maid, and he began to pick her suitors. But she had a will of her own. She was attracted to mailmen and tubercular musicians. When that cop finally appeared, Caroll Brent, Papa Cassidy was relieved. Caroll had a kind of dimwitted handsomeness, and he was devoted to Dee. Papa could die without leaving behind a bachelor girl. But he had no intention of dying.

He was fifty-five years old. The commodity he preferred was cash. He avoided paper transactions whenever he could.

"Baby."

She'd come to him in her red cape. He wanted her to go to a charity ball at the Metropolitan Museum of Art.

"It's boring, Papa. I'd start to snore."

"It's no less boring than that Hungarian orchestra you keep afloat."

"Czech, Papa. And the conductor is a genius. Milan Jagiello."

"Are you banging him, dear?"

She could have slapped Papa. But he'd only start to sniffle, and they'd both end up bawling, with Diana on his knee. She didn't want to rock in his lap. She was too old for that. She had a husband, her own orchestra, and Jagiello, the genius she was grooming to take over the New York Philharmonic.

"Papa, I'll go to your goddamn ball. But you'll have to pay a price."

His eyes began to wrinkle out like little electric lights. He could sniff a deal, and he loved to bargain with his only child.

"Gladly," he said. But it can't have anything to do with Jagiello. I hate his guts. The man's a parasite."

"No preambles," she said. "No reservations, please."

"I promise."

"Then find Milan a slot at the Philharmonic . . . guest conductor, I don't care."

"Baby, I can't. He has no talent."

"Then go to your charity ball with one of your concubines."

"Okay. I'll ask, I'll dig, I'll prostitute myself for that little prick. But you ought to find another protégé."

"He's not my protégé. He was destitute . . . I helped Milan."

"But do you have to carry a hundred musicians because of Jagiello? What kind of name is that?"

"Jagiello is the name of a king, a whole family of kings. And I have to support his orchestra. How else will he play? I can't leave him floating around in Czechoslovakia and a hundred college towns. It will never advance his career."

"I'll talk to some people. But give your father a kiss."

She was nearly as tall as Papa Cassidy. They had a similar rapacious look, like a couple of pirates who could turn Manhattan into their private farm. He wore a velour jacket that matched the color of his eyes. His clothes sat on him like a comfortable glove. He didn't have to dress the part of a financial pirate. He was Papa Cassidy. And Dee was Cassidy's daughter. Husbands were a very small item in Papa's universe. He never bothered to imagine Caroll sleeping with his own little girl. He could have gotten rid of the cop. He tolerated Caroll, liked him as much as he could like a detective in squirrel country. He wondered how Caroll could hold Diana in check. She would ride over whatever man she was with, including Papa Cassidy. And when she closed her eyes to peck him on the forehead, her eyelids fluttering with some thought that was far from Papa, he grabbed her wrists.

"Montalbán," he whispered.

Diana tried to pull away from him.

"Montalbán."

She stopped struggling and opened her eyes. "What of it? Have your detectives been following me?"

"I don't have to hire detectives. I get my information free of charge. You'd better tell Isaac to nail Montalbán on his own. I don't like Jew commissioners taking advantage of my daughter."

Cassidy let go of her wrists. The anger in her eyes unsettled him. He couldn't startle her. She had her own lunatic steel. He couldn't frighten the girl.

"I could keep Isaac on permanent vacation," he said. "It wouldn't be hard. He has enemies. He jilted Rebecca Karp. He has a Roumanian whore who makes love to him twice a year and sleeps with every bandit in the United States."

"Papa," she said. "Do whatever you want."

She whirled her body toward the door. And Papa could hear the music of her bones. It took his heart away.

"I'll expect you at nine," he shouted at his disappearing daughter. "The charity ball. Don't forget."

She met Carlos Maria Montalbán at a Newyorican café on Norfolk Street. The countermen called him "Jefe." He had a gold star in his left ear. He wore high-heeled shoes. He had a cape that was much longer than hers. She might have seduced him if she hadn't been married to Caroll. Desire was like a curious clockwork to Diana. Its only pull was inside her head. She was coldblooded about all the men in her life. She loved Caroll. And she was lending Isaac her charm to use on Maria Montalbán. He didn't hold her hand. But he began his courtship rite.

"Move in with me. You won't regret it."

"Carlos, you promised you weren't going to talk that way."

"Look, I'm not asking for a quick feel," he said. "Divorce the cop. I'll take care of you. People make fun of Newyoricans. They talk about the Cuban middle class. The miracle men of Calle Ocho, with their Little Havanas. I piss on Little Havana. And I've never been to San Juan. I have no mother country. I was born on Norfolk Street. That's enough."

"You were in Vietnam," she said.

"Vietnam? A lot of beer and smoke."

"And Joe Barbarossa," she said. The romance went out of Montalbán's eyes.

"Yeah, Joe. My own blood brother. He was always doing favors for the Embassy chiefs. He was their number-one delivery boy. And a thief. I ought to know. Joe worked for me. I sold hash to half the Marines in Saigon. I was their own little supply sergeant. And Joe was my collector. We were a terrific team. But he started ripping off my other collectors. And he stole from the till. I had to give him an extra allowance so he'd stop stealing . . . but what's it got to do with me and you?"

"I'm curious . . . about Joe. My husband used to bring him home to dinner. But he never talked about himself."

"That's because every time he opens his mouth he has to admit two or three more crimes."

"Does he still work for you?"

"Never. He belongs to the big israelita. Sidel. I think he's waiting to whack me out. That's his specialty. Whacking people. And I have to dance around Joe. I could get him busted. But what's the good of it? The israelita would send someone else. And Joe at least is a familiar face . . . has he been bothering you, trying to bite your ear? I'll have to tell him I'm your fiancé. That will cool him off."

"You're not my fiancé."

"Yes I am. I announced it to everybody."

"Carlos, I'm going to leave the table."

"Not so fast. We have to talk about books. I need your Monday Morning Club. I need libraries for all my little ones."

"The chancellor is your cousin. He'll get you books."

"Alejo? He can't even supply my district with toilet paper. There's a shortfall in the whole system. Alejo has no books."

"And so you steal them from other districts."

"Joe steals. Not me. I'm still the supply sergeant. I trade pencils and rulers. I give. I get."

"Carlos, you can borrow books from the Monday Morning Club."

"I never borrow. It's not in my nature. Borrow means you're in somebody's debt."

"Then what can I do?"

"Marry me and read to my little ones."

"I'm already married," she said.

"I'll forgive you. But I'm not so crazy about that cop of yours. He put one of my teachers into the hospital. It's a bad sign."

"Then why would you want to marry his wife?"

Maria Montalbán began to smile. He had gold rings on his fingers. He had a gold watch. He had a silver tiepin and a golden tooth. He occupied the biggest table at the Newyorican café. Where were all the children he was supposed to abuse? The only children she had met in the district adored Maria Montalbán.

"I'll help you open all the libraries you want. I'll find you books. I'll read to the children if you like. But that's as far as it goes."

"A professional lady," Montalbán said.

She was getting fond of his gold tooth. His hand brushed hers. I'm in love with Caroll, she started to sing, like Little Red Riding Hood living on nursery rhymes. She'd been imagining herself in bed with Maria Montalbán all this time. It was like a curious disease that had invaded her system. She hadn't been pursuing Maria for Isaac's sake. She was following her own mad dream.

And then Maria broke the spell. He took a handkerchief out of his pocket, dangled it like some coy magician, dropped it on the table, and asked Dee to open the handkerchief. There were watches and rings and bracelets inside, all gold. This wasn't about children, Diana realized. It was about plunder and patronage. The libraries had been some excuse to get near Dee. He wanted her as his concubine, kept in gold. He did steal from the children, he stole from their mouths, or he wouldn't have had such colossal booty. And now she foraged like a spy.

"Lovely," Diana said, picking out a ring she couldn't help admire. It hadn't come from Cartier. A Newyorican goldsmith must have hammered it together in Maria Montalbán's own streets.

"Take another," he said.

"No, Carlos. I couldn't."

"What's a little gold among friends? You don't have to live with me . . . not right now. I'm a patient man. Drink your coffee, dear."

She took another ring and a bracelet with a kind of coldbloodedness she didn't even know she had. "Carlos, who's your jeweler?"

"Would you like to meet him, dear?"

"Yes," she said.

"I'll arrange it. Next week."

And he had to run off to his various occupations, the schools he had to supervise, the lieutenants he had to scold, the rubber bands he had to collect. He pulled his cape around his shoulders. In his high heels he was just Diana's height. She watched him strut to the door. The whole café acknowledged Carlos. Old men sought to grab a piece of his cape.

"Don't touch the material," he said.

And then he was gone. Diana felt bereaved for a moment, though she couldn't really say what she had lost. She was richer by two gold rings and a bracelet. She left the café in her red hood, the wind beating down upon her back. She wasn't comfortable in the forlorn streets of Loisaida, which had a pair of feuding princes, Isaac and Maria Montalbán.

A gang of warrior girls fell upon Diana at the corner of Norfolk and Stanton. The girls had painted hair. They looked like Lower East Side Indians. They flailed at Diana, called her a bitch, their mouths like chimneys that could manufacture balls of smoke. They grabbed Diana's purse, but they weren't satisfied.

"Beg for your life, bitch."

And then a hand got between them, wearing a white glove, and it parted these warrior girls, flinging them across the gutters, while it grabbed Diana's purse.

"Joe Barbarossa, what took you so long?" Diana said from under her hood.

"I was cleaning my glove . . . you shouldn't be here, Diana.

Not with Maria. He gives you some rings, and then he sets you up with a gang of cuties, so they can stage a little war dance and steal them back."

"How do you know Carlos gave me some rings?"

"Diana, he's always giving rings to uptown girls. It's a habit with Maria."

"Did he give out rings in Vietnam?"

"All the time."

"And what makes you so sure I took them from Carlos?"

"Jesus Christ, the café is bugged. There are microphones in the flowerpots and the espresso machine."

"Vietnam Joe," she said.

"I can't take chances. Maria has a criminal mind. And he might have hurt you."

She watched the little scars near his mouth. They revealed much more than his eyes, which were a dead blue. But the scars seemed agitated. His entire jaw danced.

"Isaac shouldn't have let you into this. It's not a party. Maria makes up his own rules. He could cut your throat."

"Or shoot Isaac under a bridge."

"That wasn't Maria's work. He'd have shot Isaac *and* ripped his throat."

"And what's a man like that doing as the superintendent of a school district?"

"Maria's an angel. The superintendent before him was caught undressing a little girl."

"Please don't say that," Diana said.

"It's true."

"I don't want to hear it. It's sordid."

"It's still true . . . come on, I'll give you a ride uptown."

"I'll take the subway," she said. And she abandoned Joe.

She was late for her next appointment. She'd rented a studio for Milan Jagiello near Carnegie Hall. It had a hundred and twenty chairs. It was a loft with windows that opened onto a rat's view of the Hudson River. She felt like she was looking at a trickle of water between two enormous garbage cans. But she couldn't find another room that was big enough for Jagiello and his Czech orchestra, which hovered between sixty and a hundred and ten souls, depending on the mood of the musicians. They were like a squabbling family, with brothers, sisters, husbands, wives. Jagiello would often hire a starving Czech off the street. He had no funds. Diana had to pay for everything. But she admired Milan. He could move his arm like a magic snake and deliver Mozart, Beethoven, Mahler. He often had to tap a musician over the head. His first violin was a former mistress. He would moon at her in the middle of a performance. He couldn't survive without chaos. But Diana preferred him to ordinary conductors, who distanced themselves from an orchestra, who never descended into the pit to argue over a score.

Milan had no musicians today. He'd given them a week's rest before they toured the high schools and junior colleges of New Jersey. And he was glum away from his little colony.

"Deedee, I'm blue, really blue."

Milan was a moaner. He would wait like a little dog for Diana to suggest a meal at the Russian Tea Room, and then his eyebrows would curl at the prospect of drinking borscht around the managers and musicians of Carnegie Hall. But she couldn't tempt him.

"I'll always be a boy in America," he told her. "The big managers won't let me breathe. They're jealous of the Jagiellos."

Milan wasn't descended from any line of Bohemian kings. He was the son of a tailor. He'd starved in Prague, suffered from vitamin deficiency, had gone mad before he was ten, and studied the piano at a state asylum. He was considered a prodigy. Music professors would run to the asylum and meet with this mad boy. He was soon dining on cake. But the professors had spoiled him. He slept with their daughters and wives. He turned lazy. He took the name Jagiello. He ran off to Paris and parked at the door of an immigrant-aid society. He milked the society as much as he could. He studied with charlatans who destroyed his technique. He fled to London and then landed in the United States, where he managed to get a green card. He married an heiress. The heiress dropped him after a month. But he'd become a Jagiello and he lived within the cracks of whatever aristocracy he could find.

Milan pieced together an orchestra of gifted frauds like himself. But the sound he gave his orchestra was unique. It was a schizophrenic medley of Prague and the United States. He'd imposed his own madness on either country. Diana adored the music, but she wouldn't sleep with Milan. She had no interest in his dark eyes. And Jagiello's hands were dirty.

He'd begun to shiver.

"They won't let me graduate. They won't let me graduate."

He'd grown ugly in America. The maestro was losing his hair. His gums were turning black. She held him in her arms. He was like some fragile bird.

"Talk to Dammler. Please."

Ivan Dammler was president of the Philharmonic. Dee had slept with him once, long before she'd discovered Caroll in Central Park. She could feel Dammler contemplating her daddy's millions while he closed his eyes. But he had more than money on his mind. He'd confused Dee with some femme fatale or dominatrix. And Dee was neither one nor the other. She was her daddy's girl, who collected lost boys like Milan and Isaac or Maria Montalbán.

Milan wouldn't stop crying.

"The blinis will fatten you up," she said. "Come on. I'll reserve a table near the door and we'll look at all the movie stars."

But he was beyond the comforts of the Russian Tea Room. She saw that in his dark eyes, which were like circles shutting out all the light. Milan had arrived at the end of his own imperial line. He was an American now, one more native son, without any kings in the closet.

"I'll kill myself, Diana."
She slapped his face. "Shut up."
"I can't play for children all my life."
"Don't I get you college towns?"
"Children," he said.
Dee slapped him again. She undressed her Jagiello, held him in her arms, his scrotum like paper skin against her thigh. Perhaps she was a damn dominatrix. Because it soothed Milan to be without his clothes.
"I'll talk to Dammler. I promise."
And she put him to bed like the toy conductor he'd become. She wasn't barren. She had a child. His name was Milan. She kissed his forehead and put out the light.

13

She wouldn't wear a gown in the great hall of the Metropolitan Museum of Art. She had no purple veins to hide. She wore a summer dress in March, her ankles bound up in Spanish leather, her breasts high against her throat.

Her daddy wore a cummerbund and a proper coat. She could have been taken for his concubine. Because she was wicked around Papa Cassidy, clutching his arm, ignoring him, or stroking his ear. He flourished near his daughter. He'd preferred Diana's company since she was a child.

"Where's the cop?" Papa asked.

"You'll have to ask Susan, my secretary. She knows his schedule."

"It's a fine thing when a wife loses track of her husband."

"Stop scolding me. You couldn't even remember my mother's birthday."

"I remember what needs remembering. How's Maria Montalbán?"

"Good, Papa. He wants to marry me."

"With Caroll's permission, I hope. But Cardinal Jim might not like it. He's kind of old-fashioned. He won't recite another wedding Mass."

"Oh, I wouldn't bother Jim. I'd bring you into church, Papa. You can recite the Mass."

"Baby, I'm not a priest."

"Papa, get off my back."

And she whirled away from her father, who seemed forlorn without Diana's touch. But she was free of him, in some neutral country under the enormous ceiling. Men began to drink up that perfume of her skin. She had a glass of champagne. Diana hiccupped, and her breasts moved higher and higher, and she missed Caroll and thought of Maria's rings. She hadn't realized it was a charity ball for children. Alejo Tomás was here, chancellor of the City's schools, with a host of his superintendents, including Maria Montalbán. He'd kept all his grace in this mad shuffle. He hadn't sacrificed his high heels or the gold star in his ear. She felt a hand on her shoulder. It belonged to Ivan Dammler.

"You've been avoiding me."

"Ivan, I could never do that. I was going to make an appointment with you at the Philharmonic."

"What's the occasion? Ah, let me guess. It's the Czech genius, Milan Jagiello."

"You could let him audition, for Christ's sake."

"Audition for what? Assistant janitor? I wouldn't lend my orchestra to the likes of him."

"You've never seen him conduct."

"You're wrong. I've heard him and his home-relief society. It's a fabulous kindergarten class. Beethoven and Mickey Mouse."

"That's unfair," she said.

"I don't have to be fair . . . sleep with me."

He had such a look of terror that Diana couldn't laugh.

"Sleep with me . . . and I'll give your Czech a chance."

"Ivan, I'm not that terrific. And if there was ever something between us, we wouldn't be bargaining like strangers. I'll get that audition without you."

It was a lie, of course. Ivan could block whatever move she

made at the Philharmonic. Her daddy would have to threaten the entire board of trustees. And Papa didn't like Milan any better than Ivan Dammler did. So she'd have to seduce the trustees one by one, which she might have accomplished in her bachelor years; she no longer had the taste for it. She had to carry an orchestra on her back.

She was bored by the men who gaped at her and was about to leave when Maria took her arm and started to dance with her in the middle of the floor. She didn't resist. "It's not salsa," he said. "But I can do all the gringo trots."

"You're a gringo yourself."

"Yes. That's the cross every Newyorican has to bear. A child of two cultures."

"Poor Maria," she said, but she held him tight in the great hall of the Metropolitan Museum of Art, near the mummy room, where all the Egyptian gods and goddesses lay. The band was never good at these charity balls, because no one was encouraged to dance. The musicians stood like grim dolls in evening clothes that could have been waiters' pajamas. They must have worn the same pajamas from gig to gig. Milan Jagiello should have been the band leader. Then they could have had Czech tangos at the charity ball, a real Vienna waltz, and some salsa from Milan's own dark days in Brazil, where he starved for a month with most of his orchestra, who had to sell their shoes and their shirts.

"The cardinal's awful fond of you," Maria said.

"Yes. He married me at his cathedral . . . he said the Mass."

"I told him I wanted to live with you."

Her eyes widened, but she wouldn't pull away from Maria. "What did he say?"

"He laughed. He said you were a big girl and could take care of yourself. And he could excommunicate me if I went too far . . . I always got along with Cardinal Jim. I hope he'll marry us one day."

"He wouldn't marry any woman who was living in sin."

"He'd make an exception for you."

"No. He never marries people twice."

"Let me handle Jim. I spent half my life being paddled by priests . . . ah, princess, you aren't wearing my rings."

"I intended to return them at the next meeting of the Monday Morning Club."

"What's the rush? I haven't introduced you to my jeweler yet. He's a remarkable man."

And he spun Diana around among all the moguls of Manhattan until half the population must have thought she was Maria's girl. Dee didn't care but Papa Cassidy would be mad as hell. He couldn't discharge a school superintendent, not even with all his millions. And Dee had her own millions to fight him off.

She was dancing with Maria Montalbán, his fingers playing on her ribs. And then she saw Caroll in his detective clothes. He hadn't bothered to dress for the ball. He hadn't combed his hair. His shoes were caked with mud. His eyes were very raw. He must have been drinking in Central Park. She couldn't keep track of him anymore. She didn't even know his schedule at Sherwood Forest. She had to ask her secretary to plot the lines of Caroll's day. Susan must have told him about the ball.

"Caroll," she said, when he was almost upon her. But he didn't even go to her with his bloodshot eyes. He twisted Maria around and started to dance, clutching Maria's fingers in his own policeman's paws. Maria smiled. He was ready for Caroll Brent. He didn't have the slightest look of bewilderment. He danced with Caroll. "Ah," Maria said. "The husbands' waltz. One-two-three, one-two-three." And Caroll stopped, almost as suddenly as he began. He let Maria's fingers out of his paws and punched him. Blood flew from Maria's mouth, but he continued to smile. "One-two-three, one-two-three," he said, as he sank into the floor.

Diana screamed. "Caroll, don't." But Caroll leaned over Maria and punched him some more. The cardinal had to come. The cardinal and Alejo Tomás and Papa Cassidy and a couple of bankers. It took all five of them to free Maria Montalbán, who slid out from under Caroll, patted his swollen mouth, and walked away from the ball. Diana looked at Papa Cassidy and Cardinal Jim. She couldn't meet Caroll's eyes. She followed Maria out of the great hall.

14

No one, not even the Acting Commish, seemed to know what to do with Caroll. Sweets called Isaac at Beekman Downtown. Isaac was having his usual feast of lime jello and didn't want to be disturbed. But he picked up the phone and growled, "Isaac here."

"How are you, Commish?" Sweets said.

"I'm not the Commish. You are. I'm Citizen Sidel."

"And I'm your decoy. Because your spooks are all over the place. I can't control them. Neither can you. Caroll Brent just assaulted Maria Montalbán at the Metropolitan Museum of Art."

"What was Maria doing at the Metropolitan? Attending a smoker for superintendents who sell cocaine?"

"I hear he was rubbing his dick against Caroll's wife. But that still doesn't give him the right to assault a civilian. I told you to keep your vendettas out of my hair."

"Where's Caroll?"

"Inside the holding pen at Sherwood Forest."

"You put him in the cage at his own precinct?"

"To teach him a lesson. We took his gun and his shield. But you can let him out of the cage."

"Did you have to humiliate him?" Isaac said, outside the comforts of any lime jello.

"I could have done much worse."

"What happens now?"

"We keep it in the house. He gets a departmental trial."

Isaac groaned again. "He hits that son of a bitch and you crucify him?"

"Isaac, I saved his ass."

"Your ass, you mean."

"No, the Department's. Not that you give a shit. You have your own agents. You shuffle them around from your hospital bed. And I have to clean up the mess . . . now run to Sherwood Forest like a good little boy. Should I get you a limousine?"

"No thanks. I don't want Oliver Cromwell biting Caroll's back."

"You appointed Malik, I didn't."

Martin Malik, aka Oliver Cromwell, was trials commissioner of the NYPD. He headed the Department's internal system of justice. Malik had his own courtroom on the fourth floor of One PP. Malik was a Moslem and a Turk. He'd been an assistant D.A. in the badlands of the Bronx when Isaac picked him up. A trials commissioner was almost always a member of the "minorities." He had to judge other policemen. And the Department would be a little more immune to charges of racism if the chief judge was Latino or black or Chinese. Isaac chose a Turk. He liked Malik's aggressive style in the Bronx. And Malik reminded him of Turhan Bey, a lost movie star out of World War II. Turhan Bey had appeared with Maria Montez in version after version of Scheherazade. Isaac wanted his own Arabian Nights at One PP. He was hopelessly romantic. But Malik was no lost movie star. He carried a Glock in his pants. He was the darling of Internal Affairs. Captains and deputy chief inspectors trembled around Martin Malik, who could deprive you of your pension for the least infidelity.

"Malik doesn't like Caroll," Isaac said. "He thinks Caroll's a pretty boy."

"He's a pretty boy himself."

"But that won't make him any fairer to Caroll."

"Isaac, you can always convince Malik to resign . . . after you return to the Department."

"I don't want Malik to resign. But couldn't we just stop the proceedings? I'll talk to Caroll. I'll get him to apologize."

"Isaac, no one interferes with Malik. He'd break my hump for tampering with his court . . . go and collect Caroll, will you, please?"

But Isaac was dreaming of Martin Malik. He'd have to blackmail Malik, but he didn't know how. Former chief judges at the NYPD had become foundation presidents, district attorneys, lieutenant governors, partners in the biggest law firms. And Malik could become Oliver Cromwell to all the United States.

Isaac barely had the heart to shave himself. He put on his baseball suit, trudged downstairs, hailed a police car out on the street, and rode up to Sherwood Forest. He'd have to get to Malik somehow. Malik could topple Isaac's own little Monday Morning Club. Caroll was like a child in the thick of a dream. Isaac would have to extricate him *and* build a case against Maria Montalbán.

He entered the precinct. Weiss, the old duty sergeant, was part of Isaac's club. Weiss should have retired. But where would Isaac get another folklorist of Central Park? Folklorists were hard to find. Sherwood Forest's own history would die with Sergeant Weiss.

"Hello, Sarge."

The old sergeant saluted him. And Isaac was mortified. Because he could remember when Weiss didn't have such wrinkled skin. Isaac began his career as a cop at Sherwood Forest. And Weiss had been the first partner Isaac ever had. It was a glorious six months with the squirrel patrol. Isaac could read Kafka and

Kant while he toured the Ramble, with that incredible light coming off the snow. The Park became Isaac's cloister. There was no crime, except for an occasional bandit who drove through the park to avoid a bit of traffic. Isaac preferred the north woods, where he could step off into Harlem, attend a rent party, or eat a bowl of ice cream at Swallow's, on a Hundred and Twenty-fifth Street. But the first deputy commissioner, Ned O'Roarke, picked him out of the Park, and Isaac joined the Irish Mafia at NYPD. Weiss had been there before Ned O'Roarke, Weiss had been his own fucking Virgil, his particular guide. Isaac could have gotten him a job at One PP, but Weiss preferred the big desk at Sherwood Forest.

"How's Caroll?"

"He won't talk to anybody . . . or let us buy him lunch. Isaac, it's criminal to lock him in there."

Isaac went to the holding pen. Caroll stood against the bars, which were painted blue. His coat was torn. One of his shoulder pads hung out like a mottled piece of intestines. His face was scratched.

"Did they hurt you, kid?"

Caroll didn't answer. There was nothing in his eyes for Isaac, no gift of remembrance, no anger. Weiss opened the cage. And Caroll stepped out into that little cluttered world of the Central Park Precinct. Isaac led him toward the captain's office. "Cap," he shouted, and Captain White came out of the office in a dark pullover, looking scared. His eyes couldn't seem to focus on the Pink Commish.

"Who scratched the kid's face?"

"Isaac, it wasn't my idea to put Caroll in the cage."

"Who scratched the kid's face?"

"We did."

"Get out of here. I'm borrowing your office."

White walked into the hallway, shuffled around like some feckless creature. He was a stray dog in his own precinct. Worse than a dog. Isaac walked into the captain's office with Caroll and shut the door. He sat in the captain's chair. But Caroll wouldn't sit.

"Caroll, I did my first tours in Central Park, I ever tell you that? With old man Weiss. We were the original Batman and Robin. Weiss would run his ass off and fly down from the trees. And I was the boy wonder who could chase a lousy pickpocket for miles. Batman and Robin. I'd wear a mask sometimes. I ever tell you that? . . . you been drinking, kid? Had a tough night?"

Caroll knocked the baseball cap off Isaac's brains. It was worse than a declaration of war. Isaac picked up the cap.

"Wheelchair," Caroll said.

"What?"

"Rubino's wheelchair. I met Sal in the Park and he told me about your Monday Morning Club. It has nothing to do with books. It's one more blind for your secret service. Did you have to become Maria Montalbán's pimp, with my own wife as the bait? Couldn't you get another chippy?"

"I had to use Diana. I didn't have a choice. Montalbán's crazy about her. Dee will draw him out. Don't worry. I picked all the meeting places."

Caroll knocked the baseball cap out of Isaac's hand.

"Punch me, kid," Isaac said. "I can take it."

"You'd love it too much . . . good-bye, Isaac."

"We have to talk," Isaac said.

"Like you talked to Blue Eyes before he got killed?"

Isaac started to blink. "Malik," he said. "Malik will go for your pension. Internal Affairs will dance on your head. They'll tie up Fabiano Rice and Sal Rubino and the vig."

"You're jealous because Sal is on my side."

"Yeah, I love the way he whistles in your ear. There's a rat in my organization, otherwise Sal wouldn't know all my moves."

"Maybe there's a whole bunch of rats, nibbling on your toes."

"Then I'll nibble all the nibblers. But that won't save your pension."

"I'll join the Marines."

"The Marines wouldn't take a bent cop. Malik has a fucking echo. That echo never ends."

"That's what you're worried about," Caroll said with a little smile. "You'll have to sit down with your Monday Morning Club in Malik's court. And Montalbán will slip away . . . Isaac, you're a rat bastard motherfucker. You're the shit at the bottom of my shoe. You're a skel with a baseball hat. You're Whitey Lockman's grandma. You're the scumbag in Becky Karp's toilet bowl."

"You're delirious, kid. Go to bed."

"Make me, Mr. Isaac."

"Ah, don't talk like that," Isaac said.

"I'd like to meet that phantom who tried to whack you out. I'd give him a couple of pointers. He should have shot you in the ear."

"The phantom could have been a she," Isaac said.

"Let me finish. Your brains would have started to leak. You wouldn't have made it to the hospital."

"You would have saved me, kid. You would have covered my ear with your own hand."

"You're wrong, Mr. Isaac. I would have shook your rotten head until your blood and brains leaked out. Because you deserve to die."

"You had your chance," Isaac said. "You found me under the bridge."

"I'm almost as dumb as Blue Eyes. I should have walked away and sung myself a happy song."

"But you didn't."

"I'll know better next time . . . you shouldn't have recruited Dee. You should have left her alone, you son of a bitch."

Caroll walked out of the captain's office, with Isaac hopping behind him. But Isaac had no wind. His heart was like a broken black pump that could barely deliver blood. His lips turned pale. He managed to clutch Caroll's coat in that corridor between the captain's office and the holding pen. Caroll spun away from him. "Don't you ever touch me again."

And he started to choke the Pink Commish, grabbing the collar of Isaac's jersey, until half the precinct fell on top of Caroll—Captain White, old man Weiss, an anti-crime girl, and Joe Barbarossa, who'd arrived with his white glove and managed to extricate Isaac. Caroll was still struggling. Isaac coughed and coughed. Caroll flung old man Weiss into the women's lockers. Barbarossa and the captain drove Carroll back inside the cage like a mad lion. The captain was a little delirious. Barbarossa had to do most of the work. He handcuffed Caroll to the bars of the cage, helped old man Weiss to his feet, and found a bottle of Coke for Isaac the Brave.

"Ah, don't lock him in there," Isaac said. "It hurts me to see him like that."

"He'll survive," Barbarossa said.

And Isaac had to wonder if it was Barbarossa who'd socked him under the bridge. Joe was a tracker in Vietnam. He could have followed Isaac into the dark, or waited for him in the shadows of Sheriff Street. Perhaps he was in league with Wilson and McSwain, his two favorite dykes. Perhaps there was a club inside the Monday Morning Club. Joe could have been on Sal Rubino's payroll. It was logical. It made sense. But would Barbarossa have socked him without saying hello?

Isaac felt like a wounded baby. He started to cry. He missed his worm. The worm had been his best companion.

Barbarossa grabbed Isaac with his gloved hand. "It's all right, chief."

Isaac kept bawling. "I shouldn't have punished you, Joe. You could have made captain by now. You could have been with the First Dep . . . and I exiled you to Sherwood Forest."

"You had to, Isaac. I was a bad boy. And it could have been worse. You never gave me to Malik. Malik would have closed the door on me. I don't have any regrets."

"Will you look after the kid?"

"I'll diaper him for you."

"I'm the bad boy. I messed with his wife."

"It was the only way to Maria Montalbán."

Barbarossa put Isaac in a police car and had a rookie drive him to Gold Street. Then he got Caroll a cup of coffee and a candy bar.

"Either you eat, or I stuff it down your throat."

He went into the cage with Caroll and removed the handcuffs. But Caroll couldn't seem to hold the coffee cup. And Barbarossa had to feed him with that white glove.

"You saw her with Maria in his fucking café."

"Yeah," Caroll said.

"And you watched his handkissing routine."

"More than that. He gave her some jewelry."

"Two rings," Barbarossa said.

"And a necklace."

"No, it was a bracelet."

"You're right . . . you listened to their conversation."

"Every word."

"I know. I bugged the place for Isaac. I planted the mikes."

"It was Rubino who told you about Maria and the wife, wasn't it?"

"Yeah, Isaac has a rat in his Monday Morning Club. The rat tells Rubino everything."

"And you think I'm the rat."

"You or Weiss. Or Wilson. Or McSwain. Or the Cap. But why doesn't Isaac disband his Monday Morning Club?"

"That's not his style . . . he has to leave us in place. He can't get to Montalbán all on his own."

"So he'll risk another round of bullets under the bridge. Joe, did you glock the Commish?"

"Yeah, I'm the phantom. I hit him with all I had. Then I kissed him on the mouth . . . don't be stupid, Caroll. Isaac's our general. I wouldn't whack him out. And I wouldn't rat on him."

"But you'd let him borrow my wife."

"That's none of my business."

"You were my partner, Joe. You ate at my fucking dinner

table. I took you in for weeks at a time when you had the blues. I covered for you when you started to hallucinate."

"I don't hallucinate. I have a touch of malaria. It comes, it goes. You can never get rid of tropical fever . . . I'm sorry about the wife. But it's not my shit. It's Isaac's. I'm only following orders."

"While I follow my wife."

"And go crazy. You should hit her once or twice."

"I can't," Caroll said.

"It could do wonders for you. She'd get into line and drop the Monday Morning Club."

"I can't."

They were both whispering. The captain had gone back to his office and Weiss was behind his desk, but Caroll and Barbarossa couldn't stop whispering. It was a habit they'd picked up at Sherwood Forest.

"You started drinking, didn't you? After you saw her with Montalbán. And you wanted to run into the café and waste the bastard. But you started to drink."

"I had ten whiskeys. More than ten."

"I could have given you some Thai stick."

"It's not the same thing," Caroll said.

"If I let you out of the box, will you go home?"

"I don't have a home. I get in the way of all the servants. I have to tiptoe around them like a fucking guest. Did you ever hear of a mansion inside an apartment house? You slept in one of the rooms, for Christ's sake."

"Yeah, I almost got lost."

"I took a room at Lincoln Tower."

"You're the one who's hallucinating."

"No. I like the place."

It was a flophouse on Central Park North. It had its own secret address, because most native New Yorkers never even knew there was a Central Park North. Barbarossa and Caroll had busted a child-pornography and prostitution ring at the hotel.

But all Caroll could think about was the view from the window, or he might have murdered the child molesters. He was just above the trees, and the Park floated under him like a fabulous moving curtain. Barbarossa wanted to off the three molesters, who had their own studio and shop at Lincoln Tower behind a fake fire door. But there was a child in the room, a girl of twelve or so, who was sitting naked on a couch with a smile that could chill a man.

"The girl, the little girl," Caroll had whispered to Barbarossa.

"Partner, she won't have much of a memory for the motherfuckers. And if we walk right out, she'll never recognize us. Who will know, partner, who will know? . . . I have a terrible itch."

Caroll covered up the little girl with a blanket and arrested the three men. But the D.A.'s office wouldn't indict. "It's an illegal search and seizure," said Corcoran, the young assistant D.A.

"Jesus," Barbarossa said. "They were standing with their cocks out and photographing that little girl."

"You'd still have to show probable cause. Was the door open?"

"No."

"Did the girl scream?"

"No."

"They'll laugh us out of court . . . you should have gone to your superiors and gotten a warrant. What were you doing in that hotel?"

"We had a hunch."

Barbarossa couldn't say that he'd gone to the hotel to tease a little Thai stick out of a dealer, that he was smoking the Thai with Caroll, and had wandered through the fire door.

"I told you, partner. We should have offed them," Barbarossa had said once Corcoran was gone. But Caroll kept returning to the hotel. He'd "borrow" a room for a couple of hours. The manager wouldn't let him pay. He'd sit and watch that crazy curtain of leaves. And now he'd gone back as a permanent, paying guest.

Barbarossa brought him to Lincoln Tower in his own car.

"Partner, go home to the wife. Talk to her. Slap her around and cuddle her. You'll feel better."

"I can't," Caroll said. And he went inside the Lincoln's battered front door.

Part Four

15

The City had begun using Caroll's hotel as a holding pen for families without a roof. It was filled with the homeless. A deputy commissioner from the Department of Human Resources arrived at the hotel with an enormous ledger and knocked on everybody's door, including Caroll's.

"What are you doing here?" the deputy asked. "You're not a family. I'll have to evict you."

Caroll took the ledger out of this deputy's hands. "I'm a paying guest."

"That's impossible. We've taken over this hotel."

"I'm a paying guest."

The deputy showed Caroll his badge. "I've requisitioned every room."

"I got here before the City did. Now get the hell out of my face."

And Caroll kept his room. The City had to edge around him. But he began to feel distressed. He had his view of the trees, he had his hot plate. He could swim in his own sea of space, while the other lodgers lived four and five to a room. He promised himself that he'd go back to the mansion, but he couldn't. He had to talk to Dee. He couldn't. He kept recalling those rings. It didn't matter if she'd slept with Montalbán or not. It was still a romance. She'd been thinking of Maria all the while she was in bed with Caroll. Maria had been on her mind. And Caroll couldn't even tell if he was sane anymore. He'd met Sal Rubino in the Park. He'd followed Dee to Maria's café. He'd started to drink. He'd planned in his head to murder Maria. But he was only a cop at Sherwood Forest, diminished by jealousy and drink. He didn't have the cunning and frozen blood of an assassin. He drank his way uptown to the Metropolitan Museum of Art. And when he did confront Dee with her dancing partner, he could hardly look into her eyes. All he could do was dance with Maria and punch him into the ground. He'd lost his shield and had to wait for Martin Malik. He had five hundred dollars in the bank. And then he'd have to borrow against his Gold Card. He'd be solvent for a couple of months, until all his credit shut down . . . and he'd go looking for another shylock.

But he had those magnificent trees from his window, a curtain across the Park that soothed him in this sad hotel. Old men lost their memories in the hall. Caroll had to return them to whatever room they were in. He climbed over garbage and human shit, wondering if Malik's court could be worse than this. But he didn't abandon the hotel. He broke up fights between the different lodgers. He was both a sheriff and a scribe, helping the sick and the blind prepare dossiers that would bring them food stamps. He lived on soup and soda crackers . . . and bottles of Four Roses. He discovered a young lady in the hall. She wore high heels and a floppy hat that hid half her face. She wasn't soliciting any of the lodgers. She didn't look much like a prostitute. She had to be a model, with a swipe of lipstick and the one delicately shaded eye that Caroll could see. He recognized her now. She was the pornographers' model. But he'd been mistaken. She wasn't such a little girl.

"I'm Delia," she said, shaking his hand when Caroll wouldn't get out of her way.

"Delia, what are you doing here?"

"Looking for locations."

"You some kind of a scout?"

"Yes. I'm in the picture business. Movie pictures."

She was fifteen, sixteen at the most, under her floppy hat. And Caroll didn't play the cop. He let her pass. And he began to feel a curious thrill, as if his own future were tied to this girl. He and Barbarossa hadn't closed the pornography shop at Lincoln Tower. It was business as usual behind the fire door. There must have been other studios and shops. And he began to realize that Lincoln Tower was a pornography mill. The Department of Human Resources was only an elaborate cover. Caroll didn't pounce. He followed Delia, always at a distance. She had liquid legs. She could navigate a stairway like nobody's business. Who the hell had taught her to glide like that?

But his persistence with Delia began to pay. He caught her talking to a man in front of the hotel. The guy had gotten out of a Cadillac. Short, with elegant sleeves. It was Caroll's shylock, Fabiano Rice.

Caroll almost started to laugh. He'd found a little symmetry in his own life. The world had its very own reason. Delia was attached to Fabiano. Fabiano worked for Sal. It was Mafia country on Central Park North. Sal Rubino had placed his pornography mill on a street that no one knew about. It was invisible to human traffic.

Caroll got into a cab and followed the Cadillac. Fabiano stopped at one of his haunts, a café on Pleasant Avenue, in the heart of Italian Harlem, which had dwindled to a one-block district. It was the safest block in New York City. Caroll entered the café. Fabiano's bodyguard hopped out like a chess piece and stood in front of Caroll.

"It's only the piccolino," Caroll's shylock said. "He doesn't even have a gun. He's going to be court-martialed pretty soon. He's harmless."

Caroll sat down next to the shylock, who offered him a salad with anchovies, a crust of Italian bread, and a clear soup with parsley and bits of egg yolk that swam around like tadpoles. It was a king's lunch for Caroll, living away from his soda crackers.

"Maestro, it's very, very good."

"I can't lend you money," Fabiano said. "Not in the state you're in. You're wearing Malik's mark. And I'd rather not appear in the minutes of his court."

"Fine. But I'd like to talk to Sal."

"Forget Sal. Sal's decided to become a ghost again. He's a little gunshy when it comes to Malik."

"Maestro, I'm surprised at you. Malik runs a police court. It has no authority outside Police Plaza."

"That's what you think. Malik will be governor one day. And he won't forget. He'd love to start a crusade against our Family. No, I can't afford you, piccolino. And neither can Sal."

"Then you tell Sal that I send him regards from Delia."

The shylock stared at the tadpoles in his soup. "Piccolino, you have a big mouth. You should start to pray that you'll survive this restaurant. The chef has a very uncommon back door. It leads to the sewage-disposal plant on Wards Island."

"You'll disappoint Malik," Caroll said. "And I don't disappear that easy. I marked Pleasant Avenue on my wall. Someone's bound to notice."

"Shut up."

"Congratulations for finding an address like Central Park North."

"Don Fabiano," the bodyguard said. "I could cut him so his mouth will never close."

"Albert, who asked you? Just stay by the window."

The shylock was jittery because the Rubinos were still at war with Jerry DiAngelis. Sal had to come back from the dead to reclaim his clan, or Fabiano would have floated in DiAngelis' direction. Jerry's younger brother was a parrot for the FBI who was in the witness protection program. His father-in-law, Izzy Wasser, a tactical genius, had suffered a stroke. Jerry had fallen on hard times. Half his crews had deserted him.

"There's nothing unkosher about Delia St. John," Fabiano said. "She's the biggest child model in Manhattan . . . and she's not even a child."

"But she happens to model without her clothes."

"Only some of the time," Fabiano said.

"Then how come she's hiding in a rat's hotel?" Caroll stood up. "Thanks for the soup and salad." He walked past the body-guard and out the door, but he wasn't finished. He took a bus down to the diamond district and waited for Fabiano, who liked to lend money to the merchants of Forty-seventh Street. The merchants were always short of cash. Fabiano arrived at his favorite little diamond market. He traveled from stall to stall, looking at diamonds, collecting his vig. Then he walked up to Forty-eighth and Fifth and entered the building where Papa Cassidy had his headquarters. Caroll didn't believe in coincidences like that. He called Papa from the lobby as soon as Fabiano had left the building. Papa broke up a meeting to take Caroll's call.

"Come upstairs, will you, Caroll?"

Caroll went through a wall of secretaries. Papa wore red suspenders and a striped shirt. Oh, you son of a bitch, Caroll sang to himself. Oh, you son of a bitch. Papa had to know about the vig. There was a marriage between Stewart Hines and Papa and Fabiano and Sal. And Caroll was on their merry-go-round. It was Papa who fed him to Sal. Oh, you son of a bitch.

"We were worried," Papa said, offering Caroll a glass of champagne.

"I'm sorry about what happened at the museum. I didn't mean to punch all those people." Papa, Papa, I should have punched you.

"Where are you staying?"

"Here and there," Caroll said. "I don't have an address."

"Think of the wife, Caroll boy. I don't like leaving Diana all alone."

With the servants, Papa, and the secretary.

"Montalbán's a bad influence," Papa said. "I'll have to show him some of my teeth. And you don't have to be frightened of that big black buck."

"Big black buck?"Caroll said.

"Sweets. He shouldn't have given you to the Turk. But Malik will be in for a surprise. You'll have my whole team of lawyers at your court-martial."

"Has Diana asked about me?"

"She's worried to death."

"But did she say anything?"

"That's the problem. She's never home. I keep talking to Susan, her secretary. She's missed board meetings. She's neglected her orchestra. Jagiello cries to me on the phone . . . I was hoping you could find her."

"I'll find her," Caroll said, "like I found Delia St. John."

All the bonhomie seemed to go out of Papa. Not even the red suspenders could bring back his good will.

"Are you hustling me, Caroll?"

"I wouldn't know how to do that, sir."

"You're hustling me. Like you hustled my daughter . . . I'll break your bones."

"Delia," Caroll said. "We were talking about Delia."

"If it's blackmail, you have the wrong customer. I never pay."

He seized a lamp off his desk, pulled out the plug, and went after Caroll. *God bless all venture capitalists.* Caroll dodged the first swing of the lamp. Papa tried to crown him, but he wasn't quick enough. Caroll grabbed Papa's wrist, and they started to dance near the wall. Caroll was always dancing with other men. There was a terrible heat in Papa's eye.

"Papa," Caroll said, "put down the fucking lamp."

The heat went out of Papa's eye. He returned the lamp to his desk. He looked like one more foolish boy in his red suspenders, almost as foolish as Caroll, who couldn't hold on to his gun or his wife, who built a nest on Central Park North, and was going to be swallowed up by Martin Malik.

"You're the one," Caroll said. "You fingered me. You're my personal Judas."

"Judas?" Papa said. "I don't sell people for silver and gold."

"That's right. You sell them for free. You gave Sal Rubino the idea to cancel my vig. Now tell me you never sit down with gangsters, tell me you don't know Sal."

"Of course I know him. You can't put up a building in New York without doing business with Rubino. He has a monopoly on all the cement."

"It was Sal who introduced you to Delia . . . or was it Fabiano Rice? You back Fabiano, don't you? You're the shylock behind the shylock. You're the banker in Sal's loanshark operation. All the time I took from Fabiano, I was really borrowing from you."

"You should have come to me first. I would have helped."

"Jesus, do you hate me that much for marrying Diana?"

"I don't hate you."

"Then why did you sell me to Sal?"

"He was going to take Delia away."

"She's a child," Caroll said. "I saw her naked in a goddamn pornography shop. She doesn't even have any pubic hair."

Papa smiled, and his eyes seemed human again. "The best fashion models shave between their legs. It turns the customers on."

"You too, Papa?"

"I was impotent. Delia restored my life."

"Your little love doll."

"Don't say that. If Sal can't get you killed, I will."

"You can't kill me, Papa. Nobody can. I belong to Martin Malik."

And Caroll got out of there. He went to the district attorney's office down on John Street and asked one of the secretaries for assistant D.A. Cork Corcoran.

"Do you have an appointment, sir?"

"No, but tell him it's the man from Central Park North. I'll be outside the building."

Corcoran was downstairs in a couple of minutes, looking piggly in his eyeglasses. "Oh, it's you," he said, squinting at Caroll.

"Who were you expecting, Cork?"

"Never mind."

"Let's talk about the People versus the Central Park North Pornographers' Association."

"Very funny."

"We had a case. We caught the bastards with their cocks out."

"Not here, Detective Brent. Not in the street."

"Don't flatter me, Cork. I'm not a detective anymore."

"Yes you are. You haven't been thrown off the Force. You're just doing a little sweetheart time. Consider it a second honeymoon."

"I'm waiting for Martin Malik."

"Everybody waits for Malik. It means nothing . . . but we shouldn't talk in the street. There are too many eyes and ears."

And Caroll followed Corcoran through a passageway that led to a luncheonette on old Dutch Street. They grabbed a corner table and stirred their coffee with a spoon.

"We had a case," Caroll insisted. "We had a case."

"You had dick."

"Yeah, a naked little girl."

"She's not so little," Corcoran said. "She could be a hundred. No one can guess the age of Delia St. John."

"Then you know about the girl."

"Wake up. She's the most notorious little cunt in the history of Manhattan."

"Not so fast," Caroll said.

"Little Delia has had half of Wall Street inside her pants. Is that slow enough for you, Detective Brent?"

"And we just happened to find her at a fucking charity hotel, Barbarossa and me."

"Very funny. Barbarossa's one of her clients. Yeah, he's had relations with the girl. Who hasn't? And you want me to indict? I don't believe in fairy tales. The girl is protected, Caroll. She has the Mob behind her. She has Papa Cassidy, she has a couple of ex-governors. It's a big can of worms. I'm not going to sink the D.A.'s office because Joe Barbarossa is on some kind of a trip, between politics and ping-pong."

"So you walk away."

"I walk when I have to walk. Caroll, it's over your head . . . leave it alone."

"I can't."

"Leave it alone."

"Sure. That's the dividing line. Central Park North. That's the land of midnight. But I'm living there now, and I don't like it."

Caroll paid for the coffee and left the assistant D.A. in his own little corner on old Dutch Street.

16

He'd gone out and shaken the feathers around Delia St. John. And he'd have to bear the cost of all his enterprise. Fabiano must have talked to Sal. Caroll was a little too close to their kingdom, roosting at Lincoln Tower. They couldn't afford to have him in the neighborhood. He wondered if Sal would send the same operator who tried to off Isaac under the bridge. A member of the Monday Morning Club. McSwain? The killer lady. The killer lady with a Glock. But it wouldn't be McSwain. He began to drink from the bottle of Four Roses in his room. He had to prepare himself for the operator. He'd cut the lights and sit behind the door with the neck of the bottle in his fist. But he'd have to finish the bottle first.

He tried to think of the life he'd had before he met Dee. He didn't have a life. A few turns in the sack with Sarah Potts of the PAL. He might even have been engaged to Sarah. But it was an engagement to nothing and nowhere. He couldn't have married Sarah. She had no music in her body, the way Diana did. He'd been comfortable talking "police" to a lady cop. He could go with Sarah to the shooting range at Throgs Neck. But that didn't make for a whole lot of mystery. She'd have a pension. So would Caroll. He didn't long for Sarah Potts.

He knew the ice man would come up to his room, shake his hand, smile, chat a little, and then glock him while Caroll was looking out the window at his fortune of trees. He wished it was Joe. He wished it was Joe. Caroll could have made something of a suicide pact. He'd have finished Barbarossa with one last magic glance.

He shouldn't have been drinking so much, not a warrior like him. He'd buy a white glove, like Joe had, a parade glove Caroll could wear on every one of his kills. Because *he* was the ice man, the secret member of the Monday Morning Club. And what if he met another Caroll coming through the door? Had he gone bananas under the bridge and shot Isaac five times without knowing it? But he didn't even own a Glock.

And when he heard the footsteps, Caroll had to laugh. He plugged his bottle of Four Roses and held it by the neck. There was a feeble knock on the door. "Come in," Caroll said, moving closer and closer to the end of his line. Isaac had a daughter to cry for him. Sweets had several children. But Caroll and Diana couldn't make a kid.

He stood behind the door, the bottle high over his head, and could see the floppy roof of a hat. It was the diva herself, Delia St. John. Caroll groaned and came out from behind the door. She discovered him with the bottle. She didn't flinch. Her eyes simply took all of him in.

"How old are you?" he asked.

"That depends on who you are and what you want."

"I'm a used-up detective, but you know all about that."

"And I'm a professional child. That's my metier."

"Cork was right," Caroll muttered. "You are a hundred years old."

"I could be a lot older than that, if you're on a great-grandmother trip. Sky's the limit."

"I'm not one of your tricks," Caroll said.

"I don't have tricks. I have admirers. And they're all perfect gentlemen."

"Yeah sure. Like the three characters who were photographing you the first time we met. The shy pornographers."

"They weren't shy. And they aren't pornographers. They work for Uncle Sal . . . and why are you holding a bottle over your head?"

"That's my business." Caroll threw the Four Roses on his bed. Delia took something out of her handbag. Caroll recognized the plastic nose of a Glock. She was pointing it at him.

His knees shivered for a moment, and then he felt a wondrous calm. He didn't care what Delia did. He almost wanted to dance.

"Here," she said. "Take it. You'll need some protection. You sure know how to make enemies, Mr. Brent."

"Who gave you the gun?"

"I stole it," she said, "from one of my bodyguards."

"That's great. That's grand. It could be a hot fucking piece." Caroll held the gun in his handkerchief and dropped it back into Delia's bag. "Now good night."

"It's not even dinner time," Delia said.

"Well, I keep peculiar hours."

"You're an alcoholic," she said.

"And what if I am? Who sent you?"

"Uncle Joe."

"Is he another one of your bodyguards, Joe Barbarossa?"

"He's my friend."

"You can tell him I'm buying a white glove . . . we'll have a game of ping-pong, just me and Joe. I'll do the Blue Eyes shuffle. I'll bend his back . . . was he trying to blackmail the pornographers? Is that why he staged that little séance behind the fire door?"

"He was helping me. And who else could he trust but his own partner?"

"Trusted me so much that he didn't mention a thing. He brought me into his web, that's all."

"It was complicated," Delia said. "Furio wanted me as his

private model. I don't give exclusives. Furio doesn't own me. But Uncle Sal was dead at the time."

"Dead in New Orleans."

"And Furio was captain of the Family."

"So Joey scared the shy pornographers, who were also Family men. Where is this Furio?"

"When Uncle Sal returned from the dead he had Furio's throat cut for being disloyal . . . and unkind to me."

"Yeah," Caroll said. "That sounds like Sal. I like his chivalry. But why are you here?"

"Joe asked me to look for your wife. She's at Chinaman's Chance. It's an after-hours club five minutes from the hotel."

"Diana never goes uptown. Her limit is Ninety-sixth Street."

"Not anymore."

She took Caroll by the hand. Her fingers were very warm. She must have had a motor that ran at high speed in March. Her blood was much warmer than Caroll's. His head was spinning from the Four Roses. He had whiskey eyes. He looked like some ghostly animal in the mirror. And Delia looked like the stars.

"I'm not going," he said. "You could have me zapped in the street."

But he followed her down the stairs, his hand in hers. Children near the landing asked for her autograph. "Miss Delia, Miss Delia." They didn't have bits of paper, so she put her signature on their sleeves. Each letter was exact. The capital D was like a universe of its own.

"Who taught you your penmanship?"

"Uncle Maria."

And Caroll groaned again. "Did you go to school in District One B?"

"Yes and no, Uncle Caroll."

"I'm not your uncle. And what do you mean, yes *and* no?"

"I'm an uptown girl. But I took music lessons in Loisaida."

"With your Uncle Maria?"

"Uncle paid for the lessons."

It took fifteen minutes to complete all the signatures. And Delia admitted that Montalbán had been her English teacher at Joan of Arc Junior High School on the Upper West Side. "Maria's girls." Gringas, Latinas, and mulattas who practiced the same florid hand. The girls would have died for him. He taught them gringo culture better than any gringo could.

"It was scary, Uncle Caroll. He knew the lives of all the English poets. He knew the poems. 'Tiger, tiger, burning bright . . . in the forest of the night.' "

"William Blake," Caroll said. It was the one poem he could remember from all his schooling.

The wind sucked under his coat on Central Park North. The trees looked damaged and desolate from the ground. The Park was one more howling. There was a Cadillac behind him and Delia.

"My bodyguards," she said. "They keep me from getting kidnapped."

He walked toward Fifth Avenue with Delia. He was incredibly jealous. Maria's girls. There was a moonscape of buildings to the left of Caroll, houses of the dead. They walked hand in hand, the Cadillac crawling behind them. They passed under the Park Avenue trestle and the moonscape disappeared. They'd crossed into some magic territory of people and red stone buildings and grocery stores and bonfires in trash cans that glowed with yellow tails. Caroll must have been on these streets before. But they'd never shimmered in such red and yellow light. The diva was showing him her Manhattan.

He brooded over Montalbán.

"Was he the best teacher you ever had? . . . did he undress you after class?"

Delia took her hand away.

"Did he get you modeling jobs? Did he introduce you to Papa Cassidy and all the bigwigs at the Board of Education?"

She slapped his face. It felt like kisses in the cold air.

"He saved my life. I was a model since I was nine. He took me out of circulation . . . he sent me to music classes."

"And you started modeling again."

"My mother was crazy. My father was dead. I had two little sisters . . ."

"Sure," Caroll said. "Maria's girls." He was miserable. Delia clutched his hand and led him into a building without a front door. He struggled in the freezing weather of the hall. Down a flight of steps he went with Delia St. John. The walls were bewitched. He could hear a curious caravan of voices. They entered a cave where a man in dark glasses frisked Caroll, but didn't bother with Delia's handbag. The cave was cluttered with men and women who drank at a broken-down bar, their faces coming out of obscurity with certain chances of the irregular ceiling light. There was no music in the cave, nothing but continual chatter. And Caroll couldn't understand the attraction of this club. Then the light fell on Maria Montalbán and a packet of Maria's girls, their faces swollen and grim. Caroll imagined them as refugees from Joan of Arc Junior High until he recognized Dee next to Montalbán, his arm around her waist, and Caroll lunged into the darkness of the cave, but wherever he emerged, it wasn't with Maria or his own wife. He kept going into the dark and coming out on some far side of the cave, emptied of people. It was like the story of his own existence, scratching in the dark, from Far Rockaway to Sherwood Forest and Central Park North. He'd had Dee. He'd had a marriage. And now Dee was one more face in the dark. He couldn't cry like Isaac Sidel. He didn't have Isaac's capacity. He might have given himself utterly to the cave, scrutinizing the light, if Delia hadn't taken his hand.

"I'm sorry," she said. "I thought Maria would talk to you. I was wrong."

"Where are they? Where's my wife?"

"They're gone, Uncle Caroll."

And he found himself back out on the street, away from Chinaman's Chance.

17

Cat in the middle, cat in the fiddle, cat on the top of the moon. She was tired of being Cassidy's daughter, patroness of the PAL. She was crazy about Caroll, but she couldn't spend her life on a single honeymoon. She could still feel the goose bumps from the time they'd made love in the old barn in back of Sherwood Forest. She didn't dare take off her clothes, because there might be a guardian or a drunken cop on the premises. Her skirt was above her hips, hiding Caroll, and she had to stifle her own screams. But a barn was only a barn.

She liked being a spy, the unpaid soldier of Isaac Sidel, ferreting in the ruins of Maria's barrios. She was the heiress, and he was the prince of the streets, courting her with all that gibberish. He wanted to marry her on top of her own marriage. She knew all about his women, "Maria's girls," who were loyal to him for years and years, in spite of boyfriends, husbands, rich uncles and all. They were prostitutes and salesgirls and single parents. But he never exploited them. Isaac said they carried drugs for Maria, and this was the "currency" of their devotion. But she didn't believe Isaac.

"They're straight, boss. I swear."

She liked to think of him as her boss, this man who policed a city in his baseball cap and a pair of knickers, who rose out of his hospital bed to meet with her in the north woods.

"All his chiquitas are mules. He makes a habit of converting them to his cause. They carry his shit and like to think that they're helping schoolchildren, like the children they were when Montalbán was their own electric teacher, a wizard with the English language."

"You could be wrong," she said.

"I'm as wrong as a calendar without Mondays. He's a thief, Diana, and don't fall for him. He has his bottle clubs, he has his cafés, but he still steals from the City."

"Who doesn't?"

Isaac started to cough. He didn't even have a sweater over his uniform. He looked like the ghost of some lost baseball season.

"Caroll's going to be punished, isn't he?" Diana said.

"He can't go around punching people."

"I was dancing with Maria . . ."

"You're never home," Isaac said. "I have to call and call."

"I'm out in the field," she said. "I'm your faithful servant. I go around with Maria. I visit his sanctuaries. He's going to introduce me to his jeweler, the man who takes care of all the gold."

"It could get hairy."

"Hairy? No, no, no. I've been initiated. I'm one of Maria's girls."

"Don't say that," Isaac said.

"But I am. Where's Caroll?"

"Living at some bad-ass hotel. Don't worry. He'll be back."

"He never even took his clothes. He's keeping company with Delia St. John. I saw them together. At a bottle club. Maria says they're practically engaged."

"Come on, she has a million boyfriends."

"She's dating my dad. Imagine, Papa and Caroll involved with the same little bitch. She could become my stepmother . . . Caroll's on the bottle, isn't he? He's gone back to his first love, Four Roses. Does Delia iron his shirts?"

"I doubt it," Isaac said. "Shouldn't you visit him? It's rough for the kid."

"Delia can rock him to sleep. I have a date with the jeweler."

"Diana, don't disappear on me."

She kissed him under the bill of his cap. "Have to rush. Don't want to be late."

And she ran out of the Park, Isaac standing under a tree like some orphan of the woods, the holy crusader against crime. Did she belong to Isaac or Maria? She wasn't sure. Maria had lent her one of his cribs, a duplex on a Hundred and Twentieth Street. She slept alone. She hadn't invited him into bed, her curious cavalier. They'd kiss with their clothes on.

"Marry me."

"I'll wear your rings. But that's about it."

She would have slept with him, she wanted to, if he'd let go of his marriage song. She was Caroll's wife. She could only consider a husband at a time. But he moved her, this man of the public schools. He had disciples everywhere. They'd stop him on the street.

"Maria, I still have nightmares about Edgar Allan Poe."

"They'll go away, Charlene."

She couldn't mistake that adoration in their eyes. He'd crawled under the secret veil of language. It had nothing to do with grammar or past and present tense. They'd discovered how to sing in Maria's classes . . .

He was waiting for her at the crib, his eyes like dark funnels. He'd grown up in a housing project near the East River. He'd gone to one bombed-out school after the other, and survived them all.

"Come on. The jeweler's expecting you."

And they went down from the crib, both of them wearing red capes, like cardinals of the realm. She was beginning to feel more and more comfortable around Maria. He clutched her hand.

They got into a limousine that must have come from the Board of Education.

"My cousin's car," Maria said. "It belongs to Alejo. I borrow it sometimes. For official business."

He would stop at certain street corners, while men and women ducked into the car and delivered packets of money to Maria. He broke each packet and counted the bills. He didn't hide his counting from Dee.

"Is that school money?" she asked.

"No. Cash receipts. You can write that down for Isaac. And don't bother to playact. The Monday Morning Club was Isaac's idea. He planted you between his piles of books. You're supposed to draw me out, so he can tap into all my circuits and build his case against the evil superintendent, the monster who takes food out of children's mouths. But it's not so simple. I can't survive on a superintendent's allowance. So I deal and deal and deal. And you can tell Isaac that he isn't the only one who has his spies."

He kissed her on the mouth.

"Maria, why did you give me those rings and lend me your crib?"

"I'm a passionate man," he said. "And I like you. I like you very much."

"I don't want to meet the jeweler . . . I want to go home."

"Your home is with me."

And the limousine stopped at a huge warehouse close to the Hudson River. Dee could taste the water and the wind and the grime. She got out of the car with Maria. They were next to a handball court. The strangest creatures were volleying savagely with a little pink ball. Women with the broadest shoulders she'd ever seen, until she realized they were transvestites who serviced the truckers of the West Side. And they were volleying in all that wind.

"Hello, Maria," they shouted through the wire cage of the court. "Is that your pet?"

"I don't keep pets," Maria said. "And mind your own business."

"We always do."

"Consuela, you owe the corporation a thousand dollars."

"I thought I was getting a rebate," the most muscular transvestite said. "Aren't we Maria's girls?"

"The don owns you, dearie. You'd better pay."

And he went into the warehouse with Diana.

"Curse me," he said. "Tell me what I did isn't on any school's agenda. But how else can I juggle the books? If a school hurts, I have to find the right Band-Aid."

"Like transvestites who exercise on a handball court."

"You shouldn't be so prejudicial. One of the girls has a Ph.D."

"They aren't girls, Maria."

"You're wrong," Maria said. "If God won't make you a girl, then you just go against nature."

"While you get rich."

"I have to eat, dear. I have to eat."

The warehouse was cluttered with school desks that were packed in leaning towers, with pianos, with plumbing fixtures, with water fountains that were high enough for a kindergarten class, with window poles, with blackboards that were already chipped, with infinite boxes of board erasers and pencil sharpeners.

Maria smiled. "Welcome to God's kitchen."

"You create the shortages, Maria. You capitalize on missing board erasers."

"This isn't my warehouse. I have to pay for each desk the City can't provide."

"Who owns this place?"

"The jeweler."

And they rode up to the roof in a freight elevator. Two men were waiting for them on the final landing. They had shotguns holstered inside their coats. They didn't like Maria. But they ogled Dee, bowing to her while the shotguns bent with their own bodies. They unlocked a wire door. A voice growled from within. "Who's there?" A voice full of gravel and spite. "Who's there?"

"The schoolteacher and a girl."

"Maria's girl?"

"Yeah, boss. Maria's girl."

"Angelo, you're impolite. Let 'em in."

Diana and Montalbán were thrust inside that door and entered an elaborate living room as large as a baseball diamond. A man sat in a wheelchair at the center of the diamond. He only had half a face. He wore white gloves to hide his wounds. His legs were covered with a blanket. Maria approached the wheelchair and kissed his hand.

"Padre, I'm a little short this week."

"You're always short. Schoolteacher, get out of here."

"But we have to talk."

"Not in front of the lady."

And Maria touched her hair and withdrew into the dark, leaving Diana alone with the cripple.

"Hello, Caroll's bride."

"Who are you?"

"The mystery man. Princess, I'm supposed to be dead. Isaac killed me. It was in all the papers. But he wasn't mentioned. He's the Pink Commish."

"You're Sal Rubino," she said.

"No, I'm all that's left of Sal. I belong in a museum."

"I don't believe Isaac shot you."

"Ask your dad."

"Where did you meet my father?"

"Princess, don't be naive. Nothing gets built in Manhattan without Sal. I own a lot of cement. Ah, ya know what I wish? That I had my legs again so I could dance with you. I don't want to diddle. Just to dance. And I have to eat my heart out. Because

—141—

you'll dance with somebody and I'll start to cry . . . how do you like your rings? The rings you're wearing, I made them myself. I used to be a goldsmith. I studied gold in school. But I got involved with cement. And I lost the feel of my fingers. I can't hammer out a ring. That's my biggest tragedy . . . and not being able to dance with you."

"What if I promised not to ever dance again?"

"Ah, you'd try to keep that promise but you couldn't. You'll dance at my funeral, you'll see."

She wanted to pick Sal out of his blanket and sway with him, but she didn't dare. He was one more wounded man in her life. One more casualty.

"Princess, did ya know your husband's been seeing a shylock? I canceled the vig. I took it on my shoulder. It was a calculated risk. I was grooming him to kill Isaac Sidel."

"Stop it," Dee said. "I won't listen."

"It's only fair."

"I won't listen."

But she didn't move away from Sal. She was bound to him in some manner she couldn't explain. It was the ravages of the wheelchair. She could only seem to care about dangerous men. Caroll had rescued her from Fred the gardener, another danger-ous man. Perhaps she had encouraged Fred a little, smiled at him, but that didn't mean he had to slash at her with a knife. And she wouldn't have allowed any other rescuer but Caroll, who had his own sad danger. She imagined him handcuffing her even before they'd gone to bed. He didn't have the bluster of other cops. She only wanted Caroll on the case. And she got Caroll. And now this lunatic in the wheelchair wanted Caroll to kill Isaac. And what about Maria? Where did Maria fit?

"Mr. Rubino, Isaac has already been shot. He came back from the dead, like you."

"There's no comparison. Isaac had a beauty sleep under the bridge. I arranged it for Caroll to find him."

"And who was the killer?"

"There was no killer. Just a hired gun."

"A gun that you'll let loose on Isaac again."

"I don't give second chances. It's up to Caroll. But he's a bad boy. He's been meddling with my property, Delia St. John."

"She's my father's property too."

"Not a chance. I introduced Delia to your dad. It's strictly cash. But not with Caroll. I want him out of her life. I could get angry. I might not let him kill Isaac for me. And Caroll's bride will become a widow. I get wicked ideas in my wheelchair . . . Angelo, come here."

She might never survive her trip to the jeweler. She didn't blame Maria Montalbán. Mr. Rubino had all the bitterness of a man who could no longer hug a woman. And when his two gorillas put their hands on her, pawed her in front of Sal, slapped her, ripped her clothes, she watched Sal and couldn't find the least pleasure on his broken face.

Part Five

Part Five

18

Old Jim had come to the Park in his cardinal's cape. He'd rather have arrived incognito, but he might have been mistaken for a bum. He had a rotten habit of picking up cigarette butts and smoking them until his mouth nearly burned. He had a rough nature. He liked to deliver his own Christian charity with a sock in the teeth. He had to scout the playing fields because Isaac's lads would practice their baseball during the worst winter storm. And he had his own Manhattan Knights to consider. He wouldn't want to lose a championship on account of any negligence. But there was no one about. The fields were as naked as a gorilla's arse.

He felt a hand on his shoulder. He jumped. It could have been one of Isaac's spies, or the Bomber himself, Harry Lieberman, who was coaching the Delancey Giants.

But he shouldn't have panicked. It was only Captain White, the vicar of Sherwood Forest, looking like a scorched rat in his overcoat. The rat hadn't shaved. He belonged to the Holy Rood of Catholic cops. Jim was their advisor.

"Lucas, you scared the piss out of me. Announce yourself, for Christ's sake."

"I couldn't," the captain said. "You were standing there . . . like in a dream. I couldn't interrupt."

And he stooped to kiss the cardinal's ring.

"Will you stop that? You're a grown man. And I didn't come here as a prince of the Church. I'm a baseball manager. I've my own team to worry about. Isaac is lurking in the bushes with his lads."

"He's a thief," the captain said.

"I wouldn't doubt it."

"He wants to sack me."

"Sack you? He's an invalid. He doesn't have the powers of a PC."

"He hates my guts," the captain said.

"Did you ever harm him?"

"He hates my guts . . . I have to retire."

"At forty-six? You're in your prime. What will ya do?"

"I'll join the Church."

"Jesus, you're one of us, as fine a Catholic as the Department ever had."

"I want to become a priest."

The cardinal squinted at Captain White. "Can't imagine you as a seminarian . . . studying the Lord's Book until your eyes are scratchy."

"I have the calling, Jim. I always did. I'll kill Isaac before he kills me."

"Kill? That's Satan's work."

"I'll do it," the captain said.

"And I'll slap your face."

"It won't be the first time, Jim."

The captain started to laugh. It sounded like an explosive cough.

"You're tired, lad. Take a rest."

"Rest? The whole Park is my precinct, Jim. I'm the sheriff here. Not sheenie Isaac."

"Ah, don't belittle the man. He's ill."

"If he's so ill, you wouldn't be here. Isaac bothers you. He'll steal the pants off your boys. I could fix him for you."

"Jesus, I will slap your face. I'll do worse."

"It's a joke, Jim. Would I take advantage of an invalid? I have to go back to Sherwood Forest and inspect the toilets."

Captain White wove around the cardinal and disappeared into a thicket of trees.

"Like a ghost," Jim said, "like a bloody ghost." He wrapped himself in his cape and left those forlorn fields.

He'd been dreaming of the Bomber again, Harry in some center field that looked like the Harlem Meer. He could chase a ball in the blackest water. And then Isaac realized it wasn't Harry. It was the Pink Commish, splashing, splashing, because Isaac couldn't swim. And while he drowned, it wasn't Marilyn who blinked at him, or Margaret Tolstoy, his errant sweetheart, or his own mom and dad, but Blue Eyes, who died under a ping-pong table . . .

Isaac had to answer the phone.

"Who is it?"

"A friend of Maria's."

"I was dreaming. What the hell do you want?"

"I hope it was a wet dream," said the voice on the phone.

"All my dreams are wet dreams. What do you want?"

"Your bitch had an accident . . . Diana Cassidy."

"Where is she?"

"Maria's crib."

"That's grand. How many cribs does Maria have?"

"Only one that concerns you, Professor Sidel. Just meet me at the southeast corner of Marcus Garvey Park. And wear your baseball pants, professor, or I might not recognize you."

Isaac wasn't in the mood for baseball pants or that white embroidered cap of the Delancey Giants. He wanted his gray fedora, but it was at his apartment on Rivington Street, with the rest of his clothes. So he suited up, the Beekman Bomber, and strode out of the hospital, with his cleats attacking the linoleum floor.

He looked like a medicine man on the subway, or some refugee from an asylum, but no one considered him strange. He was one more straphanger. He got out of the subway and stood on the corner that had been assigned to him, his pants ballooning against the wind. People began offering him nickels and dimes, figuring a crazy white man had come to beg at Marcus Garvey Park. There were no drug dealers, no rampaging gangs, and he wondered if Harlem had become a haunted house.

A cop approached Isaac, tapped him on the shoulder with his billy, and Isaac snarled, "What's your name, officer? I'm Sidel."

"I know," the cop said.

"What precinct are you from? I'll have you working the graveyard shift for life."

"Shut the fuck up and follow me."

Ah, it was Harlem, and not even a Pink Commish could matter very much. Nor did he have the strength to strangle the cop. And it wouldn't have brought him to Dee. So Isaac followed this steerer in a blue bag. The cop led him to a brownstone near Lexington Avenue.

"Go to the top of the stairs, chief. I think the door is open . . . and regards from Maria Montalbán."

"I'll break your bones, you son of a bitch."

The cop laughed. He had crooked teeth. "You're a hospital case," he said. "Good for drinking jello."

Isaac climbed toward the roof. The stairs rattled under his feet. Huge strips of plaster hung from the walls. He found Maria's crib. It was a duplex with its own garden. It had a couch and a stereo that could have been worth two months of Isaac's salary. This is where the school money goes, Isaac muttered to himself. This is ten thousand sandwiches that never got to the kids. Diana was lying in bed on the duplex's lower floor, wrapped in a red cape. Her mouth was swollen. She had little tears of dried blood on her neck. Her eyes were open. She smiled. It quickly turned into a line of black blood.

"I failed you, boss. I couldn't get Maria for you . . . I think I fell in love with him a little."

Isaac kissed her eyes. "I'll get you an ambulance."

"No," she said. "I hate hospitals."

"So do I."

"You can live anywhere, Isaac. You're always scheming . . . no hospitals, swear to me."

He called Gordon Gould, chief pathologist at the NYPD.

"I don't have to come, Isaac. You're in limbo right now. I work for Sweets."

"That's true," Isaac said. "But I'll be back, Gordon. I'll be back on the fourteenth floor, and I'll give you my own pathology lesson. I'll shove a pencil sharpener up your ass."

"You can't talk to me like that."

"I'll expect you here in fifteen minutes."

He covered Dee with a blanket. He warmed her hands with his own hot breath. "Who hit you?"

"The jeweler's people."

"Jeweler? I don't know any jeweler."

"Sal Rubino."

"You mean the dead man. And it was Maria who set you up."

"I'm not sure. He's afraid of the jeweler. I'm not sure."

"Where did Maria take you?"

"A warehouse," she said. "Stuffed with school supplies. Maria bought everything from the jeweler. He can't trust the Board of Ed."

"He gave you to Sal. And Sal must know you work for me . . . I'm such a fool. I should have closed my shop . . . they hit you. How many men?"

"Two."

"And they touched you, took off your clothes."

"No. Nothing like that. They might have wanted to, but Sal was there."

"And Maria?"

"Maria disappeared."

"He gave you. I can't forgive that."

The pathologist arrived with his medical bag. He was also Isaac's physician, but Isaac didn't believe in checkups. It took a Glock to get him off his feet.

Gordon Gould felt under her cape with hands that were as delicate as a virtuoso on the violin. He looked into her eyes. He listened to her heart, placing the cup of his stethoscope at the edge of her brassiere.

"Nothing broken," he said. "But she's suffered some trauma. I'd recommend an ambulance."

"Gordon, you'll drive her home in your car."

"That's absurd. There could be hemorrhaging. I won't take the responsibility."

"You'll drive her home."

"And where are you going?"

"To find a friend."

He helped the pathologist bring Diana down to the car. Then he returned to the crib. He called the one dispatcher he knew at the Board of Ed, a police buff.

"Gloria, I need to know Maria Montalbán's whereabouts."

She whistled into the wire. "He's a tough cookie. But I'll try."

Isaac gave her the telephone number at the crib. Then he waited with a venom inside his gut. He had spasms on the left side of his body, near the bullet holes. He couldn't heal properly. He'd always have that puckered skin. He couldn't seem to get rid of his bile. He smashed the stereo; the wires bled a blue ink. He ripped the couch with a knife and fork borrowed from Maria's kitchen.

The phone rang. It was Gloria.

"He's not in the district," she said. "But I tracked him down. He put in a call to the chancellor. There's been a revolt. Some kids took over the lunchroom at one of his sister schools uptown.

And Maria's rushing to the school. Alejo doesn't want any cops around."

"Maria is Alejo's troubleshooter. He'll restore the peace with boxes of bubble gum . . . or pencil cases he stole from another district. Gloria, what's the name of this school?"

Isaac couldn't run. The walls of his chest throbbed with each step he took. But he got to that troubled junior-high school near Paladino Avenue and the East River Drive before Maria did. The school was under the massive approach to the Triborough Bridge. It lived in perpetual darkness, without a single pinch of light, as if the architect had schemed to make schoolchildren mad. Isaac met Maria at the door of his limousine. Maria was bundled inside a mink coat. He bowed to the Pink Commish.

"Glad you could come, Isaac."

"Don't patronize me, you fucking prick. You shouldn't have deserted Dee . . . Sal's thugs gave her a beating and brought her back to your crib. One of your lads telephoned me."

"I don't have 'lads' like that."

"You shouldn't have deserted Dee."

"And you shouldn't have got her involved. She has to suffer if she's your little soldier. But I don't have time for a debate. I have to stop a riot."

"I'm going with you," Isaac said.

"This isn't your kingdom, Isaac. It's a public school."

"I'm going with you."

And they entered that piece of midnight under the Triborough Bridge.

"If you wave your pistol, Isaac, I'll smash it against the wall."

"Do you see a pistol?" Isaac said, pointing to his belt and his baseball tunic. "I'm a boarder at Beekman Downtown. I have to drink castor oil, or I couldn't go to the toilet. I shouldn't be here. I'm a delinquent. I . . ."

Isaac had to quit talking. There were children in the corridor, with eyes that held nothing for him, that were beyond the power of a convalescing police commissioner. No one cared about his uniform. The Bomber had played at the Polo Grounds, which was blitzed while Isaac was a boy policeman, and turned into a housing project where many of these children now lived, outside the shadow of Harry Lieberman or Isaac Sidel. The Polo Grounds projects. Isaac was one more antiquarian, who belonged in the Christy Mathewson Club, not with a population of young women who carried pencil cases next to their hearts. Isaac couldn't tell where the boys had gone. One or two floated in the periphery of these girls and their pencil cases. But they weren't part of the same powerful storm. These girls must have carried that lonely field of learning at this junior high. They paused near Maria, who seemed to calm them with his mink coat and high heels.

"Who's Mr. Dark Eyes?" they asked, after noticing Isaac.

"The man's a little crazy," Maria said. "Leave him alone."

They formed an escort around Maria and his ragtail twin, Sidel the hospital refugee, and delivered them to the lunchroom, which had become a barricade in the hands of these girls. Their leader, who looked a little pregnant, peered out from behind a nest of chairs. Her name was Miranda Smith. Isaac tried not to stare at her swollen belly.

"Maria," she said, "you can call the cops, but we're not giving up this room. The suckers don't know how to teach."

"You scare the living shit out of them. I mean, you are a bunch of scary girls. You've had three principals since September. Your teachers run home with nightmares. They never come back."

"They don't know how to teach."

"I'll find you teachers who can teach."

"Yeah, Maria, we gonna become bank clerks in seven years. We gonna dance for all the rich uncles. We gonna get a certificate saying we can spell. We gonna save until we can buy a color television. Is that gonna be our paradise? I'm fourteen, Maria. I already had two abortions. What kind of curriculum you gonna make for me?"

"I'm not sure. I'm part of the same paradise."

"What about him? Mr. Dark Eyes."

"He's a baseball monkey. He grew up at the Polo Grounds."

"He's from the projects?" Miranda said, laughing from inside her barricade.

"Hell, the world existed before there were any projects. Gentlemen used to ride on ponies at the Polo Grounds and hit a hard ball with a very long mallet. Then the mallets and the ponies disappeared. And you had round bats and baseball diamonds."

"You don't have to teach us baseball, Maria."

"I'm trying to make a point. History is like music. It has a flow. But it's hard to find."

"We don't even have books here," Miranda said.

"I'll get you books."

"It's worse than kindergarten, Maria. It's a zoo with black windows."

"Princess, you're right."

"I aint your princess. Don't forget."

"I'm sorry," Maria said. "I was practicing my voodoo, little sister."

"I'm not your little sister . . . does Dark Eyes do anything but sit on his ass and remember the Polo Grounds?"

"He's the police commissioner."

Other heads emerged from the barricade. "He gonna arrest us?"

"Ask him yourself."

And Isaac started to cry.

"Not in front of these girls," Maria spat inside his ear. "They'll think you're a sissy."

"I am a sissy," Isaac said. "They're right to rebel. The whole system stinks."

"That's fine for you to say. But I have to live in this house. It's the only one we have."

"Stop crying and tell me a story," Miranda said.

"I'm not a storyteller. But I can tell you the truth. I was standing under a bridge. Someone was waiting for me in the dark. A phantom. He shot me five times."

"Does it have to be cops and robbers," Maria said, "the lousy riddle of your life?"

"Maria, don't be impolite," Miranda said.

"I dreamt of an angel with a baseball bat. His name was Harry. I didn't ever want to wake up. But the doctors pulled me out of my dream. I've been sucking green jello ever since."

The whole barricade started to laugh.

"Maria, we like the crybaby."

"There were other angels surrounding my bed. They tugged at my hair. They were boys in baseball uniforms, like mine. I have a team . . . had a team, I should say. The Delancey Giants."

"Do they play at the Polo Grounds projects?" Miranda asked, softening to this bear in the white-and-gold cap.

"Not yet."

"Teach us some history," another girl said. "*Your* Polo Grounds, how much did it cost to get in?"

"Sixty cents," Isaac said. "It was during the war, the big war against the Germans and the Japs. There were ak-ak guns above the Polo Grounds, on Jumel Terrace."

"What's an ak-ak gun?"

"Anti-aircraft," Isaac said. "They were manned by civilian soldiers in little metal hats. I captured one gun when there weren't any civilian soldiers around. I sat in the gunnery chair and watched that blue sky like a killer hawk until I got dizzy and fell off the chair. I'd go from the guns to the Polo Grounds. I didn't like school. I had a better education in the streets. I stole books of ration stamps. But no matter how much I stole, I was still poor as a mouse."

"Or a girl from the projects."

Isaac started to cry again. He wasn't mourning the Polo Grounds, or his lost livelihood as a trader in stamps. It hurt him to think of the ak-ak gun, and the little glories he'd had in that chair. And he was crying for Maria's girls, who couldn't even discover their own present tense in this dark, murderous school.

Maria grabbed his arm. "Come on, Dark Eyes."

"What's going to happen to these girls?"

"Come on."

Isaac left the lunchroom with Maria Montalbán, who strolled the corridors in his mink coat, while his nostrils worked like a man sniffing out a rat. Isaac wondered where the teachers were. He saw schoolchildren in an endless drift, girls on some holy crusade against District Eleven B. And then Dr. Sampayo, the principal, ducked his head out of the teachers' toilet. He had very big ears. He was one more functionary in this dungeon by the sea.

"Maria, did you get them to leave the lunchroom? I won't be responsible. They mock me, your little girls."

"They're children, only children. And they have a simple wish to stay alive."

"Who's your friend?"

"Isaac Sidel, the Pink Commish."

"You have your own policeman, and you couldn't persuade the girls to end their mutiny?"

"It's not a mutiny, Dr. Sampayo. You'll have your lunchroom. I promise you."

And it must have been a magic chant. Miranda whistled once, waved her arms, and broke up the barricade. All the children returned to their classrooms, but Isaac couldn't find any teachers. He began to understand the design of this school. Half the teachers were Maria's mules. And the other half were hiding in the toilets, or sitting home, or selling school supplies. One of them, who looked like an unsuccessful Santa Claus, arrived with a sack on his shoulder. "Maria, I can't move a thing."

"Not now," Maria said, and this Santa Claus shuffled along the corridor with his sack.

"There aren't any teachers," Isaac said, "because they're out peddling for you."

"The economy of my district depends on pencil cases. But you wouldn't understand."

"I understand. I'll glock you, you Puerto Rican prick."

"You have a problem, Isaac. The people you kill don't stay dead."

"Like Sal, I suppose. It's not my fault if he worked a miracle."

"I hear it wasn't such a miracle."

"What do ya mean?"

"You're the detective. You find out."

"Maria, you won't be as lucky as Sal."

"I'm a made man," Maria said.

"I don't care how connected you are with Sal."

"I wasn't talking about Sal," Maria said.

And Isaac could feel a shudder where the worm had once been. "You're protected, aren't you? That's why I can't get a subpoena. The Feds are letting you run your little racket."

"I didn't say that."

"Take me to Rubino's warehouse."

"Don't be ridiculous."

"I won't touch all the shit he sells to you, all the school supplies."

"He doesn't have to sell. The jeweler's a rich man. I do him favors. He gives me pencil cases."

"Where does he get that kind of boodle?"

"He rips off other people's warehouses."

"And what are the favors you do for Sal, besides lending him Diana?"

"Don't start rapping with me, Isaac. You can't win. You went to war with the jeweler. I was in the middle. I had to give him Dee. And I introduced him to Delia St. John."

"Ah, the eternal child. I can name you ten judges who've had her on their laps . . . take me to the warehouse."

"The jeweler wouldn't like that. The jeweler might get mad."

But they marched out of the junior high, got into a cab that was waiting for Maria. It was much less conspicuous than a limousine. He brought Isaac to Sal's Hudson River warehouse, which had become a huge shell, without a single blackboard or pencil case.

"You tipped off Sal," Isaac said.

"Come on. He figured you were coming. And he likes to move his stuff around. It's much safer for him . . . Dark Eyes, how come you're on such a crusade against Maria Montalbán? Did I ever harm you, did I ever show you disrespect?"

"You're a thief. You hide behind a superintendent's salary. You steal from your own district."

"You don't get it, Dark Eyes. You're jealous, is all. I'm the new king of your territories. People come to Maria. I give them what they want. Smack. Kosher bubble gum . . ."

"And some good head from Maria's girls."

"Don't say that, Dark Eyes. I'm not a pimp."

And he walked out on Isaac. "I'm not a pimp." Isaac was left alone in that enormous shell. All he could think about was lime jello.

19

Isaac packed his one little bag and moved out of the hospital, which was more like a hotel that catered to his whims and examined whatever wounds he had.

"You're too weak," the chief cardiologist said. "You'll collapse if you don't get back into bed."

He put on his fedora at Rivington Street, bathed himself, crept around in the dust of his apartment, saw the March snow from his narrow window, found a clean shirt among his laundry, stuffed his baseball uniform into the closet, and decided to solve the case of Isaac Sidel. He'd been living like a sleepwalker ever since he first woke up in his hospital room on Gold Street. He'd have been much more alert if he hadn't lost the worm. The worm was a moralist, the worm had encouraged Isaac's descent into the unknown, the worm was like Shakespeare, breathing melodies wherever Isaac happened to go. He was miserable without the worm. His face was dark under the hat. He wore a Glock inside his pants. Isaac had never been fond of holsters.

He visited Jerry DiAngelis, who was hiding from that jeweler, Sal. Jerry had captured the Rubino clan, until Sal had decided to play Lazarus in a wheelchair. But Jerry shouldn't have fallen so hard. He shouldn't have had to abandon his little fortress on Cleveland Place and his stool at the Baron di Napoli rifle club. He'd lost his lieutenants. His captains had gone over to Sal. He'd move from bedroom to bedroom in the middle of the night. His father-in-law, Izzy Wasser, had suffered a stroke. That old Hebrew schoolteacher had been the brains behind Jerry. His brother, Ted the Nose, had become a rat for the Justice Department. Nose was in the witness-protection program, but that didn't stop him from rushing around the country like a bandit, hitting people under the aegis of the FBI. His rabbi was Frederic LeComte, cultural commissar at Justice. Isaac had been Justice's first Alexander Hamilton Fellow, lecturing to police chiefs until he decided to stop off in New Orleans and murder Sal Rubino with the help of Jerry DiAngelis. He hadn't planned the hit. He was rescuing his sweetheart, Margaret Tolstoy, who worked undercover for LeComte, as his own little gangbuster. She'd lived with Sal, slept with Sal, and betrayed him. And the jeweler would have gotten his revenge if Isaac hadn't arrived and shot Sal with a Mossberg Persuader. Jerry had been running, running, ever since that night in New Orleans.

It took Isaac two days to find Jerry's current bedroom. Jerry had lost that full, flush handsomeness of his. He was away from his wife and his father-in-law, the melamed. He wasn't even with his mistress, his *comare*, who was more like a second wife. He was miserable without the entanglements of his own people. He looked crazy, like his brother the Nose. But he wasn't crazy. He had that maddening stare of a man who had to be permanently awake.

"Isaac, forgive me, I should have come to the hospital while you were in a coma. But Sal had two of his lieutenants waiting for me."

"Forget it. I wouldn't have recognized you. How's Izzy?"

"His mind is gone. Eileen is looking after him."

Eileen was Jerry's wife. He'd married a Jewish girl and

brought the melamed into his tribe. It was the melamed who'd stolen Sal's clan away from him. And now Sal ruled from a wheelchair.

"I don't get it. You had the best captains."

"Sal picked them off. It was easy. He could play the invisible man."

"We killed him, Jerry. We walked away from a corpse. I had my own captain clean up after me."

"Where is this captain of yours?"

"Burt? He disappeared. I don't get it. We're not careless people. I would have seen Sal's hand twitch. I looked into his eyes. We killed Sal and his two cousins."

"Martin and Emile. They were likeable guys."

"Jerry, they would have shot your face off."

"They loved Margaret. That's why you're sore at them."

"Loved her so much they were willing to execute her."

"That was Sal's orders. I didn't enjoy whacking them, Isaac. It wasn't fun."

"Jerry, am I dreaming? Sal was a dead man, right? Burt took our Mossbergs and threw them into the Mississippi. What went wrong?"

"We had a silent partner somewhere."

"Sal had an angel, you mean, an angel with a hospital unit. Nothing less than that could have revived Sal. They brought that son of a bitch back from the dead."

"And killed Burt? They could have switched bodies. And Burt is lying in Sal's box."

"Burt or someone else."

"But who's this angel, Isaac? Who's clever enough?"

"Not clever," Isaac said. "He just had to have the resources . . . like two or three government agencies."

"And cooperation from the locals in New Orleans."

"Fucking Frederic LeComte. That's why you're down so far. Sal couldn't have chopped up your crews all on his own. God, I'm a dummy. It was LeComte."

"So Justice is running the Rubinos these days."

"Yeah, the Maf is dancing with the FBI. LeComte indicts you and indicts you, but he can't make it stick. You look like a banker in the courtroom. So he goes after your brother. He turns Nose around."

"Ah, don't talk about the kid," Jerry said.

"But not even Nose can hurt you. You don't have the mark of a Mafia man. So LeComte decides to destroy you out on the street."

"And what do I do now?"

"Run like you've been running. And I have to catch the fox, Frederic LeComte."

"Isaac, take care. You were glocked once. It could happen again. I think LeComte has declared open season on you and me."

They kissed like two grown men, and Isaac had to keep from crying. He was a fool with tears in his head. Jerry was the Maf, but Isaac felt closer to him and the melamed than his own army of cops. It was the Mafia that policed Manhattan. In the old days, when school concessionaires would rob children of their sandwiches and their milk, Isaac made one phone call to the melamed, and the milk would arrive with mountains of candy, donated to the children of New York from the concessionaires. The Maf had made its fortune running its own system of services. It had the rotten habit of killing people, but most of the people it killed were within its own fraternal order. Isaac had charts of each Mafia tribe at Police Plaza. He had entire family trees. He could pinpoint hit men and known gamblers (KGs), but the Pink Commish never believed in a war against the Maf. It was an invitation to chaos. All the cops in Manhattan couldn't replace the services that the Mafia provided.

LeComte would never understand. He was a "tourist" in Manhattan, even though he maintained an office at St. Andrews Plaza and several cribs. He was strictly Georgetown and G Street, the cultural commissar who had his own network of spies. Isaac could never fathom D.C. It felt like a blueprint for a city, with slums and shallow houses, and the President's own cottage on a lawn. Isaac had traveled America for LeComte, he'd lectured in D.C., he'd talked to convicts and commissioners like himself, he'd gone down the Mississippi, like Huck Finn, he'd seen mud rats and flying alligators, but he could only seem to deal with the mud rats of Manhattan.

He could have gone to D.C. and ferreted LeComte out of his hole in the Justice Department. But LeComte was never at Justice. He was much too busy dining with generals and his "cousins" at the CIA. And Isaac might have gotten lost in one of the passageways under Capitol Hill. And so he waited for Le-Comte across the street from St. Andrews Plaza, where the cultural commissar would rendezvous once or twice a week with federal prosecutors to map the end of mob rule in Manhattan.

Isaac stood in the cold three days. It would have been futile ringing LeComte's little secretary, because LeComte was a se-cretive son of a bitch. And Isaac would have lost the only "han-dle" he had, the handle of surprise. And during that third day, he felt someone knock on his shoulder. He turned around. It was LeComte's mousy little secretary, Martha Hall. "Frederic's waiting for you. Upstairs."

And so he crossed the street and climbed up to LeComte like a miserable rat. Martha had prepared a lunch. There were sandwiches on the conference table. A bottle of red wine. And Isaac's favorite desert. Almond macaroons in a bed of mocha ice cream. LeComte was a "lesson" in blue, like he always was. The sharpness of the blue stripes on his shirt seemed to pierce Isaac's eyeballs. LeComte had no mouth. He had two nostrils and a puckered pink hole in his face.

"You're a bad boy," he said, pleased with his victory over the Pink Commish. "You could have made an appointment with Martha."

"Bullshit," Isaac said. "You'd never have seen me."

"Let's have lunch."

They sat at the conference table, Isaac eyeing the macaroons.

"Go 'head, Isaac. I can't touch ice cream and cake. I have to keep my figure."

LeComte was a fucking pencil, the slimmest man Isaac had ever seen. But Isaac wouldn't argue over macaroons. Hospital life had turned him into a hunger artist. He savored the macaroons, chewed them slowly, and had his mocha with a plastic spoon.

"You revived Sal, didn't you? No one else could have done it. I left a dead man in New Orleans."

"Shouldn't incriminate yourself, Isaac. There could be a mike under the table."

"There is a mike. You bug your own offices, just like you bug mine."

"I wouldn't go near your office, Isaac. It's illegal."

"Should I tell you the model and the position of each mike?"

"More dessert?"

"Margaret's your soldier," Isaac said. "If I hadn't gotten there with Jerry DiAngelis, Sal would have killed her."

"Everything was under control," LeComte said. "I couldn't let my Hamilton Fellow commit murder in the middle of a lecture tour. I would have looked very foolish. And I can't afford to look foolish. You should have considered that."

"I didn't have a choice. Sal and his two little cousins were going to wag her fucking tail."

"She takes her chances, Isaac. That's part of the thrill. She always had a fondness for gangsters. That's why she's in love with you."

"I wasn't a gangster when I met her," Isaac said. The mocha hadn't revived him. He was still a hospital child.

"Are you going to tell me how she walked into your junior high, the Roumanian princess? She was a whore at thirteen. She'd been living with a war criminal. I had to steal her from the KGB."

LeComte must have seen that sad color on Isaac's face. He

sent Martha out for another order of macaroons and mocha ice cream.

"I was one step behind you in New Orleans, I swear. I had Sal's cousins targeted. They would have been ancient history."

"What did you do with my man Burt? Did you whack him out and substitute his body for Sal's?"

"We aren't ghouls, whatever you think. I wouldn't touch the last of your Ivanhoes. I let him have a free ticket to the country of his choice. But I couldn't dawdle while Sal was dying."

"The man was dead."

"Almost. His heart stopped on the table. But we had a team of miracle surgeons at Tulane. They pieced him together with bits of magic thread. He had no face. The walls of his chest were gone."

"Who's lying in Sal's grave?"

"We fished a John Doe out of the bayou. No one noticed. No one cared. It took a month to rebuild Sal."

"And you spent the month convincing him to become a paid informant for the FBI."

"We're a little more sophisticated than that, Isaac. Sal isn't registered with the Bureau. It would have been too risky. We just took Sal's side in his fight with Jerry DiAngelis. And Sal is grateful."

"And meanwhile you own the Maf."

"Let's just say we have a controlling interest."

The macaroons and ice cream arrived. LeComte smiled all the way through Isaac's second desert.

"Months have gone by and you can't even find that phantom who glocked you."

"I have my theories."

"So do I. It had to be a member of your Monday Morning Club. One of your own boys betrayed you."

"What about my two women?"

"Yes. Your lesbian officers, Wilson and McSwain. But Sal's

scared to death of dykes. He wouldn't have invited either of them into his own club."

"Then it was Sal who set up the hit."

LeComte covered his face with his fine long fingers, which were almost translucent in the light above St. Andrews Plaza. He could have been Dracula dressed in blue. "Don't patronize me, Isaac. Of course it was Sal. Who else would have paid three hundred thousand dollars to glock you?"

"Then you know the figure, you know the sum, and you let me wander into that little trap under the bridge."

LeComte removed those women's hands from his face. "No, Isaac. I only found out after the fact. And I've been singing your praises to Sal. But I owe you nothing. You walked out on me. You were my Hamilton Fellow. I built that whole enterprise around your unorthodox ethics. I risked my ass at Justice. And you have a shotgun party with Jerry DiAngelis. Schmuck, I got you out of jail. Your attorney was crumbling. I lent him my own legal department. I had dinner with the judge."

"You shouldn't say that to me, LeComte. I'm still a cop."

"I had dinner with the judge. When the strings are there, Isaac, I pull . . ."

"Where's Margaret?"

"Isaac, we're not playing kiss and tell. Margaret's all mine."

"I didn't ask who owns her. Is she safe from Sal?"

"No one's safe. He likes to ride rough in his wheelchair."

"But is she off the street, LeComte? Did you take her off the street?"

"You can't keep Margaret in cold storage. She gets an itch to be with a man. You ought to know that."

"Ah," Isaac said. "Then I'll have to kill Sal a second time."

"You don't have the artillery. You're a civilian now, a commissioner on the mend. And there won't be any macaroons where I'll send you."

"Then I'll learn to live without macaroons."

"You're a stranded dog, Isaac. I wouldn't be surprised if the whole Monday Morning Club works for Sal. You're too romantic, Isaac. Wake up."

"Yeah, I'm romantic," Isaac said. "Romantic enough not to like it when Sal's soldiers beat up on Diana Brent."

"You shouldn't have gotten her into your own dirty laundry . . . it's not a terrific idea to hound the superintendent of a school district."

"LeComte, is Maria Montalbán one of your informants too? He says he's untouchable."

"He belongs to Sal."

"I wonder if he's a Junior G-man."

"I wouldn't go near the Board of Ed. It's too explosive. You fuck with children and you get a very bad press . . . why'd you visit Jerry DiAngelis?"

"I had to say good-bye before you get him killed."

"I like the war the way it is . . . I've been keeping Jerry alive, steering him a step ahead of Sal without Jerry ever knowing it. And don't give me your old song about the Mafia saving New York. If the City can't run itself, bring in the National Guard."

"But the Guard can't make the necessary bribes."

"Then I'd do my bribing with bayonets."

There was a knock on the door. Martha peeked in. "Frederic, your two o'clock is here."

"Bring him in," LeComte said.

Martha Hall popped her eyes out at LeComte like a protective witch.

"Bring him in."

That elegant little loanshark of the Rubino clan came into the office, Fabiano Rice. The loan shark seemed embarrassed.

"Fabiano, you've met our erstwhile police commissioner, haven't you?"

"Yes, Mr. LeComte."

"Tell him how Sal is."

"He has black fits, Mr. LeComte, knowing that Isaac can walk while he can't."

"Fabiano," Isaac said, "kiss Sal for me, because I'll be coming after him."

The loanshark started to laugh. "He could have notched you a million times in Central Park. He had to tell his soldiers, 'Leave the loony alone. He wears knickers like a little boy.' "

"They're baseball pants," Isaac had to say in his own defense. He put on his fedora. A shadow appeared under his eyes. "Thanks for the lunch, LeComte." And he walked out of the land of loansharks and federal attorneys.

20

He was hungry again. He had a coffee milkshake at some obscure candy counter sandwiched between two government buildings on Elk Street. The owner recognized him.

"Isaac, how ya been?"

"Asleep," Isaac said.

"Harry on the handle, one two three."

He'd have to wear his fedora lower down on his head.

He went uptown to visit Dee. Neither the mocha nor the macaroons could ease his guilt. He shouldn't have brought her into the Monday Morning Club. But she was as wild as his own daughter, and eager to serve the maddening sense of justice in his head that told him Maria Montalbán was a thief.

Diana was in bed. Her eyes couldn't seem to focus. Her doctors had drugged her. But Isaac didn't notice any nurse in that phantom apartment of Dee's, like some battleship with two floors that overlooked the roofs of Park Avenue instead of some sea. The butler brought him a cappuccino, and Isaac sucked on the coffee while he held Dee's hand.

"Forget about Maria," he said. "I'll find Caroll."

Her lips moved. But she had no words for Isaac.

He wiped the dark milk from his mouth. Dee didn't stir from

her dreamscape. Isaac went down the marble staircase to the lower deck. Papa Cassidy was waiting for him, the great builder with his bushy eyebrows. Isaac knew all about his cement contracts with Sal Rubino, but Papa wasn't the only builder who danced with the Mob.

"You hurt my daughter, Sidel. It's bad enough she married a cop. You didn't have to enlist her into your secret service."

"I needed a librarian," Isaac said.

Papa slapped his face. Isaac fell to the floor. He was weaker than a little boy. His body would go on betraying him for the rest of his life. He sat on his tailbone until the butler helped him to his feet. "Thanks, Jeremy," Isaac said, wishing he had a butler of his own. But Jeremy would have had to live in Isaac's closet or kitchen tub.

The butler excused himself, walking around Papa Cassidy.

"You shouldn't have done that, Sidel . . . asking her to seduce Maria Montalbán. My daughter isn't Mata Hari. You took advantage of her. She was caught in the middle, between you and Sal."

"I didn't know Maria was Sal's little helper."

"Everybody gets his supplies from Sal. I have to kiss his ass."

"I don't get it," Isaac said. "Do you owe him money, Papa? Sal went to a lot of trouble to put his mark on Dee. Maybe he was sending a kite to both of us at the same time. Do you owe him money?"

"That's none of your business, Sidel."

"You gave him ideas about Caroll, didn't you. You let him have your own son-in-law."

"You're finished, Sidel. I'll see to it with Becky Karp."

"Papa, I love long vacations."

He patted his mouth with a handkerchief and left Dee's apartment. He was lonely. He decided to go to Jim. He could talk baseball with the cardinal. He didn't have to announce himself. He was always welcome at the cardinal's house on Madison Avenue. A monsignor met him at the door. Isaac sat in the study.

The cardinal arrived from St. Pat's. Jim went up to his bedroom and changed his clothes. He entered the study in an old sweater and a pair of brown pants. He had a cigarette and two whiskies.

"You're in a mess, aint you, lad?"

"I didn't come for confession, Jim. I'm not one of your Irish cops."

"I warned you about Maria Montalbán . . . I told you not to get involved with the public schools. Jesus, your face is all hollow." And he called to his cook. "Abigail, make the boy a sandwich . . . and search the freezer for ice cream."

But there wasn't any mocha in the house. And Isaac wasn't fond of mustard. He had to coat his ham sandwich with vanilla ice cream.

"Still the savage," Jim said. "Let it go, Isaac. Someone else can catch Maria. It doesn't have to be you."

"There is no one else."

"Aint it the truth," Jim said. "It's Isaac and the darkness, Isaac and the wind. But the dark swallows people . . . you were in a coma, man. You almost disappeared. Let it be a lesson. Ease up."

"I can't," Isaac said, putting on his fedora.

"Shouldn't wear a hat in the presence of a cardinal," Jim said. "Only the tempter would do such a thing . . . ah, leave it on. You look fatter in the face."

The cardinal had a previous engagement with a gang of Irish cops. He was the spiritual clerk of the Shamrock Society. He would hear confession, or hold a cop's hand. He would go on retreat with the Irishers as often as he could. He was a fighting cardinal who wouldn't desert his flock. And Isaac met that gang of Irishers in the hall. They hugged him like some lost member of their own little tribe. He was practically an Irishman, having grown up in an Irish Department.

Another Irisher arrived. Captain White of Sherwood Forest. He edged away from Isaac, like a startled bird. And Isaac didn't have to probe the captain's eyes. It was White. White had glocked him under the bridge, and the captain had come here to do a little penance and sit at Jim's feet.

Ah, he'd been the fool, Isaac Sidel, avoiding his own phantom, because he couldn't bear the responsibility of confronting one of his very own cops. He hadn't really wanted to know who had glocked him. He'd have to face the intimacy of that darkness under the bridge. Could White have despised him so much, like some jilted lover? It was too fucking sad to think about.

Isaac's head burst under his fedora. He took a cab to Rivington Street and sat in the dark. He didn't lock his door. He should have signed up with Old Nick. He wouldn't even ask the Devil for a whole season. Just a little jump back in time. A week, a thin week with the New York Giants, during one of the war years.

He could feel a man beside him. "Cap, did you follow me home?"

"Not exactly. I roosted with Jim for a little while."

"Tell him about us?"

"He'd have socked my face. He loves you, chief."

"But he would have heard your confession. He wouldn't break the seal."

"He'd have socked my face without breaking the seal."

"Sit down, Cap. You're making me nervous."

"I'd rather stand," the captain said.

"With your Glock?"

"It was a borrowed gun. I broke it to pieces and threw it in the river, barrel and all."

Isaac searched for the captain's eyes. He came upon an empty chamber. But the captain's voice was like the lament in his own black heart.

"I couldn't make it, Isaac. I have three sons in college."

"It wasn't about money," Isaac said.

"I kept sinking into the sand. I borrowed. I begged. I started to steal."

"It wasn't about money."

"I hated you, Isaac. Sentencing me to Sherwood Forest. Captain Midnight. I was always on the outside."

"I brought you into the Monday Morning Club."

"With Vietnam Joe and old man Weiss. I had no self-respect. I was at the bottom of your list."

"I have no list," Isaac said. "Did Sal get in touch?"

"It was the shylock. Fabiano Rice. He arranged the meet. I knew they wanted you dead. I played along. I had to prove that I could handle the caper. But then I stopped playing . . ."

"What did you do with the three hundred thou?"

The captain was silent. Isaac could see the trembling lines of his lip.

"You dummy, LeComte runs the Rubinos. He knows every fucking detail. What did you do with the money? Feed it to the squirrels?"

"I couldn't spend it. I couldn't give it to my sons. I stuffed whatever I could into collection boxes at Jim's cathedral . . . most of it is in my attic, a big suitcase with small bills."

"Did you start following me, Cap? Did you pencil in all my meets?"

"I didn't have to follow you. I followed Caroll. You shouldn't have fallen in love with that little plot of dead ground under the bridge. It was easy. All I had to do was stand in the dark."

"And collect your three hundred thou."

"I never felt better in my life . . . under the bridge. I was in control. The power was all mine."

"The power of my life or death. It's only a little thing."

"You're wrong. I never intended to kill you."

"I was in a coma," Isaac said.

"You survived . . . I had to make it look like a kill. I'm your best man, Isaac."

"Yeah, the king of the surgical miss."

"It was different after I walked away from the bridge. I couldn't share my secret. I couldn't tell Jim. I'd hide in the attic . . . but

I'm glad. Glocking you was the closest I ever got to the great Isaac."

"Did you expect a kiss?" Isaac asked.

"I had a right to a little consideration."

"I'm not a social worker," Isaac said.

"Should I give myself in? Go to Sweets?"

"No one's gonna arrest you."

"But the FBI knows I glocked you."

"Fuck the FBI. You stand in place. At Sherwood Forest."

"And what do I do?"

"Wait. Sal used you once. He'll use you again."

"And there won't be a trial? Not even Martin Malik?"

"I'll take you out of squirrel land after I get back to the fourteenth floor."

"Nah, I'd like to stay. I'm getting fond of the Forest."

The captain vanished, and Isaac was bluer than he'd ever been. His life belonged to Captain Midnight. He wasn't even a casualty of war. He was a gift of the captain's prowess with an Austrian gun.

21

He went over to One PP in the morning. The clerks and duty captains didn't know how to behave. It had been different when Isaac was a jailbird. But what were the privileges of a wounded PC? He wandered into Martin Malik's office. Malik was shorter and much more burly than Isaac, who looked like a scarecrow. Malik was the Department's in-house judge. He didn't investigate any cop, but the investigators would all come to Malik. Isaac had appointed this Oliver Cromwell. The Turk was without fear.

"I won't talk about Caroll," Malik said.

"The kid's innocent."

"He's under investigation."

"Then investigate me. I'm the guilty one."

"I can't tell Internal Affairs what to do."

"You don't have to tell. You're Martin Malik. Internal Affairs will look into your eyes and blink."

"That's called obstruction of justice. You ought to brush up on the penal code."

"You are the penal code at One PP. Martin, I need a favor. Rescue Caroll. Reinstate him."

"Should I laugh you out of my office, Isaac?"

"It's not Caroll's fault. I sent him into the bush. He was hunting down pianos with missing legs."

"And did those piano legs also have a vig?"

"Martin, I'm your man. I killed Sal Rubino."

"Do dead men ride in wheelchairs? Shame on you."

And Isaac had to start fishing with Martin Malik. "You've been seen in the company of Delia St. John."

"That's no crime. I'm a bachelor, Isaac."

"And she's a fucking child."

"Check her birth certificate."

"I don't think she has one."

"That's because she's been a minor for the last twenty years. Isaac, you appointed me, remember? I'm hard to scare."

"I could put in a leak to the *New York Times* about certain sex orgies."

"Sex orgies? I've always gone solo with Delia. Ask her yourself."

"But a leak like that would ruin your career."

"Not at all. I'd get invited on the Today Show. They'd love my Turkish smile. You're pathetic, Isaac. I'd box your ears if you weren't such a sick man. You ought to try Delia. She's a terrific health tonic."

"Martin, I'll be back on the floor one day."

"I'd like that. You're my favorite Commish."

And Isaac walked out of One PP.

He rode the subway up to Caroll's hotel on Central Park North. His room was cluttered with whiskey bottles, but Caroll wasn't there. Isaac stared at that long, long sweep of trees from Caroll's window. He ventured into the Park and hopped around the edges of the Harlem Meer. He arrived at the north playing fields. He didn't see his Giants. The fields were desolate. The wind crept under his fedora. Isaac stood on a baseball diamond. Two men approached him. They wore camel's-hair coats and black leather gloves. Isaac understood their tale. These were minor-league enforcers for one of Sal's crews. They grabbed at

Isaac, pulled on him, knocked the fedora off his head. Nothing serious. But even their child's play hurt. That's how tender he was.

"Greetings, Don Isacco."

"From the Rubino baseball club?" Isaac asked.

"No names. We didn't mention names."

They were runaways, Isaac realized. Weren't even on orders from Sal. They'd been hired to watch over Isaac, and now they wanted a little fun. They crushed his hat with their heels. They shoved Isaac between them.

"It's nice to play catch with a sack of shit."

Isaac grew dizzy. He didn't have the air in his lungs to lend himself to their game. But the shoving stopped. He recognized two gigantic paws entangling the camel's-hair coats. It was Harry on the handle. The Bomber was beating both enforcers into the ground. They whimpered. They'd never seen hands as quick as Harry's. Strings of blood appeared on the brown coats.

"Harry, that's enough. We don't have the right insurance to cover a murder rap. Let 'em go."

Harry launched them toward second base with a kick. Then he stooped for Isaac's fedora and rebuilt the crown with one of his enormous hands, as if he were perfecting the pocket of a baseball glove. Those hands of the Bomber's had a majesty Isaac would never know. There was no room for the Bomber in this civilization. He was a discarded player, coaching a children's team.

"I like to come here," Harry said. "I like to feel a diamond. That's how you win."

He was almost as ragged as Isaac himself. Grown boys who'd never recovered from the affliction of baseball. Isaac was only an amateur. He hadn't been on the field with Harry. But his affliction was almost as great.

"Harry, let's go up to the Polo Grounds."

"Don't get weird," the Bomber said.

"I want to stand there. In the projects."

"It's a waste of time."

"Let's find the old diamond."

"Don't get weird."

"Is it true that Mel Ott was only five foot two?"

"He was taller than that," Harry said.

"You should have been the most valuable player of nineteen forty-three."

"Come on. We sat in the basement all year. Musial was the man."

"You had more homers, more runs batted in. You had the big glove."

"We were cellar rats," the Bomber said. "Musial had the career. I was a war baby."

"You shouldn't have jumped to the Mexican League."

"Isaac, I'm sick of your fan's notes. I'm Harry Lieberman. I was in the majors. That's enough."

He abandoned Isaac, crossing the diamond to some universe all his own, where adorers like Isaac couldn't get in.

He plotted Sal's destruction, but he didn't have the players, he didn't have the team. He was one more isolated mensch, a commissioner without his portfolio of tricks. He could have stolen a sound truck and listened to Sal's conversation with the help of wire tits. But first he'd have to locate Sal, and the Pink Commish grew tired after walking ten blocks. He sat home and squeezed rubber balls to strengthen his wrists. He did calisthenics in the corner. His calf muscles had disappeared during his sojourn in the hospital. He couldn't seem to get them back.

He made no phone calls. He didn't have any guests. He dined at a little Newyorican café on Norfolk Street. Maria's picture was on the wall, next to Ronald Reagan. Isaac was the odd man out. He didn't mourn his loss of celebrity on the Lower East Side. It was still his Cradle. He'd been reared on these streets.

His phone started ringing. It was Sweets.

"Maria's dead."

"Dead? Did he overdose? Or cut his heart out?"

"He was glocked."

"Under the Williamsburg Bridge?" Isaac asked, with a frozen smile.

"He wasn't that lucky. It was a back lot on a Hundred and Tenth Street. Near the Park Avenue trestle. The killer's a sweetheart. He picked up all the shells. And he loves to zap people against a wall. The bullets won't tell us shit. We'll have copper slugs without a single groove."

"When was Maria killed?"

"Yesterday," Sweets said.

"And I wasn't told about it? The Crime Scene boys were all over the place . . . I could have found something, Sweets."

"That's the problem. You're one of the suspects."

"Then come over and read me my rights."

"Isaac, you shouldn't have had such a hard-on for Maria. A PC with a personal vendetta. It doesn't look so good. You're the phantom's first victim. You could have copied his M.O."

"Will you give me a couple of minutes to invent an alibi?"

"It's okay, Isaac. We already checked. You were having a café con leche on Norfolk Street when Maria took the hit."

"So now you call me, now you give me the news."

Isaac went to the morgue at Bellevue to visit Maria. The eyes were closed. The skin around Maria's wounds was a violent blue. His hands looked like pieces of leather. Isaac had wanted to drive Maria out of the schools, not see him on a coroner's table.

He called Sherwood Forest. White wasn't there. The captain was at home in Marble Hill, the little nub of Manhattan that was part of the mainland now. No one liked to remember that Manhattan wasn't such a perfect island. A little swamp had separated it from the Bronx. The swamp was filled in, and a channel was cut across Spuyten Duyvil creek to create the "island" of Manhattan. But a hundred years ago any little girl and boy could have jumped over the swamp and had their own mainland. And

White had a two-story house on Jacobus Avenue, in the Bronx's little Manhattan.

The captain wasn't so glad to see Isaac outside his door. "Couldn't you have met me at the precinct?"

"It can't wait," Isaac said. And he entered the captain's house. It had glorious chandeliers and a view of the rapids where boats had been lost in the days of the Dutch.

"Not a word to the wife," the captain said.

"Forget the niceties, Cap. Maria Montalbán was killed."

"I know. It was in all the papers."

"But the papers couldn't have told you he was glocked."

White pointed to the ceiling, and Isaac followed him upstairs to the attic. The captain was trembling. He showed Isaac his suitcase full of cash.

"I'm not interested in your money, Cap. It's Maria. Did Fabiano get in touch? Did he offer you another suitcase?"

"Isaac, on my mother's grave, I didn't go near Maria."

"It had your fucking signature. A killer's kiss."

"I wasn't there."

"Then tell me who could have copied your style?"

"I had no style, Isaac. I glocked you."

"Glocked me against a wall. Picked up the shells. Erased yourself from the crime scene."

Isaac watched the captain cry. "It's a holdup, isn't it? You want your revenge. I'll go to Sweets. I'll confess. I'll tell him what happened under the bridge. But I won't take the fall for Maria Montalbán. I won't eat your shit."

"Go to Sweets," Isaac said. "That's brilliant. You'll have murder one on your menu. You'll never see the sky again."

"Stay away from me, Isaac. You look like death wearing a hat."

"Thanks to you, Captain Midnight . . . Fabiano never got in touch after you glocked me? Not even to ask for a second try?"

"Not once."

"Ah, I believe you," Isaac said. He pulled the fedora over his eye and left that house on Marble Hill.

22

Isaac rested two days and went up to the Polo Grounds projects, near Edgecombe Avenue and Jackie Robinson Park. He couldn't conjure up a baseball diamond, or the lost walls of that playing field he'd loved. He saw high-rise monoliths with a red and gray girth, he saw housing cops in cracked leather jackets, he saw Maria's girls. A hundred of them, holding red candles and sobbing in a crooked line that moved between the monoliths. Miranda Smith, that slightly pregnant rebel leader, was with them, clutching her own red candle and leading a rebel chant.

"Who killed Maria?" she asked.

And the girls answered, "A snake in the grass."

Isaac felt like that snake. He was monstrously cold. He had chilblains on his hands. His toes were numb. He hadn't read Maria the right way. He'd scrutinized Maria's methods, watched the school supplies travel with the dope, but he hadn't looked into the faces of Maria's girls.

Who would cry for him? Isaac, the snake in the grass. He'd perched too long on the fourteenth floor, and the City had grown out from under him. Chasing crime, he'd lost his sense of the street. Harry could *feel* a baseball diamond, Isaac couldn't. He'd become an invalid long before the Cap had glocked him under the bridge. He should have followed the schoolchildren, not the school supplies.

He returned home to his crib. He exercised. Peculiar muscles appeared on his neck. He meditated in front of his own crooked wall. His chest thickened bit by bit. He was like a baby bear. He'd cry for no reason at all. He had to relearn Manhattan. He'd walk out into Maria's town, have his rice and beans, sit among all the little shrines to Maria at his own café on Norfolk Street. He sat in the middle of a red gloom, with lit candles on every shelf. He hiked up to Harlem, his breath coming back. He stood under the trestle where Maria had been glocked. He couldn't conjure up the killer or even any clues. But all that meditation must have given him some magic. He saw Maria's fur coat. The coat was walking toward the trestle. It had a head of yellow hair and the long legs of an aristocrat. He recognized Delia St. John under the dark glasses. She couldn't keep to a straight line. The children's model was drunk. Her mouth gurgled in the cold air.

He trapped her under the trestle. "Do you know me?" Isaac asked.

She tilted his fedora with two fingers and said, "You're the high commissioner."

"Where's Caroll?"

"I can't say . . . told me not to tell."

She started to hiccup. And Isaac felt strange. He wanted to hug her the way he'd hug a little girl. Delia wasn't a little girl. Now he understood her pull. Making love to her must have been like ravaging a grown-up child. But he didn't want to make Delia St. John. She was almost another daughter to Isaac, another Marilyn the Wild.

"Did you steal Maria's mink coat?"

"Maria gave it to me . . . got rid of all his valuables."

"Who killed him?"

"Uncle Sal, I think."

"Take me to Caroll . . . please."

"You're shivering," she said. She thrust her arm inside Isaac's and led him up to Central Park North and Caroll's hotel. Caroll was sleeping in that room of whiskey bottles. Before Isaac could turn his head, Delia was gone. He hadn't even asked her about Martin Malik.

He sat beside the bed until Caroll opened his eyes.

"How are you, kid?"

Caroll groaned. "Is that you, Isaac?"

"Himself."

"Go away," Caroll said, with his whiskey face.

"I can't."

"I'll strangle you, Isaac, the minute I wake up."

"Maria's dead."

"Aren't you glad? You don't have to count the missing board erasers. You don't have to track his mules. And I don't have to pretend I'm a parent at one of his schools."

"We have to find his murderer."

"Fuck you."

"You're a cop," Isaac said.

"No. I'm a man waiting for Martin Malik. The Department can eat my shield."

"You're a cop. That's all you know."

"You're wrong. I dance a lot with Delia. I go to parties. I'm her bodyguard."

"Like Joe Barbarossa."

"I bumped Joe. I'm Delia's steady."

"You have a wife."

Caroll lunged at Isaac and nearly fell off the bed. "Don't you tell me that. You got her involved with Maria . . . you lousy pimp. You peddled Dee behind my back."

"I didn't peddle her. I was trying to unwrap his machinery, all his contact points. Dee was my avenue to all that."

"And what did you discover, you son of a bitch? He was one more teacher-poet, fighting the Board of Ed. The cavalier of school supplies. He couldn't have run the schools with his dope money."

"He spent half that money on himself."

"So what? He wouldn't have been Maria without his mink."

"Then help me find his murderer."

"You were the triggerman, Isaac. Sal killed him because you were getting too close to Maria."

"How do you know?"

"Delia told me. She got it straight from the wheelchair. Uncle Sal. He's been toying with you, Isaac."

"Toying, huh? His soldiers beat up your wife."

"Dee's a survivor. She always was."

"Half her lights are out."

"I'm not going back to that mansion, Isaac. I like it here. I have my view. I have my whiskey. I have Delia. All the nabobs can love her. I don't care."

"You're a cop. You weren't made for the bodyguard business."

"Isn't that how I met Dee? Guarding her body?"

"That was different," Isaac said. "You were protecting her from the slasher of Central Park."

"Fred the gardener? He was a lamb. Dee liked to run around the Reservoir in her underwear."

"That's not an invitation to poke her with a knife."

"Did anybody die of Fred's wounds? I feel closer to Fred than to you, and I only met him twice. He doesn't vampire people, he doesn't steal their blood. He fell in love with some phantom lady. He wanted to marry her. That was his crime."

"It's like a fairy tale, isn't it?"

"No. A fucking fable. Millionairesses don't marry gardeners. But they might marry a cop."

"Dee loves you. She's hurting, kid. Can't you listen?"

"Then you lick her wounds. Get out of here."

"You stay, I stay," Isaac said.

Delia returned with two men in mink coats. They were bouncers from one of her "bodegas," those nightclubs without a license, where Delia loved to dance. They were ex-cops who'd gone through Malik's court. And Isaac had thrown them out of the Department on Malik's recommendation. They were bully boys who'd extorted money from impoverished grocers. They hadn't forgotten their former chief.

"How's Malik?" the older one asked. He had several aliases. He was called Tippy at the club. The other one was called Sam.

"Malik's well."

"Is he still stealing badges?"

"I didn't bring you to chat," Delia said. "Caroll's tired. I want Uncle Isaac out of the room."

"One question," Sam said. "Uncle Isaac, Barbarossa's done more damage than I ever did. He's popped people. He's robbed drugs. And Malik never went after him."

"That's life," Isaac said. "Joe wouldn't get down on grocers. He wouldn't sock the same old man twice."

The two bouncers went after Isaac. Caroll had to get out of bed. He still had whiskey in his eyes. He pulled the bouncers' guns from under their coats while they struggled with the Pink Commish and dug the barrels into their foreheads.

"You wouldn't shoot," Sam said.

"Don't depend on it. I'm dizzy. I might fall and start an accident. Your brains would leak."

"He's ungrateful," Sam said. "We come over to help the prick . . ."

"And he takes our cannons," Tippy said.

The bouncers walked out.

Isaac left Caroll alone with Delia. "I'm sorry," he said, and wandered into the hallway like a mud rat out of the water.

Caroll searched for a fresh bottle of Four Roses. He broke the seal. He drank the honey-colored liquid in great gulps. He landed on the bed with Delia beside him, Delia the professional child. They kissed. He didn't have to handcuff her. Delia wasn't very active. Her coldness would drive a man crazy. Delia was always somewhere else.

He would escort her to the bodegas, dance with Delia, and

discourage unwelcome guests. He was forever shoving people. And Delia took care of his hotel bill. She gave him pocket money and kept him in Four Roses, adding up the sums with a little calculator. Every single one of her gestures had become a business. She performed while she brushed her teeth. She had her "Uncles," who were loyal and loving to Delia St. John. And Caroll would deliver her to each Uncle. He had to withstand the demon glares of Papa Cassidy *and* Martin Malik, who'd decide Caroll's future with the police. Caroll had no future. He had a room on Central Park North. He had his Four Roses. He also had a wife . . .

He'd gone a little musty, but Delia dressed him in a tie from Bloomingdale's. All she cared about was a bodyguard with a Bloomingdale label. It was her afternoon with Uncle Malik. The trials commissioner was on a short holiday from Police Plaza. And Caroll accompanied Delia to Malik's condominium on Third Avenue. Malik lived in a glass tower overlooking Manhattan's high-rise heart. He was descended from a line of scholars and grocers in Alexandria and Istanbul. His papa had arrived in America without a cent and managed to start a grocery store in some lost Turkish district near Bellevue. Little Malik studied like a devil. He earned a law degree while he slaved in his papa's store. He'd never married. He had a wildness in him from all those years of labor when he couldn't afford a wife. Now he didn't want one. He'd undress Delia once or twice a week.

Malik met Delia and her bodyguard outside his door.

"Care for a drink?"

"You'll hold it against me," Caroll said. "You'll tattle to Internal Affairs."

"Caroll," Delia said, "don't talk to Uncle Malik like that. Apologize."

"To him?" Caroll said. "The hangman? I'd rather die."

"I'm not your hangman, kid. I'm the trials commissioner, that's all. I make my recommendations to the PC. But you shouldn't slap school officials and get involved with shylocks." Malik bowed in his silk robe. "I'm sorry. I shouldn't prejudice your case. Have a drink, kid. It will do you some good."

Caroll had to smile at the incongruity of it. The hanging judge had a part-time mistress who was in Caroll's hands. It was like playing with a boa constrictor. But Caroll went inside. He had a whiskey. He saw that little sky of glass and stone from Malik's tower windows. He preferred the treeline of Central Park. Malik disappeared into his bedroom with Delia St. John.

Caroll had another whiskey, went downstairs, and hiked to Park Avenue. He was going to visit Dee, but he couldn't get that picture of her and Maria Montalbán out of his head.

He stood outside Diana's building. The doorman gave him an embarrassed shrug. Caroll would always be a stranger here, the policeman who was Diana Cassidy's husband-guest.

He went around the corner to an English pub called Old Ben. The little beard of his tie fell into his whiskey glass. Bloomingdale's, he muttered. He'd have to strangle that living dead man, Sal Rubino, for letting his soldiers mark up Dee. But somehow he still liked Sal. Caroll couldn't decide whom to love and whom to hate. He belonged in that jungle of Central Park North.

A man sat down next to him. Caroll laughed. It was Milan Jagiello, Diana's protégé. His cuffs were as worn as Caroll's. His dark eyes seemed to have dead zones in them.

"I can't go up to Deedee. The doctor won't let me in. I'll lose my orchestra. And my landlord is after me."

"Aint it a bitch," Caroll said.

"Deedee forgot to sign the checks. But you could persuade her, Mr. Caroll."

"Should I sock the landlord, should I whack him out?"

"What do you mean?"

"A contract. I could kill him."

"You're crazy," Milan said, running from the bar without a drink.

And who the hell was Caroll? One more phantom who couldn't even find his phantom self.

Part Six

Part Six

23

Isaac had had his Harlem nights. Not with whores. Not with jazz bands in the cellars of Lenox Avenue. Not with chitterlings and fried okra. Not with rent parties until four A.M. Not with exotic darktown balls. He'd go on a pilgrimage to Harlem whenever Joe Louis arrived from Detroit to fight at Madison Square Garden. Louis couldn't stay at the Plaza or the Waldorf and the Pierre. The world champion had to check into a nigger hotel. Isaac would stand outside the Lenox Savoy in rain and snow to catch a glimpse of the Brown Bomber. He didn't want an autograph or a touch of Joe's hand. He wanted to see the Bomber in the window of his hotel.

He remembered that face from the *Movietone News*. Joe, sleepy-eyed, coming out of his corner in baggy trunks. Where did all that fury come from? It wasn't in the face. Joe seemed to turn inward while his body attacked, as if some crucial part of him had never entered the ring, and wouldn't dream of hurting another man, particularly a white man. Joe was performing a brutal, distant dance, removed from his own feelings, removed from himself. It scared the shit out of Isaac, watching Joe, realizing that the only place in the world Joe Louis could punch a white man and not get punished was inside a boxing ring.

The Brown Bomber never recovered from his bouts. It was like a sickness he had to bear. He boxed and boxed, but the sickness wouldn't go away. He looked drugged in the ring. And when he could no longer box, he became a buffoon, a wrestler who put on a cape like Batman and choreographed his own matches. All the fury was gone. The Brown Bomber had retreated within himself. He owed money to the United States. The taxman wouldn't leave him alone. He died like some kind of pauper with a championship belt.

Isaac must have felt a little of Joe's future when he waited outside the Lenox Savoy in all that snow. He missed those long winter nights. He'd never been fearful of that other Bomber at the Polo Grounds. Harry was a galloping horse. But Joe danced in his own killing ground at the Garden. All of Manhattan had become Isaac's killing ground. He was the commissioner of death. And the commissioner had nowhere else to go.

He had to find Sal and kill him all over again. He went to Sherwood Forest. He didn't see Barbarossa or his white glove. He didn't see Weiss. The old sergeant wasn't behind his desk. He didn't see Wilson and McSwain. His two wonderwomen weren't in the auxiliary shack. He couldn't recognize a single face. The rookies smiled at him. He was Grandpa Isaac, the absent Commish. He knocked on the captain's door. He heard an unfamiliar voice. "Come in."

Another man was sitting in the captain's chair. It was Maisley, one of Sweets' shooflies from the fourteenth floor. He mocked Isaac.

"Your man's gone. Captain White's on a month's vacation. Sweets moved out your whole Monday Morning Club."

"As of when?"

"This afternoon. Sweets can't afford you, Isaac. You're a lot of trouble."

"Where's Barbarossa?"

"Filing papers somewhere with his fancy glove. Sweets made him a clerk."

"And you're Sweets' new point man in Central Park."

"Me, Isaac? I'm the fucking heart of darkness. I swallow up old commissioners. Sweets doesn't want you around."

"Ah, Mr. Maisley, I'm glad."

Isaac had to trust his own instinct. He picked up this substitute captain and hurled him out of the office. There were terrible forking lines in Isaac's head. He dragged Maisley to the front door. None of the officers took Maisley's side. No one was certain where Isaac would land in the fickle politics of the police.

Isaac left Maisley under Sherwood Forest's little green lamps. He'd used up all his strength. He limped out of the Park, coughing like a consumptive cat. He had spasms in both his legs. Sidel, the eighty-year-old-man. He was worthless. But he went looking for Joe. Barbarossa was the last "window" he had to the streets. Barbarossa was a magician with a white glove. The NYPD was one more camp in a whole series of enemy camps. And Barbarossa defined himself against each camp. Barbarossa had no real address. Barbarossa always lived near a ping-pong table. And so Isaac had to travel down to Schiller's, a ping-pong club on Columbus, where Manfred Coen used to play. Coen had died at the far table in one of Isaac's little wars. The Pink Commish dreaded going there. He didn't like to reenact his own history. But then he remembered that he had no history.

He climbed down the basement steps of Schiller's club. He heard the constant clack of balls and the buzz of kibitzers and ping-pong freaks. Schiller's was the last ping-pong club left in Manhattan. The landlords had driven out all the other clubs, turned them into supermarkets and basement boutiques. But Schiller had a thirty-year lease and killer lawyers among his clientele. The killer lawyers would go to court to protect the ping-pong tables and the integrity of the lease. They would have been stranded without Schiller's.

Isaac walked into that archaic world. The buzzing music stopped. The freaks hadn't forgotten Isaac the Brave. He was the curse of Schiller's club. Schiller stood inside the spectators' gallery and stared at Isaac with his sad vegetarian's eyes. He was too polite to ban Isaac from the club. But he still mourned Coen after eight years. Coen had been the resident angel of the club. Nobody could replace him, not even Vietnam Joe, who often slept in Schiller's rear closet and changing room.

Isaac saw Joe at Manfred's table. The table no longer had a net. Joe used it as his office. It was cluttered with file cards and slips of paper and bottles of ink. Barbarossa conducted all his business at the table. He would help Schiller out with the rent. He would only play around midnight, when most of the "tourists" were gone. He wasn't half as good as Coen. But he never tried to replace Coen at the club. He was a cop with outside interests. Ping-pong relaxed him, but it wasn't his religion.

Isaac stopped at the table. Joe signaled to Schiller. Schiller raised his head, and the kibitzing resumed. And Isaac kept staring at the glove, which seemed to have its own existence, like a five-fingered animal.

"You have a lot of balls coming here," Barbarossa said.

"I didn't kill Coen."

"Schiller hates your guts."

"I didn't kill Coen."

"If you say it often enough, Isaac, you'll begin to believe it."

"I'm sorry about Sweets. He shouldn't have pulled you out of the Forest."

"That's all right," Barbarossa said. "I'm a clerk at the Academy. There's a ping-pong table in the rec room."

"Don't take it to heart," Isaac said. "Sweets is punishing me. He closed down the Monday Morning Club."

"He wasn't punishing you, Isaac. He's protecting your ass."

"I don't need his protection," Isaac said.

"You do. You're a walking catastrophe. Maria knew every one of our moves. You ran a fucking circus. You shouldn't have bothered with Maria. Maria wasn't big enough. He was running his schools the only way he could."

"Then why did you join my club?"

"Did I have a choice? You would have bounced me to the end of the world."

"And you were dealing dope for Maria while you worked for me."

"I did him a few small favors. But I never ratted you out."

"Who killed Maria?"

"I did."

Isaac clutched the table to keep from falling. "You're Sal Rubino's man."

"No, Isaac. You have it wrong. I had to hurt the little fuck. He owed me money. And he wanted me out of the way."

"You've been feuding with Maria since Vietnam."

"It had nothing to do with Nam. I pinched a few dealers for Maria. He decided not to pay. He sent a couple of Sal's soldiers after me. I had to whack them in the head."

"And you glocked Maria near the Park Avenue trestle to make it look like it was the same hitter who glocked me."

He didn't want to talk about White, he didn't want to talk about White. He was the custodian of his own little church, the church of Sheriff Street, under the Williamsburg Bridge.

"Isaac, I had to give Sweets' bloodhounds something to play with . . . and I didn't hit Maria for nothing. I got big dollars from Papa Cassidy. He wanted Maria dead. Everybody did. Maria was trying to reform Delia St. John, take her off the street and out of Papa's arms. There was too much of the teacher in him. Or maybe he wanted Delia to carry his private union card. He was always having crazy ideas, Isaac. Just like you."

"You left an awful lot of widows," Isaac said.

"The daughters, you mean. Maria's girls."

"Some of them might claw your eyes out."

"I'll take my chances," Barbarossa said. "But you ought to go back to your hospital room, Isaac. It's much safer there. Papa thinks you and Caroll are conspiring to rob him of Delia. He'd like to marry her. Imagine. He's offering big dollars for your scalp."

"Why don't you take his money, Joe?"

"I might."

Isaac started to cough. The table whirled in front of his head. Barbarossa had to find him a chair.

"I could never sock a sick man."

"I'll recover," Isaac said.

"You're lost without Coen. Coen made you human."

"Coen was before your time."

"But I inherited his ping-pong table," Barbarossa said. "And Coen would have saved you. Caroll can't. He has matrimonial problems. He likes to suck on the bottle."

"How did you pop Maria?"

"What's the difference, Isaac?"

"I want to know. Did you arrange a meet with him at the trestle?"

"Yeah, he brought two cowboys, two of Rubino's men. He thought he'd make a funeral party. But I slapped the cowboys and sent them home."

"And did Maria try to run?"

"No. The ballsy little bastard looked right into my eyes."

Isaac got up off the chair. "Who are you protecting, Joe?"

Barbarossa took off his glove. His fingers were as pale as a swan's belly. The hand had no life without the glove. It looked amputated to Isaac.

"You wouldn't have killed Maria," Isaac said. "Maria was your partner in crime. And you're not dumb enough to hit a man for Papa Cassidy. He's a prick. And he could sing to a hundred different agencies. What happened at the trestle?"

"I told you."

Isaac snatched the glove. Joe had a wounded look on his face. Then he smiled.

"What happened?"

"Maria was getting careless."

"You were thick with him, weren't you? Since Vietnam."

"He was telling people how he worked for the Feds, how he could kill any clown and get away with it."

"Yeah," Isaac said. "He was a made man."

"He was stealing a little too much, talking to his girls, leaving a long trail from Rubino to the Justice Department, and Sal got scared, because people might start calling him an FBI rat."

"He is a rat. And he shouldn't be alive."

"But he is alive, Isaac. And he caught Maria and me at one of Maria's cribs."

"Who was with Sal?"

"Two guys to carry the wheelchair . . . and Nose."

"Jerry's baby brother?"

"He's five years older than Jerry."

"He's still his baby brother."

"I didn't beg for my life. But they tied me up and took Maria."

"And told you not to tell."

"I didn't need any instructions, Isaac. Nose belongs to the Bureau. And he hits people for Sal."

"The man has no mind. He's an imbecile."

"Imbecile, Isaac? He's very sweet with a gun."

"And now you've retired to your ping-pong table."

"Find me a better place."

"That's not like you, Joe. You aren't a quitter . . . you're registered with LeComte. That's why Nose didn't pop you. And LeComte is pulling you out of the picture."

"You're all alone, Isaac."

"And what if I am?"

He returned the glove to Joe. He passed Schiller's gallery of kibitzers and freaks. They looked away from the commissioner of death, who coughed and coughed on that dark climb up the stairs and didn't stop coughing until he made the street.

24

He needed a magic rabbi. A cardinal wouldn't do. Jim could rattle skulls in a graveyard, and he could maneuver an army of churchmen, but he didn't have much practice in killing people. And so Isaac visited the melamed, Isadore Wasser, at the family fortress on Cleveland Place. The last captains Jerry had were ensconced inside the fortress with Jerry's wife Eileen and the melamed, who'd gone senile after a stroke. Sal's crews had tried to bomb the place. They pissed on Jerry's stairs. They left bottles of excrement, but the melamed still peeked outside his window. And Isaac was allowed upstairs.

Eileen looked haggard. That subtile beauty had gone to sleep in her. She lived in some nebulous country between a widow and a wife. Jerry couldn't call. LeComte had tapped the lines. Jerry's people would leave coded messages for her, but the codes were confusing, and she couldn't be sure her husband was alive from one day to the next.

The Rubinos would get on the wire and cackle at Eileen, swear that Jerry was a corpse, and she grew frightened of the phone. Her own captains had to shop for Eileen and run to the bank with Mossbergs under their coats. And they still had casualties. It was a maddening war.

Isaac hugged Eileen. "I saw Jerry. Last week."

"Last week? That's like a million moons ago."

She fell into Isaac and cried against his chest.

"Don't worry. I'll talk to the melamed. He'll help us break the Rubinos."

"Isaac, he can't remember when to pee. You'll upset him. His mind is gone."

"Ah, then I'll kiss him for old time's sake."

He entered the melamed's room. Izzy Wasser wasn't lying under any quilt. He stood near the window, smoking a cigarette. He was dressed like a merchant prince, as if a single word from Isaac might call him into action. His forehead was ruffled. That was the only sign of disturbance Isaac saw.

"How are you, Iz?"

"The Stalinist is here, the great police chief. You took a fall. I heard about it on the radio. I'd have written you a card, but my fingers don't make sense when I grab a pencil." And he shouted to his daughter. "Eileen, fix him a meal. He's a growing boy."

And like some power source, Eileen poked into the room with spaghetti, wine, and a dish of chocolate ice cream on a tray.

"Isaac, it's the only menu we have."

She left the two disabled warriors.

The melamed watched Isaac eat.

"Are you hungry, Iz?"

"I'm always hungry," the melamed said. And they shared the ice cream.

"LeComte is behind Sal Rubino."

"Rubino, the resurrected man . . . don't eat all the chocolate."

"Iz, Jerry won't survive if he runs. Sal will get lucky. And one day his boys will reach Jerry's bedroom before Jerry does."

"And what would you suggest?"

"Attack the son of a bitch."

"With whose army?"

"If you have six soldiers, attack with the six."

"That's an invitation to slaughter."

Isaac couldn't seem to catch a note of the melamed's senility. Iz reasoned better than Isaac, even with his broken gaskets.

"There won't be any slaughter if we pinpoint Sal's weak spots and move on them one by one."

"One by one," the melamed said, spooning up the last of Isaac's chocolate ice cream. "And we lose all the DiAngelises . . . I'm better off stealing ice cream from your dish." The melamed blew his nose. "I have to wear a diaper because I've started to pee in my pants. I can't fight Jerry's war. My leg would be leaking all day."

"Let it leak."

"I'm an old man. I had a stroke. I still can't tie my shoes."

"I'll tie them for you."

"I'll look at you and forget your face," the melamed said.

"I'll remind you, Iz."

"I'm not Julius Caesar. I'm only a melamed."

"The best in the business."

"You flatter me, Isaac, because I gave you ice cream."

"I hate chocolate," Isaac said.

"Then why did you eat it?"

"I'm hungry," Isaac said. "I'm hungry all the time."

"Like me . . . I'm better off hiding from Sal."

"That's not the melamed talking," Isaac said. "That's another man."

"I am that man . . . go home, Isaac. I have to change my diapers."

Isaac kissed the melamed, said good-bye to Eileen, and went down into the street.

He had no more avenues. He only had the Glock in his pants, and he wasn't in the mood for target practice. He was eating six and seven times a day. The hunger pains would return in the middle of a meal. He drank wine and Mexican beer, frightened that he would starve. His freezer was stuffed with mocha ice cream. But Isaac couldn't sit in his flat. He traveled from restaurant to restaurant, like some phantom pirate ship, Sal receding from his mind. But there were photographs of Maria in every window. They were like the flags of his own inconsequence. He couldn't nail Maria or keep the little man alive.

And once, during a midnight attack of hunger, after his seventh meal, he came out of his Newyorican restaurant on Norfolk Street and was tossed into a panel truck by several pairs of hands. The surliness around him only increased his hunger. He wasn't blindfolded. His captors looked into his eyes with the least regard. They bounced him up and down the ribs of Manhattan and brought Isaac to one of the Rubino warehouses.

The warehouse was cluttered with blackboards that looked like the remains of prehistoric wingless birds. Isaac already missed his next meal. Sal's soldiers sat him on a stool.

"Where's Sal?"

"You think Sal will save you?"

"No. But I'd love to bite his face."

They held Isaac's own Glock against his eye. He dreamt of macaroons and grilled salmon and endless ice-cream cones. Two figures came toward Isaac. Neither of them was in a wheelchair. It was Jerry DiAngelis in a beautiful white coat and the melamed, wearing an old sweater. The Glock was returned to Isaac's pants.

"Jesus, you didn't have to trick me like that. I'm hungry. I might have had a heart attack."

"Ah, but we had to know if you were Sal's pigeon."

"Yeah," Jerry said. "You visit me, you visit my father-in-law. You come with big ideas. You could have been Sal's pet pigeon, trying to smoke us out."

"He hired one of my own men to glock me."

"That's only circumstances," the melamed said. "It wouldn't hold up in my court of law."

"So you bring me here, pretend that your soldiers are Sal's, and what did you expect me to do?"

"Beg for your life, say it was some mistake, how close you were to Sal."

"And did I pass your fucking test?"

"Isaac," the melamed said. "You shot Sal and Sal resurrects himself."

"Jerry shot him too."

"But Jerry didn't have LeComte behind him."

"And you think I asked LeComte into the neighborhood, you think I invited him to New Orleans?"

"It's possible. You were Justice's own Jewish boy."

"Then why don't you glock me and get it over with?"

"Eileen would start to cry," the melamed said.

"All that stuff about being senile. It was a big act."

"Partly," the melamed said. "Why should we advertise whatever little strength we have? It comforted Sal to think my brains were out the window. He pisses on us, but he hasn't destroyed the house. And I worry about Eileen."

"He wouldn't touch Eileen."

"Rubino," Jerry said, "Rubino would kill her if he could."

"He likes Eileen."

"That's why he'd kill her. He's a jealous prick. He wants what he can't have."

"Nose is in town," Isaac said.

"I told you not to talk about the kid."

"He glocked Maria Montalbán," Isaac said. "He's Sal's hitter. You'll have to take him out."

"Eileen would have a fit. He's the fucking infant she never had."

"And a loose wire," the melamed said. "He could start trampling the few soldiers we have left."

"He's my brother," Jerry said.

"I'd swear that Sal has already paid him to glock Izzy and you."

"Don Isacco," Jerry said. "Shut your mouth."

"The Stalinist is right for once."

"Yeah, Iz. I won't hit my little brother."

"You'll have to," the melamed said.

"Everybody gives me orders. My comare is having a break-down. I can't see my own son." Jerry had a ten-year-old boy with his comare, a beauty from Argentina. The boy's name was Raoul. The melamed had adopted him as his own grandchild, even though the boy wasn't Eileen's.

"Iz, I'm cracking up. I never close my eyes anymore. I never sleep."

"You'll sleep," the melamed said. "You'll sleep in a pine box if we don't stop your little brother and that cripple in his chair."

"I'm the boss," Jerry said. "I make the rules."

"Then make them, sonny boy, or I'm going back to my blanket. I liked looking out my window at the old Police Headquarters. I was enjoying my senility . . . Isaac, you should never have moved to Police Plaza. It was a mistake. You can't guard the City from a big red tomb. It has no character."

"I agree," Isaac said.

Jerry started to pull on his own ears. "I can't believe it. The two biggest brains in town bawling over some dump with a round roof. Iz, I was in the basement of that old Headquarters. Should I tell you how many cops punched me in the teeth?"

"Leave us alone," the melamed said. "Me and Isaac have been to paradise. Both of us came back from the dead."

"So did Sal. And you didn't trust Isaac an hour ago."

"I had to see with my own eyes," the melamed said. "I had to borrow a warehouse and bring him here . . . children, we have to do a little damage to Sal."

25

It was a war like any other war, but the Rubinos didn't realize any of the little shocks. The melamed's war was without machine guns. No bomb exploded in a Rubino café. No acountants were kidnapped. No crews were wiped out. A Rubino rent collector might get knocked on his ass by a runaway car. His receipts would disappear. But the rentman would suffer no real damage. A loanshark who'd just lost his wife would leave a little note and hang himself. How could the Rubinos tell that the loanshark's letter had been composed by the melamed himself, who had a wondrous imagination and could mimic the psyche of any man? The losses multiplied, but they were hard to grasp. The melamed picked away at the outer edges of Sal Rubino's empire. There wasn't a sudden drop in revenue, just a gradual fall that no bookkeeper ever noticed. Jerry DiAngelis stuck to his rhythm of hopping from bedroom to bedroom. The melamed stayed near the window at his old address. The same bottles of excrement arrived. The Rubinos would sing the same dirty songs on the melamed's phone. The war seemed to have the same old clock.

And then the circuits started going insane. Money was stolen from the usual "letterboxes." Loansharks were hanging themselves with a frightening regularity in all five boroughs. Scaffolds were falling on the heads of too many bagmen. Rubino soldiers were electrocuting themselves inside their houses. It was Sal who discovered this rise in the Rubino mortality rate. He was the one who had to scribble checks to all the widows and show up at funeral parlors in his wheelchair. He had his accountants go through the books. He started to panic. He wheeled himself through all his closets, where he kept bags of money in case of catastrophes. Sal would never be short. But the sight of all that money couldn't soothe him. He had to soothe himself. He dialed the melamed's number.

"Is that you, Isadore?"

"Yes," the melamed said.

"I hope you didn't mind the bottles of shit. Let's have a meet."

"Whatever you say, Sal."

"I'd like to bring you and the son-in-law back into the Family. We're one tribe, Isadore."

"Whatever you say. But I can't climb down the stairs. You'll have to come to Cleveland Place."

"Not a chance. I'm tied to my chair."

"My captains will lift you, Sal."

"I'm scared of heights."

"Then we have a problem," the melamed said.

"I know. You've been murdering me, Isadore. You've been murdering my men."

"War is war."

"You didn't have to put a rope around the neck of people who never pulled a trigger. You didn't have to fuck with electrical wires. I could live with a straight execution. Your captains against mine."

"You and your boyfriend LeComte have finished off most of my captains."

"LeComte isn't my boyfriend," Sal said.

"Then call yourself a canary," the melamed said and hung up on Sal.

Sal set the melamed's house on fire. The windows shattered. The chimneys fell into the street. No bodies were found. But Sal hadn't meant to touch the melamed. Just to leave him without his precious window. He wouldn't persecute an old Hebrew schoolteacher. Kill him perhaps, but not with fire and smoke. He had his headhunters out looking for Jerry DiAngelis and Isaac Sidel, who'd visited the melamed two days before Sal's loansharks started hanging themselves. He couldn't imagine a hell without Isaac. Isaac had to suffer along with Sal, like a fellow musketeer. That was one of the few blisses he still had. He couldn't lie down with a comare. He was a broken stick. It took three men to undress him and carry him into bed. He hired putanas to crawl between his legs, but he couldn't stay hard, even when he manufactured fantasies of Margaret Tolstoy. He'd had miraculous dreams while he lived with Margaret. And it poisoned Sal to know he could never live with a woman again. He felt like ripping out their heads. He wanted to wound Margaret Tolstoy.

It was three in the afternoon and Sal had an appointment with Ted the Nose, who'd become the chief enforcer of his clan. It gave Sal some delight that Jerry's brother worked for him, that he'd split the DiAngelises in two. The Nose had been an FBI informant. And Sal had borrowed him from the United States, with the blessings of Frederic LeComte. He was bashful about his new friend, but he would have been in purgatory, reciting the prayers of the dead, without this LeComte. LeComte was no less a gangster than Sal. The government was twice as bent as the Rubinos. It bothered Sal. You couldn't even trust the United States.

Ted was older than Sal, older than Jerry, as old as Sidel, but he had the deranged eyes of a damaged boy. He couldn't really function without the cooking of Eileen DiAngelis. And he couldn't do jail time, so he joined the FBI. He was the only man in America who could frighten Sal. Sal had worked with other loose cannons. But there had never been a cannon like the Nose.

"Should I take out the melamed, Sal?"

"He's practically your father-in-law."

"I didn't marry Eileen. My brother did. And he turned Eileen against me."

"You did rat on your brother to the FBI."

"I never gave them nothin' big. Just the little things."

"Don't go near the melamed. The melamed knows about you. He's got Isaac on his team."

"Then I'll take out Isaac."

"Not until I say so, kid."

"I'll take out Isaac."

"Show a little discipline, will ya? You'll get Isaac when the time is right. I want you to mop up whatever cannons the melamed has left. Take five or ten of my boys and go through each fuckin' territory until you find a cannon."

"I'll find them, but I'll do it alone. And then I'll take Isaac."

Sal couldn't argue with such a crazy cannon. The Nose had one or two myths inside his head. For him Isaac was the ultimate bad guy, who lived between Jerry and LeComte, who played with all the technicalities of the law, and mocked Nose's condition as the weaker brother who sang to the FBI. As soon as Nose left, Sal dialed the Pink Commish. No one picked up, and Sal put his phone on automatic dial. Two masseurs worked on him, oiling his scarred trunk, molding the horned flesh that he wouldn't allow any comare to see. He almost had an erection, dreaming of Margaret Tolstoy.

Three of his soldiers put him into the tub. Angelo, his new lieutenant with one glass eye, washed the oil off Sal's back. It was a woman's job, and now it had to go to a man. A board was placed over the tub and Sal had his broiled baby lamb chop, prepared by Sal's own cook who slept in a cot near the kitchen and was on call twenty-four hours a day. No one knew when Sal would decide to eat.

Angelo had to feed him, because Sal couldn't hold a knife or a fork in his mottled red hands. It was after six, and Sidel's phone went on ringing. Sal's soldiers returned him to his bed.

The tycoon arrived at seven. Papa Cassidy in a blazer that was so blue it seemed to swallow up every color in Sal's bedroom. Sal had no love for this man. There was nothing but dollars between them. At least with Isaac there was that shared history of Margaret Tolstoy. Papa Cassidy looked like a commodore away from the sea. One of his eyebrows twitched.

"I can't get to Delia," Cassidy said.

"Relax."

"We're supposed to be married."

"Relax, Papa. I'll start to pee if you don't stop."

"I'm impotent without Delia."

"I'm impotent all the time," Sal said.

"I can't bear to think of her with another man."

"That's easy. I'll waste all her boyfriends."

"You can start with Caroll."

"I don't kill son-in-laws. Besides, he's a cop. And what about Malik? I can't kill him. The girl has a celebrated class of clients."

"I paid you a lot of money to get rid of Maria."

"That's different," Sal said. "The little monkey was stealing from us and making trouble."

"He wanted Delia for himself."

"No. Not for himself. Maria never liked you."

"I'll pay double for Caroll."

"Out of the question. I happen to like the kid."

"I could find another contractor."

"That contractor would come back to me. And I'd have to blow your fuckin' brains out. You'd better learn to live with Caroll."

"Then deliver Delia to me."

"All right. I'll try. But I'm her guardian. I can't ask her to marry against her own will."

"I'll pay triple."

"Papa, she could cheat on you, marriage or not. And you don't have to triple the price. I'm drowning in money."

"That's not what I hear," Cassidy said.

Sal began to root under the covers. "Explain yourself."

"DiAngelis is killing your people and making a grab for the whole Family."

"He's a cream puff, that Jerry. He's running so fast, he has to shit in a paper bag. But why are you rankling me, Papa? It's dangerous."

"You shouldn't have hurt my daughter."

"Didn't we talk about that?"

"You shouldn't have hurt Dee."

"I had to make Isaac miserable. That's my only passion. You should never have let her work for the big Jew."

"Then kill Isaac for me. He's behind Caroll."

"I am not killing Isaac," Sal said. "I will make him suffer. But he doesn't rest until I rest. Understand? Good. Now I'm entitled to my beauty sleep. Good-bye, Papa."

"You'll deliver Delia?"

"Papa, if I have to say good-bye again, I'll deliver you."

Cassidy left, but Sal didn't have his beauty sleep. He put on white gloves. He still had enough touch in his hands to grasp a pair of tweezers and toy with the stones in a brooch. He was the jeweler, after all. And the stones had come from a hot collection he'd given to Margaret Tolstoy. He loved to destroy the elaborate settings, a stone at a time. But he could only work for five minutes. His hands would grow feeble and the tweezers would fall out of his grasp.

His telephone console had been dialing Isaac's number for hours. The big monkey wouldn't answer the phone. And then a little after midnight the console lit up and Sal nearly jumped out of his skeleton. He heard Isaac's voice coming through the speaker.

"Sidel here."

His face was twitching.

"Who is this?" Isaac asked.

And Sal managed to mouth his own name.

"Ah, my favorite corpse," Isaac said.

"I could shoot out your eyes any day of the week."

"That's not like you, Sal, threatening me on the telephone."

"It's not a threat . . . Nose is after you, Isaac. Watch your ass."

"He's with your Family now."

"He's a crazy cannon," Sal said.

"Like Captain White."

And Sal was twitching on both sides of his face. "Fabiano made the connection, not me. I met the man once. I knew he couldn't kill you . . . Isaac, I had plenty of my own cannons."

"They wouldn't have gotten near me. You had to use a cop."

"Yeah, a cop with a guilty conscience. He had a gun in his hand and holy beads in his pocket."

"How's Margaret?"

"Margaret? I haven't been next to Margaret."

"That's strange. You've been dancing with the FBI."

"Don't insult me, Isaac."

"I wouldn't insult LeComte's prize rat."

"You broke me to pieces, Isaac. I'm on borrowed time . . . I'm only happy if I make you miserable. But Nose is too efficient. He wouldn't run to a cardinal and cry. I know your business like my business. And I wouldn't want to be alone in this world without you."

"Thanks for the proposal," Isaac said. "But I'm too old to get married again."

And Isaac hung up the phone before Sal could say "Nose."

He dreamt of Margaret offering him such kisses that he was moaning in his sleep. He had to endure that pitiful fall into wakefulness. It was three in the morning and he woke the entire crew that attended to him. His soldiers dressed Sal and put on his shoes. Angelo looked at him out of his one good eye.

"You oughta rest, Sal."

And Sal couldn't even squeeze Angelo's throat, because his girlish hands might split. And if he spat in Angelo's eye the venom would be so terrific, Sal might blind his best man. He looked at himself in the mirror and got scared. One of his ears was like an insane flower that had curled back inside his head. His mouth moved in all directions. Most of his chin was gone. But his left eye had all the brilliance of a burning house.

Angelo carried him to the wheelchair.

His soldiers brought him down to the garage. He sat on the cushions in his white limousine, wearing his soft gloves. Sal's fleet of four cars drove into the dark of Manhattan. There was constant traffic on the radios, which had all the police bands and could anticipate any attack. The windows were bulletproof and each limo had the horsepower and armored plates of a small tank.

His fleet was indestructible. He rode uptown to a bottle club at the borders of Central Park where Delia loved to dance. He had no trouble finding her. She was with Caroll the cop. It was five in the morning, and Delia was dancing all by herself, half naked, her long legs hovering over the floorboards. It infuriated him to watch. He'd never dance with Delia, her energy would never be his. He threw everyone out of the club, except Delia and Caroll. He cut off the music, but Delia continued to dance.

"Sweetheart," he said, "I'm an old man. I could fall out of my wheelchair, watching you."

Delia stopped. "You killed Maria, Uncle Sal."

"Sweetie, it couldn't be helped. He had a big mouth. He was telling everybody he was a G-man."

"Papa Cassidy was jealous. He paid you to kill Maria."

"Hold it," Sal said. "Who reads all your contracts? Who bribes the City inspectors to keep this club open? . . . I want ya to marry Papa. Come on. It'll get kinky. You'll be Caroll's mother-in-law . . . tell her, kid. Tell her to do it."

"Papa's a prick," Caroll said, wobbling from all the whiskey.

Angelo nibbled on Sal's ear. "We could teach the little cop some manners, boss."

"Don't whisper," Sal said. "It makes my ears ring. I have a lot of metal in my skull. It's like a tuning fork . . . Delia, I could make you marry Papa. It's called force majeure. I read that in a law book. It means the unexpected, the force outside the fuckin' order of things. I'm that force. Me. Sal. Aint that right, kid?"

"You're Uncle Sal," Caroll said.

"And you're the boy what had to guard pianos for Uncle Isaac."

"I am," Caroll said. "And you're the boy whose soldiers socked my wife."

"I'll waste him," Angelo said.

"Shaddap . . . who's a boy? I was baptized in hell by Uncle Isaac. I came back."

He wheeled himself next to Delia, his hand stinging from the effort. "You'll marry Papa. That's it. The case is closed."

He signaled to Angelo, who picked up Sal and carried him out of this bottle club, Chinaman's Chance, his legs dangling like useless sticks. He was worse than a boy. He was a baby in Angelo's arms. He'd had no appetite for Delia while she danced. He couldn't stop thinking of Margaret. She was a grandma practically, with veins in her legs. She couldn't even dance, as much as Sal remembered. She ruined Mafia men all over America. He'd tried to kill her in New Orleans. The woman had seduced his little cousins from Dauphine Street, Martin and Emile. The dopes wanted to marry her, even after Sal had warned them about her relationship with the FBI. And now Martin and Emile were dead. And Sal missed Margaret as much as he ever did. It was fuckin' fate that brought him to a wheelchair.

He traveled down from Harlem with his fleet of four cars. But he didn't want to get back into bed. He'd only dream of Margaret, and he had to break that spell.

"Where we goin'?" Angelo asked.

"Cruise," Sal said. "I'll tell ya."

The sun came up around Sal, right through the filtered green glass of the windows, and blanched one of Sal's knees. He started to shake, and Angelo put his arm around him.

"Boss, do you want your blanket?"

"Shaddap."

He found himself on Park Avenue. "We'll stop," he said.

"Right here, boss?"

"Yeah, I'm gonna visit the lady."

"Lady, boss, which lady?"

"The millionairess what you slapped."

"I don't remember slapping no millionairesses."

"Cassidy's daughter, you dope."

"What's her address?"

"Park Avenue," Sal said.

"Boss, that's not an address. I need the number."

"Take out my little book. Look under Caroll Brent. She's Caroll's bride."

Angelo removed a black address book from Sal's pocket. He leafed through the book, his fingers trembling. "Boss, there's nothin' under *B*."

"Look under Caroll, you dope. I never put in last names. It might incriminate me."

Angelo found the address. He carried Sal out of the car. It was half past seven. Diana's doorman looked suspicious. "Do you have an appointment, sir?"

"Just say Sal Rubino . . . Angelo, have the boys bring up some flowers. The best. A big bouquet."

"But the shops aren't open yet, Sal."

"Then find a fuckin' shop that's open."

Three of the soldiers rushed out.

"Miss Cassidy will see you, sir," the doorman said.

"Of course she'll see me . . . Angelo, put me in my chair."

And Sal rode upstairs with Angelo and another soldier. The elevator man had a blue birthmark on his cheek. Sal couldn't take his eyes off that mark. He had the urge to tip this poor elevator man a hundred dollars, but he didn't carry his own cash.

Angelo rang the doorbell. A butler welcomed Sal's people. Sal and Angelo went up a tiny elevator inside the apartment itself, while the other soldier climbed the stairs. This elevator had golden ribs and panels made of cherrywood. The car swayed slightly inside its shaft. Sal closed his eyes. He could have been on a rockingchair ride. And then he felt a rude shove. He opened his eyes and he was in Diana's bedroom. Caroll's bride was under the covers, wearing a dark blue gown. Her face was almost as pale as Sal's. And when he saw the slight, slight bruises on her cheek, Sal started to sniffle. He couldn't cry. He didn't have the constitution for tears.

"Apologize, you dope," he said to Angelo.

Angelo began to hide his hands. "I'm sorry," he said.

Sal bumped into the bed. "It was Isaac. He started the war. I . . ."

Diana smiled. "I've been waiting for you," she said. "I was hoping you'd come . . ."

"Mrs. Brent, I have no feelings in my legs. Isaac murdered me. I can't cough. I can't cry . . ."

"Shhh," she said, taking Sal's gloved hand. And suddenly he started to bawl. His face was all wet. He could have killed Angelo for seeing him like that. Caroll's bride fell asleep. He took back his hand.

They returned to the hall. "Lend me a hundred dollars," Sal said. Angelo and the other soldier reached into their pants. But this elevator man had no blue birthmark. And Sal was disappointed. "Save the hundred," he said.

They got into the elevator. The monkey was wearing gloves, like Sal. He heard two claps. He wasn't stupid. He could recognize the little fuckin' song of a silencer. The car descended into the basement. Angelo and the soldier were lying at Sal's feet. The glass eye had fallen out of Angelo's head. The door opened. The melamed was waiting outside the car, clutching a giant bouquet. The flowers were as blue as the midnight sun.

"Hello, Sal," the melamed said. "Glad you could make it."

26

Rubino has no real chain of command. He'd been like a succubus around his Family, the man in the wheelchair who inspired dread, "the black Christ" who'd had his own Calvary out in the swamps somewhere. Fabiano Rice might have rallied Sal's crews, at least for a little while, but Fabiano was found in his own toilet, with a plastic bag knotted over his head. Sal's captains ran to Pennsylvania and the marshlands of New Jersey. The loansharks stopped collecting. Sal's cement companies decided not to deliver cement. There were no reprisals. Jerry DiAngelis began walking the streets in his white coat, without a single bodyguard. Sal's crews fell into line. The captains returned from the marshes and kissed Jerry's hand. They couldn't bear to live without the Family. And Jerry DiAngelis was the Family now. They might not have felt so humiliated if Sal had been killed. Then they would have grieved for him with the full respect of the Rubinos. But Don Salvatore was alive. The melamed had kidnapped him in his wheelchair.

They weren't fools. Don Isacco was back in business, not as the PC, but as Jerry DiAngelis' war counselor. There were editorials about him. "None of us can be certain about Sidel. The Pink Commish was in a coma two months ago. He's on sick leave from the NYPD. But no one at Police Plaza could put an end to the war inside the Rubino crime family. It took a wounded policeman away from his desk. And we have to ask: why hasn't Her Honor welcomed the Commish?"

Becky Karp summoned him to City Hall. "You've had your vacation, Isaac. It's time to put on your badge."

"Your commissioners have been sending me little kites, saying how this old man ought to retire."

"You're not an old man. And those were somebody else's kites. Just put on the badge."

"I'll make trouble," Isaac said. "I always do."

Her Honor began to smile. She still had the muscular attraction of a former beauty queen. She clutched his hand. "Come on. A quickie. To seal our pact . . . or are you faithful to Margaret Tolstoy?"

"I haven't seen Margaret in months."

But he wouldn't go down into the bunker under her office and reveal his wounds to Becky Karp.

"I'll wear the badge, Becky, but that's it."

"You cocksucker," she said. "You're crazy about that slut. Get out of my office, Commissioner Sidel."

He got his badge from the property clerk, put on his fedora, and returned to One PP. No one dared look under his dirty old hat. His cadre of sergeants shivered in his presence. Sweets had returned to the First Deputy's rooms. Isaac watered the plants, singing to the begonia that climbed his wall. He made no appointments. His own duty sergeant knocked on the door and handed Isaac a lunchbag filled with macaroons and mocha ice cream.

"I don't remember ordering any lunch."

"It arrived, Commissioner Sidel, sir."

"Call me Isaac."

There was a note inside the lunchbag. *Congratulations. We have to talk. Frederic LeComte.*

Isaac threw the note into his wastebasket. He feasted on LeComte's little lunch, licking the mocha off his fingers and devouring the macaroons. He was melancholy about his prodigious appetite. He couldn't spend his life moving from meal to meal.

His phone rang. He picked up the receiver and barked, "Thanks, Frederic. I enjoyed the lunchbag."

"We have to talk."

"I'll put you in my book. How about next Christmas?"

"Stop it."

"Well, I can give you a minute and a half."

"Not on the phone."

"Why? It's your agency that's bugging my lines. Your own eavesdroppers wouldn't care."

"Not on the phone."

"Ah, don't be so timid. Your client's in Jerry's hands. And you don't like it."

"Isaac, I can close you down. Your badge doesn't mean shit on the Hill."

"But I'm not on the Hill, LeComte. I'm at Police Plaza. And I can keep the federal government outside my walls."

"Don't bet on it. I have some tough artillery. And you're a lonely policeman in a dying town."

"Ah, faith," Isaac said in that brogue he liked to adopt at Police Headquarters. "Manhattan's been dying for three hundred years . . . all right, love, meet me at Sherwood Forest in an hour."

"I don't want an entire precinct to know our business."

"LeComte, we have no business. I'm allowing you ten minutes of my time."

Isaac hung up on the cultural commissar and prince regent, who had his hands in a hundred different pies. Isaac had embarrassed the hell out of LeComte. LeComte's star, Sal Rubino, wasn't supposed to get kidnapped—not by Jerry DiAngelis, who'd survived four federal indictments, *and* Sidel, the first Hamilton Fellow.

Isaac went downstairs to the fourth floor and pulled Martin Malik out of his little courtroom. Malik was wearing his judge's robes, with a Glock peeking out of the black skirts.

"I'm in the middle of a trial," Malik said.

"I know. You're a hard worker. I'm reinstating Caroll Brent."

"That's your privilege, Isaac. You're the PC."

"I want the bloodhounds off his back."

"Talk to Internal Affairs."

"No," Isaac said. "I'm talking to you, Malik. I'll appear at Caroll's trial. I'll defend him at every fucking point. You'll look like the silly prick you are."

"You can always fire me," Malik said.

"I wouldn't dream of it," Isaac said. "But you'd better stop seeing Delia St. John, or I'll arrest her for prostitution, for running illegal nightclubs, for selling contraband whiskey, for sodomizing old men, and I'll pinch her while she's in bed with you."

Malik blushed under his black robe. "You bastard."

"Better believe it," Isaac said. "Now go on back to persecuting my policemen."

He walked out of One PP. His chauffeur, Sergeant Malone, was waiting for him. Malone could barely make out Isaac under the fedora. It was grand to have Isaac on the fourteenth floor, but Malone wished he could see the lad's eyes.

"I'm going up to the Forest," Isaac said.

Malone put on the sirens and raced uptown in the PC's black Dodge. He'd lit candles at St. Pat's all through the dark nights of Isaac's coma. But it wasn't the same lad. Some of the juice had gone out of him.

Isaac waltzed into Sherwood Forest without a word for Malone. Old man Weiss was behind the big desk. Isaac had put his Monday Morning Club back into place. He'd pulled Weiss out of retirement, rescued Barbarossa from a room of filing cabinets at the Police Academy, returned White from a phantom station in the Bronx. But White had gone on retreat with Cardinal Jim.

He found Barbarossa upstairs in the weightlifting room. Vietnam Joe was doing bench presses. Isaac could have seized the barbell and forced it down on Barbarossa's throat.

"You Japped me, didn't you, Joey?"

Joe set the barbell down on its rack, sat up, and pulled on the fingers of his glove.

"You're LeComte's little nephew, aren't you, Joe?"

"Did I have a choice? You were always under some bridge. LeComte had me by the balls. He caught me whacking out some dealer."

"But you're indestructible, Joey. You're not supposed to scare. That's why I kept Malik away from you. I'd tell myself, 'Let Joey steal. Let him kill a couple of bad guys. Joey's my pathfinder in the woods. Joey will come through.' But you're a piece of shit."

"Then why didn't you let me stay a clerk at the Academy?"

"You're *my* piece of shit. No one else can have you."

And Isaac walked out to the auxiliary shack and his two sweethearts, Wilson and McSwain. They were ferocious and beautiful, and they troubled his mind. He had to accept that they preferred to mate with women rather than any man. He was always shy around them, because he couldn't understand their mystery. He wouldn't flirt with one or the other. They loved Isaac as they would love some decrepit, cumbersome bear with brains.

"Boss," Wilson said, "what's on the agenda? Are we ruining somebody today?"

"I'm going out to meet LeComte. Follow the fuck. Intercept him. I don't want Frederic on my tail."

"Can we hurt him a little?" McSwain asked, and Isaac was tormented by her smile. He would have married McSwain if he'd had another lifetime, and draw her back to the company of men. But Isaac had never divorced his first and only wife, the Countess Kathleen, who was developing real estate in Florida among the crocodiles. He'd married her when he was nineteen. And she'd supported Isaac, while he struggled to become a cop. She was five years older than the Pink Commish.

McSwain pulled him out of his reverie. "I'd love to tap that Junior G-man."

"He's a pussy," Isaac said, and the girls frowned at him. He couldn't seem to find the right vocabulary with Wilson and

McSwain. "Just lead him in the opposite direction. Nothing rough."

He hugged them like he'd hug a fellow cop. And then he stood outside Sherwood Forest, but there was no Frederic LeComte. He started to walk, and LeComte came up behind Isaac in dark glasses, like a mafioso.

"Where are we going?"

"To the Ramble," Isaac said.

"That's strictly gay territory."

"No. There are a couple of bird watchers. It's a sanctuary, LeComte."

"Someone might see us," LeComte said.

"It's too dense. That's why I picked the Ramble . . . hold my hand."

"Why?"

"Hold my hand. I don't want people to think we're gay bashers . . . or cops."

LeComte gripped Isaac's hand, and they walked through the Ramble like two little girls. Isaac would get lost in the Ramble when he was a rook at Sherwood Forest. The paths seemed to circle around themselves into an infinity of rocks and sky and trees.

"Where are all the gays?" LeComte asked, his eyes searching the grass.

"They're hiding from us, Frederic. Keep quiet."

They stumbled upon a gazebo and LeComte immediately sat down. He took his own paw away from Isaac.

"I need Rubino. You'll have to give him back."

"Send a registered letter to the melamed and see what happens."

"That's not funny," LeComte said. "You don't want to be on my bad side, Isaac. It could be dangerous for you."

"Will you indict me, Frederic? You already tried to have me killed."

"I told you. I wasn't involved with that. It was Sal's idea."

"You gave him the green light."

"Don't be stupid. I wouldn't execute my own Hamilton Fellow."

"Yes you would. You gave him the green light. He's your rat, LeComte. You take responsibility for whatever he does. And you don't walk out of the Ramble until you admit it."

LeComte started to laugh. "My own Minotaur. I have a compass, schmuck. I can leave your little labyrinth whenever I want."

"I put a tail on you, Frederic. My best girls."

"Ah, Wilson and McSwain."

"They'll walk you into oblivion."

"And you'll face a fucking FBI alert . . . I want Rubino. I can't afford to have him kidnapped, Isaac. He's part of my prosecution team."

"Yeah, like little Maria. You and Sal sold him a bill of goods. You let him think he was with the Bureau. And then Sal used your own hitman to get him killed."

"I don't have any hitmen."

"Sure," Isaac said. "The Nose isn't your people."

"He's in the witness protection program."

"That's some protection. He's been keeping the coroner busy . . . making corpses left and right."

"You couldn't stand Maria," LeComte said. "You should rejoice."

"I was wrong about the little guy . . . Frederic, you shouldn't have gone into my house."

"Your house, Isaac?"

"I don't mind the bugs. You can monitor my office every day of the week. But it was pretty dumb to reach into my Department and start recruiting cops."

"I didn't reach," LeComte said. "I wouldn't touch a New York City cop."

"What about Joe Barbarossa?"

"That's different," LeComte said. "That's a unique case. The man happens to be a homicidal maniac. He took out one of the Bureau's best undercover cops."

"You mean one of your G-men was dealing drugs on the side. Barbarossa wasted him. And you were in a dilemma. Your troops would have looked bad if Barbarossa went to trial. You grabbed Barbarossa for yourself."

"It's your fault . . . letting a cop go around killing people."

"If he whacks a couple of bad guys, why should I care? He delivers his own rat poison . . . should I speak a little louder, LeComte? Should I talk into your wire?"

"I'm not wearing a wire," LeComte said.

"I'll bet you aren't," Isaac said. "Make sure you edit the tapes. Because as soon as you produce them, I'll have my own lads mark off the missing loops. And some judge will ask what the great LeComte was hoping to hide."

"Schmuck, I had my own men watch the hospital. I kept you alive. I discouraged Fabiano Rice from finding another hitter."

"I'd love to talk to Fabiano about that. But Fabiano's dead . . . gotta go, Frederic. It's time for me to sit with Sal."

"Wait," LeComte said. "I'll trade you Margaret for Sal Rubino. I'll give her to you, Isaac."

Isaac peered out from under his hat, his whole face like a piece of spitting fire. "You bloody dog. She's my fiancée. I don't want her in this discussion."

"Wait. I'll sign her over, Isaac."

The Pink Commish took out his gun. "I'll waste you, LeComte, right here, in the middle of the woods. The birds will shit on your skull."

He got up and walked out of the Ramble.

27

He moved among the Maf like the war counselor he'd become. All the little soldiers knew he'd engineered the seizing of Sal. The melamed could no longer make battle plans. And Jerry was no strategist. It was Isaac who had one of Jerry's soldiers planted on Park Avenue. Sal was a fickle son of a bitch and might want to atone for having his men slap Dee. It was Isaac who'd telephoned Dee, got her out of her slumber, told her to let Rubino into the house. It was Isaac who had the elevator man drugged and stationed the melamed in the cellar to greet Sal. Corner punks began pulling on his clothes. "Don Isacco, get me into the Family, will ya?"

He had to swat at them like flies. He was the PC. He went from the Park to a little brownstone near the Eighty-ninth Street stables. The brownstone looked deserted. The windows had been covered with boards. Mattresses were piled on the front steps. The mailboxes had been ripped out of the wall. The inside stairs were strewn with bits of colored glass that looked like the scattered beads of a kaleidoscope.

The brownstone had been one of Jerry DiAngelis' most valuable "beds" while he was running from Sal. Isaac climbed over the mattresses, knocked on the door, and let himself in with a silver key. A couple of Jerry's captains saluted him. They had cause to celebrate. Sal Rubino was upstairs in their own prison. And the police commissioner of New York was part of the Family. They were unstoppable now, the new Rubinos, without that crazy Sal.

He sat in his wheelchair, the sick snake. He wouldn't allow Jerry's soldiers to undress him. He hadn't washed in days. He wouldn't eat. He dreamt of Margaret, not his lost estate. And then he looked up and there was Isaac.

"Satisfied, you prick?"

But Isaac was trembling under his clothes. He hadn't made a personal appearance at the kidnapping. He couldn't afford to reveal himself to Dee's doorman. He was too recognizable in the kingdom of Manhattan. And this was the first time he'd seen Sal since New Orleans. Sal had paid a terrible price. His skin was taut around his temples, as if he'd been scalped. He had tiny wisps of hair. The point of his nose was gone, and his nostrils were like two macabre holes. The Phantom of the Opera without a mask. Sal slumped in his chair like some creature who'd withdrawn into his private eternity.

"I asked you, are you satisfied?"

"Yeah, Sal, it's always a pleasure to chat with you."

"Finish me, for fuck's sake. I don't want one of Jerry's people to sock me in the head."

"No one's socking you, Sal. You're valuable to us the way you are."

"Us?" Sal said. "Jesus, I forgot. You're in the Family."

"So are you."

"Me with my lion's heart and a body that you butchered . . . do I get to sit in my wheelchair in front of all my old chiefs? You don't have the right to abuse me just because I'm a cripple."

"You're our trophy, Sal, our spoils of war."

"Kill me, Isaac. I'm a vegetable."

Isaac fed him some soup. Then he undressed Sal, carried him over to the tub, and bathed him with a big sponge. Sal was a patchwork of sewn-together skin.

"Some trophy," Sal said.

"You would have killed Margaret. I had to come to New Orleans."

"Don't mention Margaret. I'm in love with the lady."

"Sal," Isaac said. "She's my fiancée."

He rubbed Sal's brittle bones with a towel, dried him, and returned him to the chair.

"Watch out for the Nose," Sal said.

"Nose is shitting in his pants since we copped you."

"He's still a cannon."

Isaac walked out of the debris, bits of glass crackling under his feet. He went down to the melamed's fortress, which was being refurbished after Sal's firebombs. The house on Cleveland Place was cluttered with captains who ran through the halls with bags of money. There were millions lying about. And all that cash made Isaac uneasy. He hadn't helped the melamed and Jerry to increase their fortune. He loved them and didn't want them to die.

Eileen was morose. She couldn't have her own children and she wanted to adopt Jerry's little bastard, Raoul. She didn't concern herself with the South American beauty who called herself Alice. But Jerry had to pay a price for his comare.

"You'll bring me Raoul," she said.

"Have a heart," Jerry said, standing in his white coat. "You can't ask a mother to give up her own child."

"I do ask."

"Eileen, we're in the middle of a war."

"The war is over."

And she walked out of the room, leaving Jerry to sulk among his captains and his father-in-law.

"She's been worried about you for months," the melamed said. "That's how the worry shows. She makes unreasonable demands, that daughter of mine. But she'll bite my head off if I say a word."

Jerry handed Isaac a money bag. "That's your cut. Count it."

"I can't take your dollars," Isaac said.

"You have to take it, or I'll look bad . . . one of my people working without a reward."

"I'm the police commissioner," Isaac said.

"It's just a title."

"I can't take the gelt."

"The Family's more important than Police Plaza. Tell him, Iz."

"The man likes to be a pauper," the melamed said. "Respect his wishes."

"No," Jerry said. "I'll mark it down in my book. Isaac's cut goes to the Delancey Street Giants."

"The Giants aren't supposed to be rich kids," Isaac said. "Give it to the Polo Grounds."

"What Polo Grounds?"

"The housing projects."

"That's nigger country. I'll look bad."

"You have some black soldiers," Isaac said.

"But I can't give them such a big piece of the pie."

The melamed looked at Jerry. "It's not for the soldiers themselves. It's for the children at the Polo Grounds."

"Yeah," Isaac said. "Maria's girls."

"I'll still have to clear it with my nigger platoons. And what about Italian children in the Bronx? I'll look bad if I leave them out."

"Jesus," the melamed said. "Give Isaac's share to Maria's girls and forget about it. I'm going to bed. I'll have another stroke if I keep listening to you, Jerry."

"I'm not finished," Jerry said. "Isaac's getting too close with Sal."

"Ah," Isaac said, "one of your babysitters dropped a dime on me. Sal is undernourished. I have to feed him."

"I hope he dies," Jerry said. "You undressed the man. I say that's getting too close."

"Well, he can't scrub himself. And your babysitters are help-less fucking morons."

"They offered to bathe him," Jerry said.

"He doesn't want to be undressed by strangers."

"I'm dying," the melamed said. "Do we have to keep going back and forth? Isaac bathed Sal. It's no sin."

"What about the Nose?" Isaac said.

"Nose is nothing without Sal."

"He'll surface again," Isaac said. "Hit him, Jerry. That's my advice."

Isaac brooded under his fedora. He'd rather have coffee with the melamed than police an entire town. But he did police Manhattan while he was with the melamed. It was Jerry's sol-diers who caught child molesters and bandits who preyed upon the old. "It's for Don Isacco," they'd mumble, offering cat burgl-ers to the nearest precinct. And Isaac got used to having mafiosi kiss his hand.

He avoided Sweets, who didn't approve of Isaac's dance with the Maf. But the black giant trapped Isaac while he was watering his begonia.

"I'll have to resign," Sweets said.

"I didn't steal a penny. I haven't done a thing."

"Sure, boss, tell me you never kidnapped Sal."

"You wouldn't even care if LeComte wasn't so pissed off."

"That's correct. But we have to work with the FBIs. And I'm sick of hearing you on tape with Jerry and the melamed . . . how can I dig into the Rubinos if you're a member of the clan?"

"Dig," Isaac said. "Dig all you want."

"Isaac, you'll have to choose between Jerry's people and ours. And please don't threaten Martin Malik."

"I didn't threaten Malik . . ."

"You did. You want to take Caroll Brent out of hock, then do it without involving Malik."

"Ah, shit," Isaac said. "I forgot about Caroll."

"He's a bad cop."

Isaac put on his coat and slid the fedora over his head. "Excuse me, Sweets. I gotta go."

And Isaac was out the door.

Sweets stood in the PC's office that he'd vacated a week ago, with the plants, the twin flags of the United States and New York City, the oak desk that had once belonged to Teddy Roosevelt. He'd rather have Isaac in this office than some glom the mayor brought in as a public-relations man. Sweets didn't want the job. The Pink Commish moved across the seas of Manhattan with his own unfathomable music.

Part Seven

28

Isaac arrived on Central Park North with his own little SWAT team, Wilson and McSwain. He didn't want to be alone with Caroll. Isaac had let him drift in that broken hotel while he went to war.

"Hiya, kid."

Caroll opened his eyes. He didn't like to be woken out of a whiskey sleep. He recognized Isaac and his two Monday Morning girls, Wilson and McSwain.

"Come on, kid. You're going to Sherwood Forest."

"What about Malik?"

"I cut out his heart."

"And who the fuck are you, Isaac?"

"The Pink Commish."

"God, I dreamt about it last night. You're back on the fourteenth floor." He lunged at Isaac, knocked off his hat, and pulled him by the ears until McSwain seized Caroll and handcuffed him to the bed.

"I'm not working for you, Isaac, never again."

"And what will you do? Guard Delia and live in this rat's hotel?"

"It's none of your business, Isaac. I like the view."

"Free the kid."

McSwain removed the handcuffs and dragged Caroll into the shower. She held him under the water until he lost his whiskey eyes. He started to shiver and curse and scream. And then it was Isaac and Wilson *and* McSwain who had to hold him. Caroll slipped, and they all fell into the shower, rocking against the walls like angry children, Isaac with pools of water in his pockets. But holding Caroll like that, Isaac felt he was struggling for his life. He had to climb out of his own ruin.

The girls pulled Caroll from the shower, limb by limb. Isaac looked into Caroll's brown eyes. "You're going back to the Forest, you hear?"

He handed Caroll his shield and his service revolver. And then he whispered to McSwain. "You'll chaperone the kid . . . I've got things to do."

He returned to Police Plaza. He watered his plants. He dreamt of the Polo Grounds, and that blazing green grass of center field was more vivid to Isaac than the shoes or shirt or wristwatch of a policeman. One of his sergeants walked in and wrenched Isaac from all that grass.

"There's a babe downstairs. Calls herself Delia. She's making a ruckus, says she has to see you. But I can't find her name in your calendar book."

There were no names in Isaac's calendar. "Let her in. She's my guest."

Delia marched into Isaac's office with her hair curled in pockets around her head. "You closed all my clubs."

"I did."

"You're a cocksucker."

"That's what Becky Karp says all the time."

"Who's Becky Karp?"

"Jesus," Isaac said, "don't you ever stop dancing? Becky Karp's the mayor of New York."

"Oh, *that* Becky Karp," Delia said.

"I might open one or two of your cellars . . . if you behave. I don't want you going near Caroll Brent."

"He's my bodyguard," Delia said.

"He's a policeman. He can't take gratuities from little girls like you."

"I'm not a little girl."

"Then why do you dress like one?"

"My customers won't allow me to grow up, Uncle Isaac."

"Then it's a tragedy," Isaac said. "You'll have a mid-life crisis before you're twenty-five."

"I am twenty-five. And I'm going to call Uncle Malik. Uncle Malik won't let you bully me."

"Call him," Isaac said, handing Delia the phone. She started to cry.

"Uncle Malik won't talk to me . . . where's my Uncle Sal?"

"He can't help you," Isaac said. "Sit down."

He removed a gallon of mocha ice cream from the little freezer he kept behind his plants. He broke a spoon trying to dig out the ice cream from the bottom of the container. He had to chip at the mocha with a knife. He gave Delia a bowl, and they started to eat.

"No Caroll," he said. "And you can have one club, Chinaman's Chance."

"One club? I'm not Salome. I need the exercise . . . will you visit me, Uncle Isaac?"

"Ah, I wouldn't want to make your other uncles jealous. And I don't dance. I have a wooden leg."

"I like wooden legs," Delia told him.

She was playing the child again. But Isaac was immune to her charms. He'd sworn himself to Margaret Tolstoy. He waltzed Delia out of the office with his wooden leg. And waiting for him, in his anteroom, was the melamed, wearing a dark suit like some undertaker. The sergeants hadn't known what to do about Iz, who had a special relationship with their chief. And so they let the melamed sit until Isaac discovered him with his own eyes.

Isaac didn't have much choice. He brought the melamed into his office.

"Nice plants," the melamed said. "You must talk to them every day."

"You had to come here, didn't you? Should I give you a gold shield, Iz? Would you like your own desk in my office? I can make you a deputy commissioner, I can swear you in."

"I am your deputy commissioner. I always was. But I'm not rash, Isaac. I had to get in touch."

"You could have given me a tinkle on the telephone."

"I don't trust telephones."

"Damn you, Iz, my office is wired. LeComte has his bugs all over the place."

"I'm not worried about LeComte. It's Jerry I'm worried about. He's planning a banquet with Sal's old captains. And I don't have to tell you who the guest of honor will be."

"He's out of his mind," Isaac said.

"I can't reason with Jerry. He says Sal belongs to him."

"We didn't capture Sal to exhibit him like a monkey. It will cause bad blood. Those captains might decide to free the son of a bitch . . . sympathy is a fucking contagious disease."

"I agree."

"And where is the son-in-law?"

"On Eighty-ninth Street with Sal."

"Will you ride up with me, Iz?"

"No, no. He'll think we started a conspiracy."

"Then I'll drop you off at home."

"Your own troops might get suspicious."

"Jesus," Isaac said. "You're already in my office. How cozy can you get?"

And he called for his driver, Malone.

Isaac arrived at the rubble of Jerry's brownstone in less than half an hour. Jerry's soldiers shrugged at him as Isaac climbed the stairs. He could hear Jerry shout from the top floor.

"Dress him, will ya?"

Isaac peeked over the banisters and saw two soldiers trying to fit Sal into a tuxedo.

"Leave him alone," Isaac said.

Jerry stared at the Pink Commish. "I didn't invite you."

"I don't need an invitation," Isaac said.

"This is my house."

"Good. But I have the key. Leave him alone."

"He has to wear a tux," Jerry said. "I'm taking him to a bene-fit."

"Then you'll have to kill me," Isaac said.

Jerry dismissed the two soldiers, his eyes burning with anger. "You talked to the melamed. My own father-in-law's a rat."

"I love this," Sal muttered, his head rising out of the chair. "I'll go to the party, Mr. DiAngelis. I'll count the faces. I'll see who's loyal. I'll have my revenge."

"No one asked you, Rubino."

"Come on, Isaac. Dress me."

The anger had gone out of Jerry's eyes. "I can't disappoint the captains. I promised them Sal."

But he left the house, sulking in his white coat. "I'm the fool of the Family."

Isaac heard little popping noises and then footsteps on the stairs. He wondered if Jerry had decided to come back. But those weren't Jerry's footsteps. He saw Margaret coming out of the stairwell in a short brown wig. She was carrying her spacegun with a silencer. And Isaac almost had to laugh.

"LeComte sent you," he said.

"Isaac, you couldn't expect him to fall asleep. I'm his best man."

"I'll bet you are," Isaac said. "I suppose you whacked Jerry on your way in."

"No," she said. "Jerry wasn't in the deal." She kissed Isaac in front of Sal, with the Glock in Isaac's belly. And Sal was feeling murderous. He didn't want a rescuer like Margaret making kiss, kiss, while he had the faint hope of an erection in his pants.

"And you have all the angles, don't you, dear?" Isaac said. "You whacked Jerry's soldiers and you'll have to whack me too."

"That wasn't in LeComte's scenario," she said.

"But Jerry will think I had it all planned, so you'd better kill me."

"Wait a minute," Sal said. "Don't I get to say something?"

Margaret ignored him. "I couldn't kill you, love. You know that."

"And what if I didn't let you take Sal?"

"Then we'd have to rewrite the scenario," she said.

A G-man came up the stairs, a blue-eyed Mormon who'd been elected to carry Sal down into LeComte's car.

"Nobody touches me," Sal said, "nobody but Isaac." He bit the Mormon's hand. "I'm a snake. I'm a fuckin' snake."

The Mormon put a blanket over Sal's head, picked him up in his wheelchair, and carried Sal and the chair out of the house.

Margaret ran her finger across Isaac's face. And then she vanished with the Mormon and the wheelchair. Isaac was left with the corpses of Sal's babysitters. He shouldn't have fallen in love with an FBI girl.

LeComte was waiting for him at the bottom of the stairs. He grinned at Isaac.

"It's always nice to see my Hamilton Fellow."

"Fuck you, Frederic."

"You had your little caper. Fun is fun. But now we're playing hardball. You had no right to steal Rubino. I stole him back."

"Grand," Isaac said. "And now the war will start again. Babies will be shot in the street."

"We're holding Rubino under wraps. The melamed can have his territories. I'll catch Jerry another time. But we keep the wheelchair. We keep Sal . . . kiddo, walk me to my car. You can say good-bye to Sal and your sweetheart."

"She's not my sweetheart anymore. She was going to glock me."

"Not a chance," LeComte said.

Isaac walked out with the cultural commissar to an empty street.

"Where's my car?"

A schoolbus turned the corner and stopped in front of Isaac and the commissar. The door opened with a pneumatic hiss. The melamed stood behind the door.

"Don't be bashful, boys. Come inside."

There were soldiers at the windows, their cannons aimed at LeComte's eyes. LeComte stepped into the bus.

Isaac started to walk away. The bus moved alongside of him.

"Sonny, do we have to shoot off your toes?"

"Shoot," Isaac said. "Iz, you staged the whole fucking thing."

"We can't have a dialogue like this . . . people will notice."

"You knew LeComte was coming for Sal."

"I had a hunch," the melamed said. "And I acted on it . . . we have Margaret, remember. We might hurt your fiancée." The old man turned pale. "Sonny, I'm getting excited. I'll have another stroke."

"Ah, we wouldn't want that," Isaac said with his policeman's brogue and climbed aboard.

29

The bus brought him to a bingo club on Pleasant Avenue, in Jerry DiAngelis' Harlem domain. Margaret had a mouse under her eye. Sal was wearing a dark tuxedo. LeComte was sandwiched between two of Jerry's cannons.

The bingo club was filled with Rubino captains, their wives and mistresses, their children, their bodyguards, and saintly halfwitted boys who served as good-luck charms. There was a priest in the entourage, the nephew of a particular captain. There was the Rubinos' private baker. They'd all come to hiss at Sal, their fallen chief.

It's a circus, Isaac muttered. But no one kissed his hand at the bingo club, no one called him Don Isacco. He wasn't a war counselor tonight. He was a captive, with Sal and LeComte and Margaret Tolstoy, whose mouse grew green under her eye. He couldn't bring himself to clutch her hand. He felt as if he'd been cuckolded by the FBI.

He watched the thick, swollen faces around him, all the celebrants, and then he noticed a boy who didn't play with the other children at the club. It had to be Raoul, Jerry's own little bastard. The woman next to Raoul must have been Alice, or Alicia, Jerry's comare, a big blonde who looked more Levantine than Latino. But Isaac couldn't really fathom any racial mix. Raoul was an outcast among the Rubinos. His eyes were like two enormous marbles in his head. And behind the boy was Eileen DiAngelis, like some bountiful witch at the proceedings, with her own mad claim on Raoul. Isaac almost pitied Jerry, who was caught between his comare and Eileen. Some crazy instinct must have driven him to invite them both. Perhaps he needed his two women to preside over the dismantling of Sal Rubino. But it was still a circus.

Jerry wasn't the ringmaster. He didn't have the gift of speech. He was splendid in his white coat. But he couldn't sway an army of bandits and their wives and children, legitimate or not. It was the melamed who stood on the dais at the bingo club, his face slightly twisted from the stroke. One arm trembled. But he was the Family poet. Next to him were Sal Rubino and LeComte, sitting on little black chairs.

The melamed silenced that circus with a single twitch of his eyes. "Brothers and sisters," he said. "I brought you a gift . . . your old friend Sal. Look at him. Don Rubino with his own FBI man. Ah, I forgot. I'd like to introduce Frederic LeComte, prince of the Justice Department, who indicted Jerry four times."

The captains and their women laughed and shouted, "Fucking Frederic LeComte."

The melamed held out his fingers. "Four times."

The children clapped. LeComte played with his knuckles. Sal's head started to wag. Isaac had the urge to climb up onto the platform and sock the Hebrew teacher. But he sat with Margaret Tolstoy and Jerry DiAngelis and Raoul and all the Rubino captains. He'd have to create his own Mafia within the walls of One PP.

"Brothers, sisters," the melamed said, "all the while he was your padrone, he was babysitting with our enemy, Frederic LeComte. Ask him to deny it."

Sal's head stopped wagging. Spittle flew from his mouth. His left eye seemed to circle the ceiling. He was on another planet.

"Maybe," the melamed said, pointing to LeComte, "maybe the Justice Department's own little commissar will enlighten us. Speak to us, Commissar. We're civilized men. We won't bite."

LeComte continued to crack his knuckles. "I have nothing to say."

"That's because you're married to Mr. Rubino. And you had the wonderful idea of controlling our Family, of sitting behind Rubino, pulling him like a puppet, and laughing at us with all your FBI men. But you're not at the Justice Department right now. You're at a banquet of the Rubinos . . ."

The captains grinned with sausages in their mouths. Their mistresses and wives hurled paper cups at Sal Rubino. And Isaac wondered if he was at some madcap convention and not a bingo club in the bucolic little corner known as Italian Harlem.

The melamed raised his arms. "Brothers, I'm an old man. Please don't disgrace our Family . . . after all, we escaped our misfortune. We found out who this Sal Rubino was. And the FBI isn't our padrone. Eat, enjoy yourselves. We have no more business with these people."

And like a magician, he closed a curtain around himself and the two men in the chairs, and when the curtain opened, Sal and LeComte were gone. The melamed came down from the dais while the captains danced with their wives and mistresses, having already forgotten Sal. But a commotion had started around Jerry D. Eileen tried to steal Raoul from his mother.

"I'm your wife," she told Jerry. "The children of all your whores belong to me."

But big blond Alice had her own volition. "Darling," she said, "when he's on top of you once a month, he closes his eyes and dreams of me."

The two women attacked, their fists in each other's hair. The melamed and Jerry were paralyzed. It was Isaac who parted Eileen and Alice, who took their blows, and allowed each of them to cry on his shoulder, while Raoul trembled near the melamed, his huge eyes absorbing all those crazy adults. And then the melamed's own bodyguard collected the boy and his mother and drove them downtown in Jerry's sedan.

The banquet started all over again.

Isaac stood in the corner with Jerry and the melamed.

"You had to bring both women?" the melamed asked.

"Ah," Jerry said, "Raoul wanted to meet the FBI man." And he walked off, celebrating with his own captains. Isaac was left all alone with the melamed.

"I love that disappearing act," he said.

"Speak plainer," the melamed said. "My mind's impaired."

"Impaired, huh? I think the stroke did you some good . . . what happened to LeComte and Sal?"

"I'm no murderer," the melamed said. "I gave the rat to the FBI. I set him free. How can he harm us, Isaac? His own captains saw him on the stage with LeComte. He's a walking dead man."

"He already died once."

"But you can only have one resurrection. That's all God allows."

"And I suppose you're God's special priest."

"No. I'm a melamed who had to sit on his son-in-law because that son-in-law doesn't have the brains to plan ahead."

"You're the strategist, all right. You used me, Iz. And it's not the first time. You show up at my office with crocodile tears. You knew that LeComte was listening to our conversation. And you knew he would try to get Sal back from Jerry. So you let him pounce, and then you bring LeComte and Sal to your little captains' party."

"It was the only way," the melamed said.

"Why didn't you trust me?" Isaac had to ask.

"You're a cop."

"I'm your fucking war counselor. I swiped Sal in the first place."

"You're a cop. Sooner or later you would have turned on

us. You don't have a choice. LeComte would have applied the pressure."

"I didn't turn," Isaac said.

"Sonny, not even you can fight the whole United States."

"What about Margaret?" Isaac asked. "She might have gotten hurt at the house on Eighty-ninth Street."

"Be a little charitable. She killed three of my men."

"She's still my fiancée. And you set her up."

"Isaac, did I put her on the platform with LeComte? I kept her out of the picture. She can go on sleeping with gangsters and busting their brains. I have nothing against Madame Tolstoya, believe me."

"And Nose?"

"He'll stay in the woodwork. He doesn't have Sal to sponsor him. And what can I do? Jerry won't let anyone touch the kid. How can I get between two brothers? . . . but I'm tired of talking, Isaac. Enjoy yourself, please."

"LeComte will hunt you down," Isaac said.

"You don't understand the psychology of the FBI. LeComte wouldn't want to advertise his appearance at our party. He'll land in a pile of shit if his bosses ever learn he was kidnapped for a couple of hours."

"The man's his own boss," Isaac said.

"You're mistaken. That's the beauty of this government. There are always bosses . . . good-bye, Isaac. I don't envy you. A police commissioner with a talmudic bent. We're both antiques."

The melamed went off to calm Eileen, and Isaac was like an outcast at the party. He couldn't find Margaret. She must have slipped away with that mouse under her eye. He walked out onto Pleasant Avenue without a nod from the Rubinos and breathed the air of one more Harlem night.

30

They sailed away with Sal, Margaret on one side of him, Frederic on the other. And Sal had such bitterness he could have swallowed LeComte's head, eaten all the cartilage, and spat out an ear or two with LeComte's yellow blood. "I'll kill DiAngelis. I'll kill the melamed."

"You'll do nothing," LeComte said. "Those were your captains, Sal."

"So what? I'll get other captains."

"That's not the point," LeComte said. "The melamed owns your Family. It's all over, Sal. I have to cut our losses."

"And what about me?"

"I haven't let you down," LeComte said. "I took you out of the sausage factory in New Orleans. I put you back together. I haven't let you down."

"And now I'm Mr. Frankenstein," Sal said, squinting at Margaret. He'd have gone to the FBI college in Quantico, he'd have educated his wheelchair to run over bankrobbers, if only Margaret would live with him again. But how could he expect her to respond to such a Frankenstein face?

He started to shiver. The bitch took him in her arms, rocked him like the baby he was, and it was LeComte who ruined it, ruined it with his words.

"What's wrong, Sal?"

"Shh," Margaret said, and he could sniff that perfume of her body. It was like a long, savage hit to Sal, the awakening of something he'd rather not wake to. He could have made love to Margaret, in spite of all his brittle bones, the scrotum that was hiding in some little shelf. Sal was his own idiotic flower. But LeComte ruined it all.

"Don't you get it, Sal? The melamed doesn't have to wrinkle you."

"I'm already wrinkled."

"Listen, you can't walk the streets. If you surface, your own captains will kill you."

"I can hire a coupla cannons."

"And those cannons will kill you. You're marked, Sal. It's all over."

"The Nose is still mine," Sal said.

"I'm taking him off the market," LeComte said. "The man's a danger to everybody. I'll send him to some halfway house in Atlanta where he can sit for life."

Sal started to laugh. "You can't find the Nose, can you?"

"We'll find him," LeComte said.

"And you can't figure who he'll hit next. The mayor of Atlanta, the melamed, or you yourself."

"He's in his own shitstorm. He can't crawl anywhere without my help."

"And what about the shitstorm I'm in? I'm not living in any of your halfway houses."

"We'll find the right solution," LeComte said.

Sal twisted around and stared into LeComte's eyes. "Who's going to be my babysitter?"

"Margaret," LeComte said.

And Sal could have cried. "Did you have to bribe her with some silver?"

"Shh," Margaret said, bathing him in perfume.

Isaac felt lost without his Family. He couldn't locate the right tribe at One PP. He had the Irish, but they'd all gone gray around the ears. Being in their company was like being at his own wake. He tried not to think of Margaret. The wind howled against the glass on the fourteenth floor. The sun arrived, and Isaac was in the thick of spring. His Delancey Giants were scheduled to play the cardinal's Manhattan Knights in the North Meadow. And the Commish was much more excited about that game than any of the material that passed in front of his desk, even though it was the Bomber who piloted Isaac's Giants. Harry was the Giant's horse.

Isaac looked up and saw his own first deputy commissioner.

"Thanks, boss," Sweets said.

"Why are you thanking me?"

"For giving up the Rubinos."

"I didn't give up anything. The melamed threw me out of his clan."

"I don't care," Sweets said. "I'll light a Jewish candle for him."

"You only light candles for the dead."

"It's my candle, boss."

And the black giant disappeared from Isaac's office. But Isaac didn't have any peace. One of the downtown brokers of the Democratic Party, Saturnino Gomez, had made an appointment to see him. Gomez was president of the Harry Truman Club and an ally of the schools chancellor, Alejo Tomás. He'd been an outfielder with the Chicago Cubs for a week in 1954. Isaac envied Saturnino that one little week. And he tolerated all of Gomez's intrigues because of that.

"We want you to run for mayor," Saturnino said.

"Don't be ridiculous. The chancellor hates my guts."

"He's not a problem. He can be convinced to like you . . . he knows about your work in One B."

Isaac had been doing penance. He'd visited the schools in

Maria's district, he'd attended sewing classes like one of the pupils, he'd talked to Maria's girls about the anarchy of lower Manhattan. He had no practical advice. He was a visionary, like Maria had been.

"Get married at fourteen," Isaac had said to the girls. "Go for it. But don't drop out of school. Question your teachers. Don't let them fill you with lies. You were put on this earth to dance, to make love, not to become money machines, not to sell your body and your mind. If you have to steal to feed yourself, then steal, but don't take any pleasure from it."

School principals had to tolerate the Pink Commish. The girls fell in love with Isaac, brought him apples they'd baked with their own hands, and Saturnino Gomez wanted him to become the next mayor of New York.

"Rebecca can't win."

"But she won't like it if you pit me against her."

"Tough. She'll never get the Latino vote . . . the Newyoricans are crazy about you," Saturnino said. "You're our candidate."

"What will the Republicans do?"

"They're feeling out Martin Malik. He'll kill Rebecca at the polls. The iron judge of the Police Department. We need you to fight the Turk."

"I'll think about it."

"Don't think too long. We might have to kidnap Malik from the Republican camp."

Gomez left. Isaac wouldn't give up his rooms on Rivington Street for Gracie Mansion. He'd have to kiss babies, woo builders like Papa Cassidy, demand toilets for the poor. He'd survive better at One PP.

His chauffeur brought him uptown to Diana's building. But when he arrived at her duplex, a funny little man met him at the door. Isaac handed him his hat.

"I'm not the butler. I'm Milan Jagiello. I live here."

The apartment was flooded with musicians. There were tubas and bass fiddles on every sofa. Isaac had to navigate around them to get near Dee. But Diana was out of bed. The bruises had disappeared from her face. She hugged Isaac. There was nothing vague in her eyes. She'd recovered from Maria and that punching party Sal's men had prepared for her.

"Dee, it's a madhouse."

"Milan lost his lease. I had to take him in."

"And his whole bloody orchestra?"

"Why not? I like having them here. It's lonely without Caroll."

"The kid hasn't come back?"

"He's not a kid."

"I'll break his bones," Isaac said.

"You'll do nothing."

"He must be living at Sherwood Forest. Ah, Dee, I messed your life . . ."

"I'm fine," Diana said. "It was the man in the wheelchair. He cured me. Sal Rubino. One of his bully boys carried him up to my bedroom. I was in a fog that morning. He started to cry. He touched my face . . . I had a chill."

Isaac groaned. "Sal the faith healer."

"No, Isaac. It's much simpler than that. He was very kind."

"The man's a snake."

"My father's getting married," Dee said.

"We were talking about Sal."

"His new bride is Delia St. John. Papa's furious. Cardinal Jim refuses to marry him at St. Pat's. I might not attend the wedding. I'm older than she is."

"You can't be sure about Delia."

"She's also Caroll's mistress."

"Not anymore," Isaac said. "I'll talk to Caroll."

"Don't you dare. Leave Caroll alone."

Isaac cursed himself on the way down to the lobby. He'd driven Delia into Papa Cassidy's arms, and he couldn't deliver Caroll. He dismissed his chauffeur and entered the Park at Woodmans Gate. The North Meadow was packed. Isaac saw his Giants and the Manhattan Knights in their long red stockings.

Cardinal Jim was chatting up the umpire. He had a monsignor in the coaching box. He had priests with baseball bats. And his Knights had the smooth look of golden boys. They hadn't lost a game in two seasons. The Giants were a bit bedraggled, like the Bomber himself, who had stubble on his face.

"I can't sleep," Harry said, as Isaac approached.

"Ah, we'll steal Jim's pants."

"I'm not interested in Jim's pants. I have two catchers with broken thumbs. And my outfield hasn't clicked. I've been away from the diamond too long. I can't breathe . . . will you coach these kids if I fall on my ass?"

"I'm with you, Harry," Isaac said, and he caught the cardinal winking at him. "I'll be back."

Isaac met with Jim under the wire roof behind home plate. "What about a friendly wager?" the cardinal asked. "Your lads are much improved."

"But I don't have the Church's cashbox behind me."

"Wouldn't involve the Church in this," the cardinal said. "I could lend you a few dollars, love, out of my own pocket . . . or you could always borrow from the melamed."

"That's unkind," Isaac said. "There are no money matters between the melamed and me."

"I've been hearing different," the cardinal said. "I was told that the melamed had pensioned you off to the Police Department."

"Then I'm a charity case," Isaac said. "But I'll bet a hundred on my boys."

"A hundred dollars? Aint that steep?" And Jim's eyes sparked in his head. He clapped Isaac's hand. "It's done." And he returned to the Manhattan Knights.

Isaac felt like some orphan, with a team that was his and also wasn't. He hiked up to the stands behind first base. His Giants took the field. The Knights were a head taller, but they couldn't seem to solve the Giants' curious shift. The Bomber had arranged his boys in a zigzag pattern that smothered whatever ball the Knights could hit. Isaac began to enjoy himself after the second inning. And then he discovered a face down on the field, behind the catcher's cage. It was Teddy DiAngelis, the Nose, watching Isaac and the Giants. Isaac's innards shrank. He could almost feel the ghost of his worm pulling at him.

He came down off the stands like some trampoline artist walking on twisted boards. He passed the cardinal, who was screaming at his Knights because they couldn't uncover that elusive hole in the jagged infield of the Delancey Giants. He passed the Bomber, who rocked on his feet, and got to Nose.

Teddy Boy laughed with his button eyes and imbecilic bliss. "I could sock the cardinal," he said. "I could take out five or ten of your brats, Mr. Isaac."

"What the hell for?"

"To make you unhappy . . . you turned my people against me."

"You have no people," Isaac said. "I'll walk with you, Nose, anywhere. But leave the cardinal and these kids alone. You don't have any grievances against Jim."

"I'll take the cardinal," Nose said. "And then I'll take you."

"Not a chance. I'll chew off your head."

Nose stared at Isaac. The thought horrified him. "Say good-bye to this world."

"I don't need good-byes."

Nose had his Glock, and pushed it against Isaac's ribs. "Come with me, mister." He led Isaac away from the diamond and into the north woods.

"Ask God to forgive you."

"He wouldn't."

Nose seemed troubled. "You gotta ask."

And then Isaac saw Caroll. *Kid, why haven't you gone back to your wife?* And with him was Barbarossa. They must have followed Isaac from the playing fields. Ah, he was living with chaperones.

Nose turned his eyes like the gadgetry on a tank and found the two detectives. He clutched Isaac to his body and removed most of himself as a target. "I'll kill this man," he said. "I'll kill this man."

Caroll wavered. Barbarossa shot Nose in the tiny patch of forehead that was available to him. Isaac heard the crush of bone. But Teddy Boy didn't fall. His knees dipped. There was blood on the side of Isaac's face. Nose had been glocked in the head, and he wouldn't sit down. He shot Barbarossa. He tried to shoot Caroll. But Caroll dropped to the ground, crept around Isaac, and emptied his service revolver into Nose, who danced with the force of each bullet, hugged himself, as if he could wipe away his wounds, waltzed deeper into the woods, clutched at the sky like some circus bear, and pitched facedown into the grass.

"How's Joe?" Isaac demanded. "How's Joe?"

"Pissed," Barbarossa said from the ground. "I cracked his head and nothing happened."

It was the cardinal who arrived first from the playing fields. He'd listened to all the little devilish explosions and ordered the umpire to stop the game.

He looked at the blood on Isaac's face. He looked at Caroll. He looked at Barbarossa and the corpse in the grass. "Sonny," he said to Isaac, "you planned the whole thing. Did you have to upstage my Knights with a shootout in Central Park?"

He looked at Barbarossa again. "Jesus God," he said to Caroll. "Will you call an ambulance?"

31

It was Medal Day on the steps of City Hall. A patrolman from Brooklyn South blew taps. Isaac couldn't control himself. He cried and cried. He always felt like a buffoon on Medal Day. It was Sweets who had to protect the Pink Commish.

"What am I going to say to all those widows?" Isaac asked.

"You'll say what you have to say."

It was Sweets who was chairman of the honor board, Sweets who wrote the citations for the living and the dead. And Isaac had to sing about all the heroes to mothers, fathers, widows, children, and wives.

He stood near the mayor and Cardinal Jim. He gripped the podium that had been placed at the top of the stairs. He wanted to swoon. The First Dep was behind him, clutching the seat of Isaac's pants. Isaac's mouth opened, but he couldn't deliver his own phantom speech.

The cardinal had to rescue him. "Boyo," he whispered in Isaac's ear, "move your arse." He nestled into Isaac's space and stared at all the onlookers. "Dear Heart, it's a sorrowful day and a proud one for the City of New York. A policeman who was killed or injured in the line of duty tells us something—that there still is a line of duty, and that each day men and women officers risk their lives to uphold this line. I come here not as the honorary chaplain of the Police Department, which I am, but as an adopted son of your City, as a mourner and a celebrant, and a surrogate for the commissioner, Isaac Sidel, standing at my side, who was wounded at the start of winter, and risked his own life but a few scant weeks ago, by drawing a maniacal killer away from a crowded field of young lads in Central Park until two of his finest men, Detectives Brent and Barbarossa, could destroy this maniac. Barbarossa was wounded in the gun battle. This aint the first time. He's the most decorated cop in New York. And it was Brent who fired the last shots . . . but your commissioner, who has seen other cops fall, is much too noble a man to speechify while *his* cops have gone to the grave. So I will have to do it. I'll bear the burden. I'll be the one who tells you that your lads didn't die in vain. They protected God and New York from heathen criminals, they held the line. . . ."

There was clapping and crying. The mayor hugged Cardinal Jim, who edged away from the podium and whispered to Isaac once again. "Sonny, you still owe me a hundred dollars."

Isaac didn't answer. Rebecca tugged on the microphone, addressed the audience, but she didn't have a cardinal's music. There was no lilt to her voice. She was in a town where the mayor was only one more puppet within a narrowing arc. It didn't matter that she'd memorized all the citations, that she presented the medals of deceased officers to their widows with a mayor's kiss, that she pinned metallic bars on the chests of officers who'd earned the combat cross.

The audience watched Isaac, not Rebecca Karp. He shook the hands of decorated cops. Barbarossa had five other bars on his chest. He wore a blue bag, with one of his arms in a sling. He looked like a total misfit in his uniform. *My best boy.* And when Caroll came up to him with his own blue bag and the gold-and-green bar of a combat cross, Isaac felt ashamed. It was Caroll who had to finish Isaac's business and whack out Teddy Boy. And he couldn't stop crying.

"Jesus," Jim said, after the presentations. "Will you get a grip on yourself? You're a grown man."

"I don't owe you a hundred. The game was canceled."

"Because of you and that rotten corpse."

"Nose was a good Catholic," Isaac said. "Not a heathen. He prayed all the time."

"Heathens can pray," the cardinal said. "The Lord is deaf to them."

Isaac was gloomy until he saw Diana. She'd come to celebrate Caroll, that lost husband of hers. Make the peace, Isaac muttered, but he'd stopped trying to interfere. He wasn't so welcome in their lives. Ah, he'd have to get some ping-pong lessons and play the ghost of Blue Eyes.

But Isaac saw another ghost, the ghost of a very old man in an impeccable dark suit and a shirt that was blazingly white. It was Izzy Wasser, he who'd had the stroke. But the melamed seemed to dance on the steps of City Hall. He had much better balance than the Pink Commish. And he wasn't ashamed to appear among so many cops.

"I couldn't come to the funeral," Isaac said. "It wasn't proper."

"Isaac, you didn't miss much. Those lousy medical examiners mutilated Nose at Bellevue. We had a hard time getting the body back. Our lawyers had to ask and ask."

"Iz, I don't make the rules. Nose got caught in a criminal investigation, dead or alive."

"It was a very small funeral," the melamed said. "Considering Nose was a government spy. Whatever pals he had in the witness-protection program didn't come. Eileen cried for the baby."

"And you?" Isaac asked.

"Me? I didn't shed a tear . . . maybe we shouldn't talk in front of all the brass. I wouldn't want to compromise you on Medal Day."

"It's okay, Iz. You kicked me out of the Family. I'm clean. But I was wondering how Nose knew I'd be at the baseball diamond. He was never that bright. He had to have a steerer."

"And you think the steerer was me."

"I didn't say that, Iz."

"I'm clairvoyant," the melamed said. "Sonny boy, I can read your eyes. You have a terrific imagination. But it happens that you're right. Nose called Eileen. I got on the wire. I told him your whereabouts. I have your itinerary, Isaac. Just in case . . ."

"You pointed the finger, Iz."

"Not so fast. I paid a visit to LeComte. I let him know all about the baby's intentions. And LeComte called Barbarossa. So you see, Isaac. It was all taken care of . . . I had to get rid of Nose. He would have menaced us sooner or later. And Jerry didn't have the heart."

"And what if I didn't survive your little game plan?"

"You always survive," the melamed said.

He danced down the steps of City Hall and into the upholstered cave of a limousine. Isaac lost most of his vertigo. He could have sneaked up behind Barbarossa and knocked him around the ears for being LeComte's little man. They were probably laughing in their socks over at Justice. Had Caroll been part of the caper?

He saw Dee hover around Caroll, with a starkness on her face, like some disjointed doll. Ah, he was the dollbreaker. Him, Sidel. And he fled from the scene of his own crime . . .

She'd never been so bashful around a man. Caroll was the only cop in the city who could look magnificent in a blue sack. "I missed you," she said. She had no idea how to woo a husband. "I wasn't in love with Maria . . . can't we go somewhere and talk?"

He brought her to a trattoria in Little Italy where he would have lunch after his excursions to Police Plaza. The padrone let him have a corner table so they could sit in peace.

"Where are you living?" she had to ask.

"Different places . . . I moved back into Lincoln Tower. But don't tell Isaac."

"That whores' hotel?"

"It's my home," Caroll said. "I bought a hot plate."

"But you have a home . . . with me."

"I'm not Park Avenue," Caroll said. "I never was."

"If you're allergic to Park Avenue, there are plenty of town houses on the market. I can—"

"I don't want town houses. I don't want butlers. I don't want dinner bells."

She started to cry. "You should have warned me about all that when you proposed."

"I didn't propose," Caroll said. "You did."

"Well, I couldn't wait. It would have been a century before you decided on your own."

"Your father set me up, Dee. He can't bear it that you're with another man."

"Papa suffers so much that he's marrying your fiancée."

"Don't exaggerate," Caroll said. "I was Delia's bodyguard, that's all."

"Did you handcuff her to the bed, Caroll, like you handcuffed me?"

"I didn't come here to talk details." He stared at Diana's purple eyes. "I suppose you were an icebox with Maria Montalbán."

"I wasn't an icebox, but I didn't sleep with him. I wanted to, but I couldn't. We kissed. We—"

"Shut up," Caroll said. His legs were throbbing. He slapped her. "Ah, shit," he said, getting up from the table. "If I have to hit you, what's the use? You were with Maria. You were one of his girls."

He handed the padrone twenty dollars and took a cab uptown to his crib. He'd learned to control his whiskey ways. He never drank at Sherwood Forest. He only nibbled late at night.

Barbarossa was in his room when Caroll arrived at the hotel. Vietnam Joe had started sucking on Caroll's Four Roses. He looked funny with a sling.

"There's a Colombian coming to town with an awful lot of product. I can't take him alone. Not with this contraption," he said, pointing to the sling. "But with you, kid . . . it's a piece of cake."

"Let it rest, Joe. You're wearing the medal of honor."

"You didn't tell Isaac, did ya? He was looking weird at the ceremony."

"What would I tell him, Joe? That I got a phone call from LeComte to rush over to the North Meadow. I had to grab you away from your ping-pong game. It was a phony deal. We come out a couple of heroes and Isaac could have been killed."

"The man has no life. He's in love with that FBI bitch. The Roumanian princess, Margaret Tolstoy. She puts out for a hundred mobs."

"Stop it, Joe. You have no right to talk about him."

"Yeah, he kills Blue Eyes. He almost kills you. He sends out your wife on a mission to make it with Maria."

"Stop it," Caroll said.

"I'm speaking the truth, kid."

Caroll seized the Four Roses and jumped on Barbarossa. But he wouldn't wrestle with a man in a sling. "What makes you so fucking holy? You rip off dealers before and after Medal Day. What do you do with all the money?"

"I have my expenses," Barbarossa said.

"You sleep at Sherwood Forest. You don't even have a place to wash your clothes. So don't criticize Isaac. He isn't LeComte's errand boy."

"Gimme the bottle," Barbarossa said.

"No."

Barbarossa took his arm out of the sling, reached into his coat, smiled, and held his Glock to Caroll's head.

There wasn't a beat of terror in Caroll's eye. "Go on, Joe. Show me how good you are with a gun."

"Don't push me, kid."

Barbarossa took back the bottle and walked out of Caroll's crib. And Caroll was left all alone with that deepening view of the trees and a bit of metal over his heart.

32

He'd become Isaac of the public schools. He'd make pilgrimages into the heart of Manhattan, address most of Maria's girls. He memorized passages from William Blake. "I wander thro' each charter'd street," he sang of Blake's London town. "And mark in every face I meet . . . marks of weakness, marks of woe."

His favorite camping ground was a junior-high school on Montgomery Street where Maria had had his headquarters and little Rosen was the assistant principal before he tried to hang himself. Rosen must have healed. The local board had appointed him acting superintendent of District One B. Isaac had grown fond of the little man. They would have coffee together in the superintendent's office. Both of them loved the Lower East Side and had an incurable constancy to schoolchildren.

"I shouldn't have been so hard on you, Rosen."

"It's your job. You're police commissioner."

"But I didn't understand Maria . . . he had the curse, like you and me."

"He bent the law, Commissioner Sidel."

"I do it every day."

"I know," the little man said. "But that's our secret."

And Isaac would visit every single class, wearing a broken-billed baseball cap, and sometimes his fedora, like a Dead End Kid. He wouldn't condescend to the children, tell sugared lies.

"It's getting too expensive to breathe."

"Then why should we bother with poetry, Mr. Isaac?" asked one of Maria's girls.

"Because if you can see through all the haze and read a wonderful line, then you'll know you're still alive."

"What if we don't want to be alive?"

"Ah, then I can't help you."

He'd often cry into his own hat after one of these séances in the classroom, thinking of so many girls *and* boys without a real future.

"I want to be an undercover cop," said another one of Maria's girls.

"You'll have to finish school and take a long test . . ."

"And if I pass I'll get a big pension."

Maria's girls started to laugh.

"What's a charter'd street, Mr. Isaac?"

"A street that has no room for children, that's more interested in money than boys and girls, a street where mothers have no milk."

"Hey, that's where I live."

"It's Newyorico, man."

"What can we do about it, Mr. Isaac?"

"Make a big stink. You scream and scream until somebody has to hear."

But Isaac couldn't even hear the echo of his own screams. He went down into the street. A limo was waiting for him. It belonged to Becky Karp. "Get in," the mayor said. And Isaac climbed into the back seat.

"Where are we going, Rebecca?"

"To Papa Cassidy's wedding breakfast."

"It's kind of late for breakfast."

"It'll be a surprise."

"I'm not dressed for a wedding," Isaac said, putting on his baseball beanie.

"Papa will forgive you. You're the Pink Commish."

Isaac began to dread the ride.

"Saturnino Gomez will be there, Gomez and his crowd, from the Harry S. Truman Club. I couldn't face them without you, Isaac. You're Saturnino's dark horse. He thinks you're going to steal the primaries from me."

"I never told him I would run for mayor. But you'd better worry about Malik. The Republicans are grooming him."

"I don't give a fart about the Republicans. Malik is just a screen."

"Should I put on a waiter's coat at the wedding and sing that I'm for Becky Karp?"

"Some singer. My own PC is mute on Medal Day. The cardinal had to bail you out. I don't like it. You may be a fat cat to your own men. But no one has nine lives in my administration. Remember, you work for me."

"Sweetheart, how could I forget?"

"You still have that whore on your mind, Tolstoy . . . she took you out of my bed."

He'd been visiting Becky Karp several times a month in her bunker at City Hall until Margaret Tolstoy popped back into his life, she who called herself "Anastasia" when she was a little girl. He couldn't even kiss another woman, and he hadn't seen Margaret since the melamed's bingo party. Ah, he'd never survive the curse of a childhood romance.

They arrived at the Ritz-Carlton. Papa Cassidy had reserved the roof. Isaac had never been to a champagne breakfast at noon. The bride wore a white breakfast gown with some kind of tail. Her long legs seemed to own the Ritz. Delia was the girl who could destroy an entire town. He didn't think it had anything to do with acrobatics. She couldn't have been so nimble with a hundred different men. It was the lost child in Delia, that perpetual state of puberty. You'd never grow old in her arms.

But a pall seemed to enter the room with Isaac. It wasn't his fault. The whole roof garden shunned Rebecca Karp. And Isaac realized that the bigwigs of her Party weren't going to reelect her. She didn't have a Chinaman's chance.

Isaac began to wonder why people were kissing his hand. And then he saw Saturnino Gomez. Saturnino dipped his knees to Isaac and stole him away from Becky Karp. The Pink Commish didn't like it.

"You're deserting her, aren't you?"

"Hombre, she's a drowning ship."

"I'm her police commissioner."

"The lady tried to put you in limbo, on permanent sick leave."

"I'm in limbo right now."

"Isaac, please. You're the next mayor of New York. It's been decided."

"Not by me . . . Gomez, how did it feel when you played for the Chicago Cubs?"

"I'm talking strategy, and you want a trip down memory lane."

"How did it feel?"

"Like shit. I was a Newyorican rookie. The old-timers pissed on my shoe . . . Isaac, I have much more fun at the Harry Truman Club. And you're our candidate."

Isaac ran from Saturnino Gomez, but he couldn't avoid all the handkissers.

"Your Honor," a tall dark woman whispered in his ear.

"Go away," Isaac said.

His vertigo came back. Isaac never cared for roof gardens. He couldn't escape the bride and groom. "Uncle Isaac," Delia said, lacing her arm in his. Papa Cassidy wore a ruffled shirt, like a highwayman. Isaac didn't have to imagine their conjugations in Papa's king-sized bed.

Papa pawed at him. "Let's bury the hatchet."

"Why, Papa? You never liked me."

"It's all in the past," Papa said. "You're my angel, Isaac. If you hadn't closed down Delia's clubs, she might never have come to me . . . I know who my friends are. Caroll isn't here. Not even my daughter. The cardinal wouldn't marry me in his rotten cathedral. He'll suffer, believe me."

"Well, I'm here as the mayor's guest. Be nice to her."

"I am nice."

He winked at Isaac and led his bride toward Saturnino Gomez. "Hold on to Becky," Isaac muttered into the side of Papa's face.

He was about to retire from the roof when he saw a ravaged man. It was Rubino in his chair, with Margaret behind the wheels. The politicos kissed his hand and bowed to him, like they'd done to Isaac. Rubino had lost his captains, but not his cement companies, and cement was king of New York City's "crops." Isaac wanted Anastasia. Her hair was blond today. He wondered how many wigs she had in her closet.

Delia kept saying, "Uncle Sal, Uncle Sal." And Isaac couldn't tell which misery was worse—seeing Margaret at the wedding breakfast or not seeing her at all. She wouldn't glance at Isaac. Her eyes were faraway moons. Isaac felt a claw on his arm.

Rubino had wheeled himself over to the Pink Commish. "You're alive and Nose is dead. That's quite an accomplishment."

"LeComte orchestrated the whole affair. So you can thank your master."

"You don't have to insult me."

"I'm sorry, Sal. Just give me Margaret and I'll never insult you again."

"She's not mine to give. Margaret's on loan from D.C. And Justice aint getting her back. But you have compensation. I proposed you for mayor. I talked to Gomez."

Isaac's pager began to sing. "Excuse me," he said. He unclipped the device and saw the number of Central Park Precinct in the little blue screen. One of the waiters brought him a telephone. He dialed Sherwood Forest. Caroll came on the line. Isaac had a nasty premonition in his bones.

"It's Captain White, isn't it?"

"Yeah," Caroll said. "Killed himself."

"Don't let anyone touch him, kid. Not the fingerprint boys, not some sleuth from One PP. You're in charge until I get there."

Ah, he should have figured on White. Cap didn't have the temperament to be an assassin. White had his own worm that ate at him. As Isaac got onto the elevator, Margaret turned to look at him, and those faraway moons seemed to form a hook right into his gut. He had to clutch his belly on the ride down from the roof. His driver was waiting near the hotel.

"Sherwood Forest, Sergeant. Lights and siren, please."

And Sergeant Malone brought him into the Park . . .

Isaac could keep away his own lads, but not the cardinal arch-bishop of New York. Jim was waiting for Isaac in the captain's office. White's head lay on his desk, in some terrible slumber. His eyes were open. His left ear looked like a bloody balloon.

"It's my fault," Isaac said. "I shouldn't have left him alone. He needed counseling . . ."

"I counseled him, Isaac, as much as any man could."

"You knew about what happened under the bridge . . . before I ever did."

"Indeed. The poor sod didn't really confess. He'd talk around it at one or two of our gatherings. 'I'm Mr. Midnight.' I had to measure the man. I knew he wouldn't try it again. There was some danger, Isaac, but I wanted him to tell you. He waited too long. And he couldn't recover from that wait."

"Will you bury him?"

"Jesus, the Church would never allow it. He'll have to lie in some unholy grave."

"But will you pray for him?"

"I can't."

"Will you, Jim?"

"He'll be in my thoughts. That's all I can say on the subject . . . take care of Caroll. He's gloomy without his wife."

"I shouldn't have enlisted Dee."

"You're an enlister. That's what you are. And I wouldn't run for mayor if I was you. We'd fight all the time. I'd have to show you who's boss."

And Cardinal Jim walked out of the office.

It was Caroll who'd opened the door and found Captain White, after hearing a great boom that shivered the walls of Sherwood Forest. It was Caroll who'd had Isaac paged, who'd helped put the captain in a body bag, and then returned to his crib. He had his Four Roses. It was too early to nibble. He looked up. Isaac was in the room, wearing his baseball hat.

"White was the phantom hitter, wasn't he? He socked you and then he felt sorry. It was a secret you shared with the Cap and Cardinal Jim . . . ah, he was cracking up. I could see his scared eyes. He had the stink of the dead."

"I forgot all about him, kid. I blanked him out."

"He was a leper. A cop who shoots another cop . . . and I'm the skel who saved your life. I ought to give my medal to Le-Comte. He dropped the dime, I didn't. I ran to the baseball field. I went for the Nose. It was my glory assignment."

"Ah, you did what you could."

"I betrayed you, Isaac. I was a little soldier for the FBI."

"I'm still breathing," Isaac said.

"You live inside a whole circle of betrayers. That's all the family you have left."

"Stop it. I hurt you. I stole Diana. You had the right. I made her become a spy."

"No one makes Dee do anything."

"I filled her head with romance. She was part of my children's crusade. You had the right. You had the right."

Caroll looked up again and Isaac was gone. One more phantom of Central Park. He sucked on his bottle. He should have joined Barbarossa's brigade. He'd rip off all the traficantes. He'd wear a white mask. He heard a knock on his door. Caroll hid the Four Roses.

The phantom had come to take back the combat cross.

"Boss, it's open. Come in."

He prayed that his eyes would focus. But he could always pretend to recognize Isaac.

"You're blotto."

It was a woman's voice.

Caroll closed his eyes. There was a man behind the woman, carrying a bunch of pigskin bags. Dee and her butler. Caroll couldn't mistake that million-dollar luggage.

"Jeremy, have a drink."

"He's not supposed to drink," Diana said. "Jeremy, say good-bye."

"Good-bye," the butler said.

And Caroll was alone with Diana in a land of pigskin.

"I'm frightened," she said. "It's a big step. Living in one little room."

"I didn't invite you."

"You said no town houses. I got the message."

"Dee, you can't live here. We have cockroaches in the hall."

"I like the view," she said. "Don't worry about all the luggage. We'll throw away what doesn't fit . . . or give it to a neighbor."

"My neighbor's a drag queen."

"That's perfect. He can wear all my clothes."

And she put both her arms around Caroll.

33

She was Margaret of the many names, who'd once been her own little princess, Anastasia of Paris and Odessa and the Lower East Side. She'd gone to kindergarten with the KGB. She'd gotten "married" when she was twelve. Her husband, Ferdinand Antonescu, gave her a platinum ring he'd stolen from a Jewish prince. Ferdinand was the emperor of Odessa during World War II. He had his own little Gestapo state, called Transnistria. While Odessa starved, he borrowed young boys from the insane asylum and fed her on their flesh. She was a whore, a mistress, a cannibal, and a wife who played with dolls and entertained generals from the German high command. She wasn't a long-legged mannequin, like Delia St. John. She had her first gray hairs when she was fourteen. She was caught between the Russians, the Roumanians, the Germans, the Poles, and certain immigration officers of the United States.

Anastasia was a complicated fiction. She had no future and no past, except for a weird idyll on the Lower East Side when she was the sweetheart of a dark-eyed junior-high-school gypsy, Isaac Sidel. She'd already done everything conceivable with a man, except bear him a child. And the gypsy would have hot flashes whenever he clutched her hand. He reminded her of

those idiotic boys whom she'd eaten in another life. His devotion
terrified Anastasia. He too gave her a ring. He was much more
serious than Ferdinand Antonescu. Like a poet who could have
been born in an asylum. But she was plucked out of that idyll,
sent back to Roumania, where she was turned into a "swallow,"
a professional teaser of men.

The swallow kept thinking of her little gypsy. He always stumbled into some killing ground. She might even have to shoot him
in the pants one day. But she'd nurse the gypsy like she was
nursing Sal. Anastasia had become Sal's keeper. She'd bathe
him, caress his dusty bones. The dry squeal in his throat might
have been an orgasm. Anastasia couldn't tell.

The small thread of history she had was somewhere between
Isaac and Sal. The gypsy had blown off Sal's face. LeComte
rebuilt Sal like some kind of monster man. His own captains
wanted to kill him. And the melamed wanted Sal's cement.
Anastasia had to wheel him to phantom meetings with his board
of directors. He couldn't visit the same place twice. The melamed had let him go free and also put a price on his head. But
Sal wouldn't hibernate. He had this maddening wish to appear
in public. And so she wheeled him to Papa Cassidy's wedding.
They'd fought over that.

"She's like a niece," Sal had said. "I can't disappoint Delia."

"The melamed has his spies. We'll last ten minutes."

"I don't care."

"Well, I'm not sentencing you to death. Should I ask Le-
Comte? He can be the umpire."

"I won't go to the Ritz-Carlton with a lot of G-men. They'll
embarrass me."

"Then I'll escort you, Sal."

He was prince of the wedding, king of all the fat cats. The
builders and brokers couldn't survive without Sal's cement. Isaac
appeared at the wedding, and the look of him bit into her heart.
He was the same gypsy who'd followed her home from school,
her troubadour with his silent songs. She'd loved Ferdinand

Antonescu, and hated him in that cannibal country of Odessa, but it wasn't like having a sweetheart in the public schools of Manhattan. Anastasia would have peed in her pants if she'd smiled at Isaac on the Ritz-Carlton's roof. She'd have abandoned the wheelchair and run away with her gypsy. But she couldn't. She was sworn to Sal. And she had to take him down on the service elevator at the Ritz, wheel him across some forlorn kitchen to avoid the melamed's men, who'd arrived on the roof with padded overcoats. Anastasia was always ten minutes from doom, no matter where she lived.

Isaac sat with the widow up in Marble Hill. He wasn't sure if White still had some blood money in the attic. He had to be cautious.

"Mrs. White, have you looked in the attic? The Cap admired my baseball team, the Delancey Giants. He was sort of our treasurer, you see. But he was always going into his own pocket. And we're solvent now. We've had some big donations. So if you should find some cash, well, it's the Cap's. It belongs to him."

Ah, God protect Isaac from his own little lies.

He had to take his phone off the hook. The news hounds had gotten hold of his number. They wanted stories about Isaac the candidate. He busied himself with his baseball card collection. *Willie Mays, 1951*, was worth a thousand bucks. But *Harry "Bomber" Lieberman, 1944*, was practically priceless, because most of the card manufacturers had stopped production during World War II. Paper was much too scarce. But there was a very small run of phantom cards in '44, a pirate edition that was never distributed in packages of gum. Isaac had finagled and cajoled to get the *Harry Lieberman*. He kept the card in a cellophane jacket. His fingers would tremble whenever he removed the card. He would touch it like some kind of totem. He'd met Anastasia in 1944. He'd sat in the bleachers at the Polo Grounds. A ticket cost sixty cents. But Isaac would crawl under the gate.

The Polo Grounds stood on a bluff between the river and Harlem Heights, a magical green box where Isaac had come into his manhood watching the Bomber dive into his own shoelaces to catch a fly ball.

He'd been dreamwalking through the Polo Grounds ever since 1945.

He'd go to work at odd hours to avoid the reporters who stationed themselves outside One PP. His name appeared in gossip columns. He was called "the future king." He ducked Becky Karp and Saturnino Gomez and realtors who were ready to make contributions to his war chest. Papa Cassidy sent him a check for a hundred thousand dollars. Isaac tore it up.

I'm not going to run, I'm not going to run, he sang to himself. But the town wouldn't let him retire into a world of baseball cards. No matter how hard he resisted, Isaac would be the next mayor of Manhattan.

His picture was on the walls of Newyorican restaurants. No one seemed to like the current alcaldía, Rebecca Karp. He couldn't walk into a café without someone kissing his hand. He was the chosen one, the guy with great expectations.

He went to his apartment on Rivington Street. His lock had been tampered with. The burglar didn't know his business. He wondered if some journalist was squatting in his rooms. Isaac didn't even take out his Glock.

"I'm home," he announced, bursting through the door.

Anastasia sat on his couch, looking through Isaac's card collection.

"It's for kids," she said.

"You're wrong. Most of the serious collectors are my age. It's an expensive habit . . . Margaret, are you on your lunch break?"

"No. I took the afternoon off."

"Didn't they teach you how to pick a lock at FBI school?"

"I'm out of practice," Margaret said. "And I was too old to take the regular course."

"But the KGB must have had a pretty good kindergarten."

"Don't, Isaac . . . I couldn't get near you at the wedding. Sal is jealous."

"Jealous?" Isaac said. "I'm your classmate who gets to kiss you every forty years or so."

"I thought you liked my kisses."

Isaac had a fit of meanness. He grabbed up his card collection.

Anastasia didn't resist. "Will you keep a room for me at Gracie Mansion?"

"I'm not running for mayor."

"I lived in a mansion once," Anastasia said.

"I know. When you were a child war bride in Odessa. But this is different. There aren't any Nazis around our necks."

"There are always Nazis," Anastasia said.

"I'll handle them."

"You're getting all gray," she said, climbing off the couch and touching Isaac's hair. That touch terrified him. She could immobilize Isaac with the run of a finger.

"Take off the wig," he said.

Anastasia removed her blond mask. She was as gray as the Pink Commish. Her hair had been cropped like a cadet.

They started to kiss. Soon they were undressing each other. She looked at the wounds on Isaac where the bullets had gone in. Her examination excited him. He was hung like a horse. Her gun and his gun lay on the night table. And when Isaac entered her, all his dreams of baseball fell away. He wasn't an orphan of the Polo Grounds. He didn't need card collections or the burnt grass of center field. Anastasia was all he required. She had one long blue vein on her leg. He worshiped that vein. He'd have killed to keep her. But she'd become Sal's nurse. He'd have to wage war on Justice to get her back. Isaac didn't have the manpower to attack the United States. He was a lonely commissioner in a chaotic town.

He couldn't pin her to the bed like a butterfly. She had sturdier wings than Isaac. So he suffered this terrible "tristesse."

She smoked a little black cigar that must have been a habit from her Odessa days and nights. Isaac sat next to her in a tangle of sheets.

"Marry me."

"No."

"I'll kick LeComte on his ass soon as I get to Gracie Mansion. I'm the people's choice. Marry me."

She put on her wig, and Isaac couldn't reconcile *his* Anastasia with that mop of yellow hair.

"Can't we have some lunch?"

"It's late . . . Sal doesn't like to be alone."

"Where do you sleep when you're with him?"

"I sleep in Sal's bed."

"Does he touch you?"

"Yeah, he touches me. He still has hands . . . don't ask me another question, Isaac. Don't."

"So I'm the beggar who has to wait, wait for crumbs."

She socked the Pink Commish, hit him flush on the mouth. And Isaac fell back, bewildered. He'd swallowed half his tongue. Ah, they must have trained her as a ninja at FBI school.

"I risked my life coming here, Mr. Mayor."

She dabbed his mouth with a handkerchief.

"Sock me again," Isaac said, "but don't go to Sal."

"It's my job. There's no pleasure. I pity the poor guy."

"Quit LeComte," Isaac said. "Quit the son of a bitch."

"Damn you, Isaac. LeComte could deport me. I have no papers."

"You're in limbo. Like me."

"Smile," she said. "You're my man."

And she kissed Isaac with such persuasion, he forgot about his sore tongue.

"I could blackmail LeComte."

"Shh," she said, and she was into her clothes and out the door.

"When will I see you?" Isaac hollered behind her.

"No questions, my silly darling goose."

Darling, she'd said. She ran down the steps, and Isaac was happier than the last time he saw the Bomber hit a home run, forty years ago, on a September day in the Polo Grounds. Forty years of grief. Without Harry on the handle. One two three.

Anastasia ran and ran. She removed her blond wig and put on a black helmet, like Louise Brooks, her favorite star, who'd arranged her own invisibility and died in that winterland of Rochester, New York, where Anastasia had seduced and abandoned Marco Ponti, the Mafia prince of Lake Ontario. She'd married the prince in a secret ceremony. But the FBI had confiscated Anastasia's wedding ring (she'd always get a receipt for the booty).

In *Lulu*, one of the first silent films Anastasia had ever seen, Louise was murdered by Jack the Ripper. Lulu gave herself to Jack and disappeared with a smile. She was a girl who went looking for death, like Anastasia. But Lulu didn't have a Glock, or a hundred different aliases and a closetful of wigs.

She was assigned to Rubino, Jack the Ripper in a wheelchair. He'd loved her and tried to kill Anastasia. He wouldn't stop giving her wedding rings. Sal had a whole continent of rings, and he'd get morose if she didn't wear them on her fingers, five or six to a hand. She took off the rings when she visited Isaac.

Sal wouldn't stop pestering her.

"Chinaman's Chance."

"I'm not taking you to a disco. It's dangerous."

"It's a bottle club."

"It's still dangerous."

"But I promised Delia I'd visit her at the Chinaman's."

Anastasia tapped him on the head, which had the texture of a lettuce leaf. "She's married, you dope. Papa Cassidy wouldn't let her dance."

"Who's a dope? I protected Delia. Papa had to sign a contract or I wouldn't give the bride away. Delia gets to dance when I say so. I'm her force majeure."

"Force majeure? That's not a person. It's an act of God."

Sal picked up his cordless telephone, cradled it in the curve of his arm, dialed with one raw finger, mumbled a few words to Papa Cassidy, and put down the phone. "It's done. Delia dances tonight. At the Chinaman's. A command performance."

"It's risky."

"Then I'll find another babysitter. One of the Mormons will take me."

"They'll take you to LeComte, you big dope."

Anastasia drove him in the taxicab she often used as a cover. She didn't care for this arrangement of Sal's. A private midnight show. She left the cab near the Park Avenue trestle and carried Sal in her arms across a moonless street, like a broken feather. All the weight seemed to have gone out of his body. She went down the cellar stairs to Chinaman's Chance. Lady Longlegs was all alone, dancing in the dark. The music seemed to drift out of the floor, like a dragon's breath. Anastasia didn't like it. The scenario was a little too neat, the cellar a little too dark. She sat Sal down in a chair, next to a mirror that had its own silver life and revealed aspects of Delia St. John.

Anastasia had her Glock. She'd shoot the mirror if she had to and drag Sal out the door.

"Uncle Sal," Delia said, her legs kicking out against the silvered glass, and for a moment Anastasia thought there were two Delias.

She didn't like it.

"I'm happy," Sal said. "I ought to live in the dark . . . I am the fucking darkness."

"When you're not the force majeure," Anastasia said.

"Shaddap. I'm concentrating."

But Anastasia didn't take her eyes off the mirror, because that glass held whatever truth there was in this lousy salon. And when she could no longer see Delia's kicks in the glass, she lunged toward Sal's chair, but it was too late. Three heads appeared in the mirror. The melamed, Papa, and Jerry DiAngelis, clutching a Mossberg Persuader.

"Better not go for the gun," he said with a sweetness in his voice. And Anastasia couldn't have glocked the three of them and also save Sal.

"It's like New Orleans, isn't it, Jerry?" she said.

"There's a big difference, sweetheart. You weren't protecting this piece of shit. He was going to put out your lights."

The melamed started to make catlike noises in his throat. "We don't have time for dialectics. Madame Tolstoya, you can walk away from this cellar, or die with Sal Rubino. That's your only choice."

"But I'll get one of you before Jerry gets me."

"I don't think so," the melamed said. "You're quick, my dear, but I have two more pistols behind your back. I wouldn't come naked to Chinaman's Chance."

"Margaret," Sal said. "Don't talk to that Hebrew schoolteacher."

"You've been doing mischief, Mr. Rubino. LeComte was supposed to retire you. That was our bargain. I gave you back your life. And you wouldn't let go of your cement. You blabbed to politicians. You meddled. You wanted to bribe our best captains."

"I'm a player," Sal said. "I can't sit still . . . but this wasn't political. I came to see Delia dance. That's my privilege. And Papa ratted on me."

"Not at all," the melamed said. "He knows where his future is . . . and it's not with you."

"How much are you paying Delia?"

Delia emerged again in that silvered glass. "Not a cent, Uncle Sal. You killed Maria. I'm Maria's girl."

"And who financed that killing? Who commissioned it? Your darling husband. Papa wanted Maria out of the way."

"Don't listen to him," Papa said. "The man is nothing but a murderous snake."

"Talk, talk, talk," the melamed said. "I'm going crazy . . . Sal, I can't let you leave this cellar. It's that simple. And Madame Tolstoya has to decide. Either she walks, or she shares a grave with you."

And then a voice seemed to shoot right out of the glass. "I'll decide who walks." Anastasia saw that bearish face. He didn't have his baseball cap or his big chapeau. He wore a dark suit, with a tie knotted around his neck.

"Jesus," Jerry said. "I can't believe it. How did Isaac get in?"

"Through the door, Jerry. Through the door."

"But someone had to tell you about our little meet."

"Papa told me. I put a tap on all his phones."

"I'll crucify you, Sidel," Papa said. "Jerry, you'll have to kill this man *and* the woman *and* Sal."

"Don't be so generous with our guns," the melamed said. "He's the police commissioner."

"Papa's right," Jerry said.

"Sonny boy, you shouldn't agree with strangers."

"I'm the boss," Jerry shouted in the dark. "And I say Isaac goes."

"He could have brought his own army," the melamed said. "Isaac, will you get out of here like a good little boy?"

"The honeymoon is over, Iz. I'm declaring war on the whole tribe, including your loanshark, Papa Cassidy."

"He's insane," Papa said. "Kill him, Jerry. I'll write you a check for six million dollars."

"Dad," Jerry DiAngelis said to his father-in-law. "I'll take my chances. Isaac is alone."

The melamed rubbed his eyes. "I like the Stalinist. I'd rather have him as a live enemy than a dead one."

"Kill him," Papa Cassidy said.

Anastasia reached for her Glock. If she blew the melamed's brains out, Isaac could hide in all the smoke. But what about Sal? What about Sal?

"Kill him," Papa Cassidy said.

And another voice came out of the glass. The rough purr of an angry animal. "Papa, when does Delia dance?"

Papa froze against the silver. "Dee? Is that you?"

"Yes, Papa. I'm Isaac's back-up man."

Papa Cassidy beat his chest. "Jerry, don't hurt my daughter."

"Nobody walks," Jerry said.

"Sonny boy," the melamed said, "are you going to kill the whole country? Let's say good-bye."

"Not without Sal's ghost."

"Say good-bye."

"He'll destroy our Family, dad."

The melamed had to push his son-in-law. Papa trudged behind them, with Delia St. John. And Anastasia didn't know what to expect. "Some show," Sal said from his chair. And she saw Isaac in the glass, without his bearish look. He wasn't that gypsy boy who'd followed her from school.

"Anastasia," he said, the mirror catching the crisp collar of his shirt, the fall of his necktie, the deep wound of his shoulders, that riven face, like a panther hurtling into the dark.

Anastasia closed her eyes.

The lights went on. Anastasia blinked. The mirror lost its magic chance. There were men and women cops in the club, with shotguns and fiberglass vests. Anastasia recognized Caroll Brent. The gypsy had come en famille. He'd staged his own theatrical at Chinaman's Chance, with cops and Cassidy's daughter.

"Anastasia," he said.

But she wouldn't answer him. She picked up Jack the Ripper off his chair. Her black helmet dropped over one eye.

The gypsy touched her hand.

"Marry me," he said.

She ran out of the club with Sal in her arms, picturing herself as Isaac's bride. She started to laugh.

"What's so funny?" Jack the Ripper said.

"Sal, I need another wedding ring."

DATE			